THE HEART OF ALCHEMY

JAMES E WISHER

SAND HILL PUBLISHING

CHAPTER 1

Otto Shenk stood in the hall outside the guest room his mother had been using and watched her pack. She'd spent the summer and most of the fall helping Annamaria with the baby. Mother had the magic touch and now Abby seldom cried. For that mercy alone he would have thanked her a thousand times.

He'd asked her more than once if she wouldn't consider just staying at Franken Manor permanently, but she always insisted on returning home to Shenk Barony. Since Mother could be every bit as stubborn as Father, Otto had been forced to accept her decision. And that meant going ahead of her to have a chat with Stephan, his rather unstable eldest brother.

He sighed and she looked up from the trunk. The fine lines around her blue eyes were barely visible in the bright morning light. She wore a velvet burgundy dress and tough leather boots. Her heavy wool cloak hung on the back of a chair nearby.

"Are you still worrying?" Mother asked. "Bad enough Axel fusses like a mother hen, I don't need it from you too."

Otto smiled and tried to keep his unease from showing. "We both love you, Mother. And given Stephan's temperament, not to mention Griswalda's, it's not beyond the realm of possibility that they might do something stupid. It's unlikely, I admit that, but far from impossible."

"It's sweet that you're concerned, dear." Mother closed the trunk and straightened. "But I've been dealing with your brother and his shrew of a wife for years. You have nothing to worry about."

Otto nodded and let the matter drop. Once he finished with Stephan, he really wouldn't have anything to worry about. The ether swirled at his command and lifted her trunk. They walked together towards the stairs.

At the bottom, Annamaria stood with the baby snug in her arms, sound asleep. She wore a fine white dress, her hair brushed and flawless. Whenever he saw her done up like that, he was reminded of that first day when they met. He'd been so full of hope for his impending marriage. How quickly she'd disabused him of his illusions. Now he viewed her and the baby the same way he did the long dining table. They were both permanent residents of the mansion and he was stuck with them.

Edwyn sat at said table a few feet away and heaved himself to his feet as they approached. Otto hardly believed it possible, but his father-in-law appeared to have gained at least another twenty pounds since trade got back to normal. His girth now barely fit in the dining room chairs.

"We're going to miss you around here, Katharina." Edwyn bowed to her and smiled, setting his many chins to jiggling.

"We certainly will," Annamaria agreed. "I don't know how I would have survived the last six months without you helping with Abby."

2

"She's a sweet girl." Mother leaned over and kissed Abby's cheek. "Once the roads clear in spring, I'll have to come again. Take care of yourself, Otto. You still look far too thin."

"Yes, Mother." Otto walked her outside into the blustery fall breeze. The leaves had started to turn on the many trees that dotted the estate. A hint of moisture filled the air and he suspected they'd have a rain shower before the end of the day.

Otto guided her trunk up onto the carriage roof where one of the guards secured it. Another opened the door and she stepped in without assistance.

"Have a safe trip," Otto said.

"Goodbye, dear."

The driver shook his reins and the carriage clattered down the path and out of sight. Otto waited until he could no longer hear the carriage, became one with the ether, and reappeared in the courtyard outside the keep of Castle Shenk.

Graves was pacing in the training yard despite the bitter wind. Only a few days' ride separated the barony from Garen, but the weather felt like Straken. They'd have to hope the frost held off or a fair portion of the apple crop would freeze.

The good sergeant hurried over when he spotted Otto. He looked older than Otto remembered. More gray ran through his dark hair and new wrinkles lined his face. Time, it seemed, had not been kind to Otto's former tutor in the way of the sword.

"Lord Shenk." Graves saluted fist to heart. Since they'd seen the power of his magic, all the guards were now far more respectful around Otto. "I'm glad to see you here. Your father and brother..."

"Yes, I heard. I've been putting this visit off, but Mother set out this morning so I can't delay any longer. Tell me, is the situation as bad as she made out?"

"Three days ago, they nearly drew swords on each other. The garrison is already starting to pick sides. I'm your father's man for life, as are most of the older guards. But many of the younger men see Stephan as the future, despite his quirks."

"You should be a diplomat, Graves. Stephan's insane and we all know it. That can be useful in the right circumstances, which these are not. Right now, all that concerns me is my mother's safety. Is she in any danger from Stephan or his miserable excuse for a wife?"

"I hesitate to say for certain, my lord. Stephan wants to be baron. That hissing harpy spends every spare second whispering in his ear. When the snows come and everyone's locked up together for five months, heaven knows what might happen. Only a miracle will see both your father and brother alive come spring. In truth, I don't know who to put my gold on."

That was even worse than Otto had feared. "If Father falls, you and any of the guards that wish to leave will have a place with me in Garen. You remember Franken Manor?"

"It's a hard place to forget."

"Come to the gate and tell them who you are. You can bunk with Axel and his scouts in our barracks."

"That's very generous, my lord. I—"

"There's a price. Whatever happens this winter, I want you to keep Mother safe. I will make the consequences clear to Stephan, but if he's in one of his rages, rational thought might be out of the question. Protect her, bring her to the capital if you must, and your future, along with any guard that comes with you, is assured. If she dies, then it had better be after you've already been killed. If it's otherwise, you'll wish Stephan had gotten a hold of you. Clear?"

"Perfectly." Graves actually looked vaguely offended that

Otto felt the need to threaten him. Maybe he hadn't needed to, but some habits were hard to break. "We all love Lady Shenk. There isn't a guard here, new or old, that wouldn't lay down his life for her."

"That's what I wanted to hear. Now, let's see if I can't talk some sense into my father and brother."

Graves walked as far as the keep door with him, pulled it open, and stepped aside to allow Otto to enter. A fire burned in the great hearth and Father's hounds lounged in front of it. One dog lifted his head, snorted at him, and lay back down. Once he was inside, the door closed behind him with an ominous *thunk*.

No running away now.

Otto straightened. He wasn't some weakling to be pushed around anymore. Let Stephan try. It would make his life immensely easier if he had an excuse to burn the life out of the madman.

Now that he thought about it, Otto could kill Stephan in his sleep easily enough, but then he'd lose Axel to the barony and that didn't suit him at all. Having a soldier as skilled as Axel sitting in a rural barony overseeing the apple harvest was beyond a waste.

Besides, Mother wouldn't appreciate it if he did anything to Stephan. Angels bless her, she still loved the lunatic.

Stretching out with the ether, he quickly located Father downstairs in the treasury. Brooding over his gold no doubt. Stephan was upstairs with his family and the servants were scattered around the keep probably in hopes of staying as far as possible from either their current or future master. His home had become a fine mess, that was certain.

He turned toward the basement stairs. Best to talk to

Father first. No need to threaten him though. Otto just wanted to hear firsthand how everything had gone so wrong.

A guard stood at the top of the basement stairs. The man wore a mail shirt inside the keep when there was no threat from outside forces. That told Otto a great deal about just how serious matters were.

The guard moved quickly to block Otto's path. "Your father doesn't wish to be disturbed."

"I need to talk to him. If he doesn't want to talk to me as his son, he will talk to me as a Crown representative."

The guard winced and looked all around as if afraid someone might overhear him. "He doesn't trust anyone besides Graves and some of the other veterans. Most days he stays holed up with that huge chest of gold. In some ways, he's gone as mad as Lord Stephan."

"Mother's on her way home. He needs to pull himself together before she gets here. Let me talk to him."

The guard weighed his options, which amounted to moving or having Otto move him. Finally, he shuffled a few feet to the right. Otto nodded and descended the narrow stone steps.

At the bottom, a pair of Lux crystals cast dull, yellow light across a fifteen-by-fifteen-foot room. A shelf held small coffers filled with taxes collected from the many little villages that dotted the barony. In the center of the room sat the enormous chest filled with gold double eagles that served as the dowry that secured Otto's wedding.

Father sat on the chest, his double-edged sword resting on his knees. He wore a full coat of mail along with his usual leather and fur. His beard hadn't been trimmed or his hair washed in weeks at least. Bloodshot eyes glared at Otto from dark, hollow sockets.

"What are you doing here, boy? I thought you had a soft place in the capital far away from us."

Considering everything Otto had been through since leaving for Garen, he'd hardly call it a soft life. Aside from the quality of his bed, there was little soft about it.

"Mother's on her way home and I wanted to see what she was returning to. From everything I've seen, calling it a mess would be generous. What happened?"

Father rubbed his eyes and let out a long, exhausted sigh. "Your brother came back from Markane even more hungry for power than when he left. It started out calmly enough. He suggested hiring more guards and getting everyone better equipment."

"But you refused," Otto guessed.

"Of course I refused! We have no enemies at the moment; there hasn't even been a bandit attack this summer. You don't hire extra soldiers just to have them sitting around collecting pay with no one to fight."

"Then why did Stephan want to hire them?"

"I'm not sure he did. It was a test to find out if I'd let him make a decision of even minor importance. I would have, you know, if only he made a good one. It went from one thing to the next: tapestries, new feather beds, new swords, you name it and he suggested we buy it. Nothing we actually needed of course. Some I blame on his wife. The pig can see her place as baroness only a breath away and she wants it bad."

"Bad enough to hurt the current baroness?" Otto asked.

Father surged to his feet as though ready to fight. "No harm will come to your mother while I live!"

Otto nodded. "That's exactly what I'm afraid of. Graves said you two nearly came to blows a few days ago. What was that fight about?"

"Whether we had roast beef or pork for dinner."

Otto stared. If he'd believed his father capable of telling a joke, he would have assumed this was one. But given his grim expression, it clearly wasn't.

"It was just the final thing that broke the dam. We haven't eaten together or spoken since. I keep to the downstairs and Stephan the upstairs. Matters can't stay this way for long. We'll have to settle it in the training yard once and for all. Once he's dead, I'll need Axel released from his duties."

Otto swallowed a laugh. "Axel wouldn't come back here if you gave him that chest and all the gold it holds. Besides, I have greater need of him."

"That's not for you to say." Father growled like a cornered wolf.

"Of course it is. Believe it or not, there are far greater matters in the world than who inherits Shenk Barony. My advice, assuming you can actually defeat Stephan, is to name his son as heir. You and Mother can raise him and Mandel. With any luck, Little Stephan will end up less mad than his father. I further advise that you dump Griswalda in a deep hole filled with sharp rocks."

Father snorted a laugh. "Choosing her as a daughter-in-law might not have been my best decision."

"So, you and Stephan do agree on something. I can't believe I'm saying this, but why don't you wait until Mother gets home? Maybe she can work out some kind of compromise."

Father thought for a moment then nodded. "If he agrees, I won't kill him until Katharina gets home."

"Fine, I'll go talk to Stephan, see if I can coax a sensible idea out of that warped brain of his. Will you meet us in the dining hall?"

"Yes."

Otto retreated back to the first floor then climbed to the second. As he drew closer to Stephan's room, the sounds of muffled shouting reached him. Sounded like Father wasn't the only one Stephan was having a fight with.

He shook his head and knocked. The fighting didn't drop in volume, but the door did open, revealing a small, glum blond boy. Little Stephan had grown about five inches since Otto last saw him. What was he now, four, five? Something like that.

"Uncle Otto, Mom and Dad are fighting again. Can you make them stop?"

It was such a pitiful request, Otto nearly said yes. The problem was, the only way to make them stop for good involved long pine boxes and deep, dark holes.

Instead he said, "I'll try. Why don't you go downstairs? Your grandfather is coming up and you can play with the hounds."

"Okay. Bye, Uncle Otto." Little Stephan darted for the stairs and was soon gone.

While they were talking, the fight ended. A moment later Stephan stalked toward the door. He wore a fur-trimmed robe and it appeared the last of his hair had fallen out. "What do you want, runt?"

"Peace. I have it, more or less, in the empire. Why is it you and Father refuse to give it to me in my own family?"

Stephan blinked and stared for a moment as if not entirely clear what Otto meant. When confused, Stephan defaulted to belligerence. "The old man should step aside. It's my time to rule the barony."

"Your time doesn't come until his ends. You know that as well as I do. Are you truly that eager to count barrels of apple brandy and negotiate deals with merchants?"

"No, it's the principle of the thing. He's old and weak, I'm young and strong. That means I should be in charge." Otto shook his head at the stupid, simpleminded thinking. "What do you care anyway? You always hated Father more than I did."

"I *don't* care, Stephan. As long as the barony pays its taxes on time and doesn't start trouble with its neighbors, you can cut Father's head off and put it on a pike for all the difference it makes to me. But I want to make it clear that if anything happens to Mother, I'll find you and skin you alive. And I have the power to make sure you're awake for the entire process. Do I make myself clear?"

"Yes. Believe it or not, I have no interest in harming Mother."

"Good. She'll be home before long. I suggested to Father that she might forge some sort of truce between the two of you. He's willing to keep the peace until she arrives if you are. Shall I tell him you have an agreement?"

"Fine. What's another week, right?"

"Right. If you win, congratulations. If you die…" Otto shrugged. "In any case, I've spent all the time on this I care to. Good morning."

Otto paused long enough to pass the word of a deal to Father before vanishing into the ether. He sincerely hoped Mother didn't arrive home to a bloodbath. But whether she did or not, Otto had done everything in his power to prevent it.

CHAPTER 2

New Year's Day had arrived and, to celebrate the formation of the empire, some genius had suggested resuming the annual gala. They hadn't had one in two years, not since before they were forced out of the Portal Compact. If they never had one again, it would have suited Wolfric perfectly fine.

He stood in the throne room and watched as the rich and powerful filed in. Beside him, Captain Borden, commander of the palace guard, eyed each group like they were potential assassins. Wolfric couldn't exactly criticize him since that was his job.

Each individual or group approached the throne, bowed, and went to mingle. In addition to the Garenland nobles, the governors he'd assigned to the new provinces had come via portal for the gathering. Even former King Liatos and his daughter had been set free for the night. Mainly so Otto could see who dared speak to him and listen in on what they discussed.

He would have ordered the gala canceled, but Otto pointed

out that an emperor needed to be seen by his people. It was also a perfect chance to eavesdrop on the nobles and merchants to discover what they really thought about the empire. Meeting and greeting, listening to them complain or flatter, all of it served a purpose.

The stiff collar of his black and gold formal uniform scratched his neck and he yanked it away. He was emperor for heaven's sake! He should be able to wear whatever he wanted and receive nothing but compliments.

When the throne room door finally thudded shut, the band started playing soft music and servants began to circulate, bearing heavily loaded trays of food and orders to keep their ears open and mouths shut. Otto had yet to put in an appearance. He would be busy spying on the proceeding via some magic or other. There never seemed to be a moment of rest for his dear friend.

Well, if Otto could do his work, the least Wolfric could do was circulate and act like an emperor. His first stop was the hors d'oeuvres table where Edwyn Franken was piling a plate high. Annamaria stood a few feet away looking stunning in a white gown, her hair done up with silver clasps. He hadn't been nearly diligent enough in visiting his old friend and that would have to change.

When they spotted him approaching, Edwyn bowed without losing a roll and Annamaria dipped a graceful curtsy. "Your Majesty," they said in unison.

"I'm pleased you both made it, though I must apologize about keeping Otto too busy to escort you properly."

Annamaria smiled and waved off his concern. "It's fine. I often go days without seeing Otto, sometimes weeks. All for the greater good of the empire, I'm sure. It is a great honor for our family that you trust him with such important tasks."

"Indeed," Edwyn chimed in. "I fear I won't be able to hand off the running of our business to him for many years."

"I say with all honesty that without Otto, not only would the empire not exist, I might well be dead several times over." Much as he would have enjoyed spending the whole evening with Annamaria and her father, Wolfric needed to move on. "Enjoy the gala."

"Be sure to pay us a visit when you can," Annamaria said.

Wolfric smiled but made no promises. He did make a mental note to arrange an afternoon visit sometime soon. He eased his way through the crowd, chatting with this governor and that baron. A couple dukes bent his ear about a promising new farming technique he couldn't have cared less about.

"Your Majesty!" He turned to find Governor Varchi plowing through the gathering like a charging warhorse.

The former general had gained about twenty pounds since taking on his new position and his hair was slicked back with some black oil. He really did look the part of a nobleman now. More's the pity.

"Governor. You're looking well. I'm pleased to see you made it for the gala."

"I wouldn't have missed it. If you have a moment, I need to speak with you about Otto Shenk."

Wolfric winced. He'd already heard all the man's complaints about Otto stealing both his mithril and the best scouts in the Northern Army. As if either of those things actually belonged to him.

"What about Otto?" Wolfric asked. He made his tone hard enough to cut glass.

"When is he planning to return my scouts?"

"Why, do you have an enemy position you need spied upon?"

"No, but they're assigned to the Northern Army. If he doesn't need them, they should be sent back to Straken."

"Let me make this clear," Wolfric said. "And I'll use small words to be sure there's no misunderstanding. If Otto wants the scouts, they're his until he's finished with them. You may consider them no longer a part of the Northern Army and therefore no longer your concern. I swear, if I hear one more word about either those men or the mithril, I'll see you reassigned to oversee the cleaning of Tharanault's sewer system. Do I make myself clear?"

Varchi had the good sense to look ashamed. "Of course, Your Majesty. I—"

Wolfric spotted an unfamiliar face in the crowd and left the governor talking to himself. He didn't know who the woman was, but the glimpse he caught of her made him want to know more.

He found her standing near the right-hand wall beside a man old enough to be her father. She wore a black gown accented with silver jewelry. Her skin was a deep bronze rarely seen in the capital. Green eyes grew wide at his approach. She and her companion both made their obeisances as he drew near.

"Your Majesty, it's an honor to speak with you," the man said. "My name is Baron Martinique St. Croy and this is my niece, Jade. When I received the invitation to the gala, she insisted on joining me. My wife has been unwell of late and willingly gave up her place."

"My pleasure, Your Majesty." Jade blushed in a most fetching manner.

"Where is your holding?" Wolfric asked.

"Far to the south, near the Rolan border," the baron said.

"It must have been a difficult journey. I trust the roads weren't too rough." He addressed this last question to Jade.

She shook her head, her long, dark hair partially covering her face as she looked down, too nervous to meet his gaze. "They were fine, Majesty. It was exciting to leave the barony and make the journey. I've always wanted to visit the capital."

"And is Garen everything you hoped it would be?"

She looked up and caught him with those deep-green eyes. Wolfric's heart skipped a beat. "It's been wonderful. We're planning to stay for the winter. Uncle rented us a villa."

"Quite a small one," the baron said. "St. Croy Barony is a modest holding after all."

Wolfric had nearly forgotten the man was there, so engrossed had he become with Jade. He forgot all about the rest of the party and spent the next two hours chatting with the beautiful noblewoman. They discussed nothing serious, just minor, safe topics. Her childhood in the south swimming in the ocean, collecting crabs with her uncle.

He in turn told her about his youth, learning swordsmanship, hunting with his father. When the gala finally ended, he found himself surprised to see everyone filing out.

"Come along, Jade," the baron said. "We've taken up enough of the emperor's time."

Wolfric wanted to say she could stay as long as she wished. Instead he said, "It was a pleasure to talk to you. Perhaps you might visit the palace again while you're in Garen."

Jade looked eagerly at her uncle, who offered a fond smile. "We certainly couldn't turn down an invitation from the emperor. Anytime you wish to see us, we are at your service."

Wolfric had absolutely no interest in seeing the old man again. His niece was another matter. Of course, as her guardian, it wouldn't be appropriate to let her come to the palace unescorted. Especially if St. Croy was an old-fashioned nobleman. Some things simply weren't done.

"You'll hear from me soon. Good evening."

Jade and her uncle bowed again and withdrew. When the night was finally over, Wolfric went straight to the library where he had a meeting with Otto. He never even thought about visiting his harem. The only woman on his mind was Jade.

৭

Otto blew out a long sigh and leaned back in his chair. Beside him, Corina and Draken likewise relaxed. The three of them sat in a room directly under the throne room. From there, they easily listened and watched as the nobles chatted, plotted, and schemed. Happily, everything Otto heard and saw indicated no one had anything detrimental to the empire in the works.

"Did either of you learn anything that concerned you?" Otto asked.

"As ordered, I focused my full attention on Liatos," Draken said, his voice thin and strained after using so much magic for so long. "Beyond a few polite greetings, no one had anything to do with him or his daughter. I see no threat."

Otto nodded. "Good. Corina?"

"Wolfric, I mean His Majesty, spoke to a number of people, but seemed especially interested in a pretty girl who showed up with an older man claiming to be her uncle. They discussed nothing of importance, though he did say something about inviting them for a meal at the palace."

"Okay, thanks, both of you. I need to talk to the emperor. You two can go home."

Draken stood, his spine popping, and bowed before heading for the door.

Corina started to join him, hesitated, then asked, "Is everything okay, Master? You've been tense lately."

Otto grimaced. Between refitting the ship and making preparations for the journey to the Celestial Empire in the spring and wondering what was happening in Shenk Barony, Otto had been somewhat out of sorts. Hopefully only Corina noticed.

"I've got a lot going on just now. Don't worry, I'll be fine. Go on. You know how Hans worries."

"Heaven's mercy, you get kidnapped once and he starts thinking you can't cross the street without getting hit by a carriage. Are we still going to Lux to check on the ship tomorrow?"

"Yes, but not until afternoon. I'll collect you at the warehouse."

She bowed and they left the listening post together. At the top of the basement stairs, she turned right toward the front gate and he went left, toward the library where he was supposed to meet Wolfric.

The guards outside nodded to him and opened the door. He found the emperor seated in one of the overstuffed leather chairs, a leg slung over the arm and a brandy in his hand. Wolfric smiled and looked around in an almost dreamy state. Hopefully it was just exhaustion. The day had been a long one.

"Otto! I trust all is well, my friend."

"No one seems to be plotting anything at the moment, at least nothing they discussed at the gala. Are you well? You seem a bit...off."

"I met a girl tonight. Pretty, charming, sweet. I hope to see her again soon. She seemed willing."

17

"You're the emperor," Otto said. "Any woman, noble or common, would want to get close to you. Has she asked for money yet?"

Wolfric frowned. "You don't have a romantic bone in your body, do you? Still, her uncle did mention their barony produced only a modest income. I really hope that's not why she seemed so interested in my conversation. Either way, I'll know more when we have dinner together in a day or two."

"I sincerely hope I'm wrong," Otto said. Of course he didn't believe for a second he was. "No doubt it would please the nobility if you took a wife and produced an heir or three. It's not like we can tell them you plan to live forever."

Wolfric's frown turned to a grin. "I can imagine the looks on their faces now. They'd probably think I was either a lunatic or an imbecile that needed to be removed from the throne with all haste. When their great-grandchildren are bowing to me, they'll know the truth."

"Indeed. At the very least, I can say with confidence that no one is plotting anything of concern to us. At the moment anyway. With the nobility, that can change over a cup of coffee."

Wolfric waved a hand. "If anything happens, I'm sure you'll handle it, just as you always do. If there's nothing else, I think I'll call it a night."

Otto nodded and Wolfric took his leave. Alone in the library, Otto made a mental note to look a little closer at Baron St. Croy.

CHAPTER 3

After a morning spent studying one of the handful of books he could find on the Celestial Empire, Otto set out for the warehouse to collect Corina. The streets of Gold Ward were quiet at this time of day and he saw only a pair of carriages, their passengers concealed by closed curtains, as he walked toward the gates.

Given his position, Otto really should have taken a carriage as well, but he found he enjoyed the fresh air, even when it held a bitter chill like today. Happily, it took little in the way of magic to keep him comfortable. The guards nodded to him as he passed into the business district. He'd made the walk often enough that they hardly even flinched at his appearance anymore. That was both a relief and a concern. As the old saying went, familiarity bred contempt.

He shook off the stupid notion for the waste of mental energy it was.

The business district, unlike Gold Ward, bustled with activity. What it gave up in wealth, it made up in energy. The streets practically vibrated with excitement. Vendors shouted at passersby in the hopes of getting a sale. Messengers ran past at full speed, ignoring everyone and everything in their quest to earn a good tip. Life, it seemed, had at last fully recovered from the effects of the war.

It never ceased to amaze Otto how resilient people were. Reports from the rest of the empire agreed that things were getting back to normal in the provinces as well. Even Straken seemed calm. Hopefully it wasn't the calm before the storm.

He reached the warehouse without incident and pushed the door open. No stench assaulted him today, thank heaven. Ulf seemed to be between experiments at the moment. In fact, he found Ulf, along with Hans and his squad, seated around a table enjoying their lunch. Everyone started to stand when they saw him, but Otto waved them back.

"Where's Corina?"

"Here, Master!" She came running out from behind one of the giant suits of armor.

"Ulf, have you seen Allen or Sin?" Otto asked.

"I believe Allen is at the tavern. Sin left an hour ago on some errand or other. Was there something I could help you with?"

"Yes, you can give them a message for me. I want them to look into a baron named St. Croy. Start with the servants, they're always good for a little gossip. Tell them I'll want a report in one week."

Ulf nodded. "I'll tell them as soon as I see them. Is this nobleman trouble?"

"Too soon to say. His niece has her eye on the emperor and I want to know more about them. If all they want is imperial favor, that's harmless enough. If it's something more, let's just say I'd like that information."

"We'll do our best."

"Good. Corina, time to go check on the ship."

Hans and his squad finished wolfing down their stew and stood.

"We're ready, my lord," Hans said.

Otto had intended to leave them to rest this trip, but didn't feel like arguing. The little group collected their heavy wool cloaks and they set out for the portal.

The trip through the portal took only an instant. When they emerged in Lux, a gust of wind nearly knocked Otto off his feet. The clouds were so black it felt like day had turned to night. No guards emerged to greet them and Otto couldn't find fault with their decision. Only the poor devils on duty could be seen at their posts on the wall and at the gate. It took both men to push the gate open against the howling wind.

As soon as they were outside the walls, the storm grew even worse. After ten paces, Otto conjured a barrier around them. It took fifteen threads' worth of ether to seal the storm out, but once he was done, they all stood up straight and walked with ease.

"I see why you didn't want to sail until spring," Corina said.

It was less that he didn't want to than it was that the storms made it impossible.

Aside from some trash blowing down the street, the city looked empty. They made the trip to the docks in record time and soon found the *Sea Star* in her dry dock. No workers appeared and no sounds reached them over the wind.

"Guess they took the day off," Hans said.

Otto muttered to himself. Given what he was paying the shipwrights, they could stand a little cold and wind. They were working inside the ship, after all.

"Lord Shenk!"

Otto turned to see Captain Wainwright waving at them

from the entrance of a nearby shed. At least it looked like a shed; it was actually the size of a small house. The workers stored their tools in it and ate their meals out of the cold.

They hurried over and slipped inside before the captain closed the door behind them. "You picked a miserable day for an inspection," Wainwright said.

"It wasn't this bad in Garen. How goes the work?"

"Good. The crew's making a quick job of it. When storm season ends, we'll be ready to sail. In fact, I've been plotting our course using that map you gave me. Would you like to take a look?"

Otto very much wanted to take a look and they all gathered around a rough-sawn table where the centuries-old map was held down by a pair of planes, a drill, and a hammer. Otto winced until he remembered it was just a copy and the original was still safe and sound in the armory.

The line Wainwright had plotted followed a course far south around the tip of the Dead Lands then back north before ending in the middle of a sea labeled The Demon's Pit. A rather ominous name that hopefully sounded worse than reality.

"Why does the course stop there?" Otto asked.

"That's where we run out of food." Wainwright scratched his scruffy gray beard. "We need to decide where we'll try and gather more."

Otto eyed the map and shook his head. So much about the area was unknown, anything he decided would simply be a guess.

"We have two choices," Wainwright said, breaking into his thoughts. He stabbed a large island about the same size as Markane. "That is the Island of Giant Beasts. According to the logbook, there's fresh water and good hunting. There are also predatory birds big enough to carry off a horse, some sort of giant lizard with a poisonous bite, and heaven only knows what else."

"Charming. The second option?"

Wainwright stabbed a second spot, a peninsula jutting into the sea. "That is the Land of the Demon Binders. The logbook said little about it and its author had no desire to learn more. I recommend we try the island."

Otto nodded. He knew nothing about demons save that avoiding them seemed prudent. A visit to Lord Karonin was called for. If anyone could advise him on this matter, she could. It wouldn't hurt to drop in on Castle Shenk as well. Hopefully things had settled down.

"We'll check in again, Captain, hopefully on a nicer day. If there are any problems, send me a message at once."

"Aye, my lord. We'll keep on keeping on. No need to worry."

Every time someone told him that, his concern only went up. Maybe he was a glutton for punishment, but he worried most when things seemed to be going well.

CHAPTER 4

W olfric paced in the dining room, his uncomfortable, too-tight formal tunic threatening to strangle him. Two days had passed since the gala and he'd finally sent an invitation to Jade and her uncle to join him at the palace for dinner. The cook had spared no effort to prepare a fine meal, the mouthwatering scent of which filled the air. Now he just needed his guests to show up.

He finally forced himself to stop and sit down. He needed to make a good impression and having them find him nervous and sweaty wouldn't do that. They'd arrive here when they got here and no amount of pacing would speed the process up.

Five minutes later the dining room door opened and the herald announced, "Baron Martinique St. Croy and his niece, Jade."

They stepped through the door which promptly closed behind them. Wolfric stood and stared at Jade. She had on a pale blue gown that hugged her curves and was just low cut enough to give a hint of treasures within.

Not wanting to be impolite, he forced his gaze away from

her to her uncle and held out his hand. "I'm pleased you could join me."

The baron hesitated then shook his hand. "It was our honor to receive your invitation."

He turned to Jade and bowed over her hand. "A pleasure to see you again, my lady."

She blushed and batted her eyelashes. "You're too kind, Your Majesty."

He released her hand with great reluctance and directed them to their seats. Neither actually sat before Wolfric. He rang a silver bell and a trio of servants entered through another door, each laden with a silver tray bearing a steaming bowl of soup and a roll. The food was placed in front of each diner, the servants bowed, and the three of them retreated to the kitchen to await Wolfric's summons.

After a couple spoonfuls of the rich broth, Wolfric peeked over to see if Jade was enjoying her meal. When he did their eyes met and she smiled.

His heart skipped a beat. By all the angels, she was beautiful.

"This is wonderful, Your Majesty," the baron said, breaking the moment.

"I'll be sure to share your compliments with the cook. Why don't you tell me a little more about St. Croy Barony?"

"Oh, it's a typical backwater barony. St. Croy Castle is built on a cliff overlooking the plains of Rolan. We raise cattle mostly and thanks to you we no longer lose them to Rolan rustlers."

"Happy to be of service." Wolfric turned back to Jade. "What do you like about the barony? Any secret places worth mentioning?"

She got a wistful look on her lovely face. "Not in the

barony, but before the war I used to go to Rolan, a little town by the sea called Blue Cove. It was the most beautiful place I've ever seen. I made another visit just before we came here, hence my tan."

Wolfric looked at her smooth skin and pictured it glistening as she emerged from the sea. What a sight that must have been.

The main course came next followed by dessert. They chatted about inconsequential things. Jade had a taste for a crystal carver from Lux and Wolfric stored the name away for later. One of his designs would make a fine gift for their next visit.

Finally the baron yawned and said, "It's been a wonderful visit, Your Majesty, but I'm about to fall asleep on your table. Perhaps we should call it a night."

"Of course." He rose and they joined him. "We'll have to do this again soon."

"I'd like that very much," Jade said.

"Indeed," her uncle agreed. "Though if we eat like this every time, I'll get fat."

Wolfric offered a polite chuckle at the poor joke and rang for the servants to guide them out. His gaze followed Jade until they were out of sight. He very much looked forward to a private meeting with her.

CHAPTER 5

When Otto appeared in his master's tower, he was greeted by her frowning face. That, more than the cold, sent a chill up his spine. What could have happened in the netherworld to put her in a sour mood?

"I hadn't expected to see you again so soon," she said.

"I was hoping for some advice, Master. I'm in the process of planning the trip to the Celestial Empire and given the distance it will be necessary to make a stop somewhere for supplies. Unfortunately, we know next to nothing about our two best options, the Island of Giant Beasts and the Land of the Demon Binders."

"Stick to the island," she said. "Even the Arcane Lords avoided the Demon Binders."

More curious than ever Otto asked, "Why? Is their magic so powerful?"

"They're demon worshipers, priests who gain power from serving one of the nine lords of Hell. We didn't fear their power and Amet, on occasion, had dealings with the forces of Hell. They had an understanding that we wouldn't meddle in their business and they wouldn't trouble our lands. The easiest way to accomplish that was to avoid them altogether. Frankly, I have no idea what they might do if you sailed into one of their ports and I recommend you avoid doing so."

That was exactly Otto's plan, but if worst came to worst and he had no choice, it helped to have some idea what they might run into.

Otto stood and bowed. "Thank you, Master."

He started to become one with the ether, stopped, and asked, "Is all well? You seem a bit... out of sorts."

"I am perfectly fine considering I'm a disembodied spirit trapped in the netherworld. Now, if you have no more questions, leave me in peace."

Otto couldn't remember ever seeing his master in a self-pitying mood. Angry certainly. Amused or annoyed at his ignorance, all the time. Still, a certain amount of depression was probably unavoidable given her circumstances.

Discretion being the better part of valor, Otto vanished into the ether and reappeared in the courtyard of Castle Shenk. There was no sign of violence outside and no pacing Graves. He took both of these things as a good sign.

A hard rap on the door brought a guard who hastened to let him in. The man wore no mail, another good sign.

"Welcome, Lord Shenk." The guard closed the door, sealing out the worst of the cold.

"How fare things between my father and brother?"

"Better, my lord. The baroness's return did wonders for the mood."

"Splendid. Where is my mother now?"

"I believe she's up in her sewing room."

"And Father?"

"We caught a thief two days ago in the village. The baron is... punishing him."

"Thank you." Otto left the guard and trotted upstairs.

He paused in front of the door to his old room. It seemed a lifetime ago that he had lived here. Certainly he had been a different person. Weak and afraid of everything, he cowered before his father and brother. When he thought back on it, he couldn't help the disgust that filled him. No wonder Father never respected him. He'd never respected himself.

Otto left the memories as well as his room behind and continued down the hall to Mother's sewing room. The door was open a crack, but he knocked anyway before pushing it open. She sat in the sun, a modest pile of socks at her feet waiting to be fixed. Her embroidery frame didn't have a new project in it yet, but knowing Mother, that would change as soon as she finished with the socks.

She looked away from her work as he closed the door and smiled. "This is a nice surprise. What brings you here?"

Otto crossed the room and kissed her cheek. "I came to count the bodies. Happily, I came up with zero."

She snorted a laugh. "Your father mentioned you paying them a visit before I got back. Did you really think one of them might hurt me?"

"You know how Stephan gets. Besides, I promised Axel I'd have a talk with everyone. Since all's quiet, I assume you worked some magic of your own."

"Hardly. I just suggested a few changes. Your father gave Stephan some of the double eagles as well as more day-to-day responsibility for running the barony. The truth is, he should have done that years ago. But you know how stubborn he can be."

Otto did know. "And how is Stephan handling his duties?"

"He hasn't killed or maimed anyone, so that's a start. I fear he's finding that being baron is a good deal less exciting than he imagined. And how are things in Garen?"

"Quiet for the moment. Abby's sleeping more and crying less which pleases everyone. There appear to be no major plots against the government, which frees me up to prepare for my next journey."

"Where to this time?"

"The Celestial Empire."

Her eyes widened. "That's an even longer trip than your last."

Otto nodded. "Nearly twice as long in fact. It may be over a year, round trip. I can't say I'm looking forward to it, but that's where I need to go regardless."

"Are you staying for dinner?"

"Sorry, I've got to get back. I just wanted to check in and see if you needed anything."

"No, we're good here. I do appreciate your concern though."

Some of the tension left him. Knowing she was safe made it easier to do what he had to. "Goodbye, Mother. Be well."

He became one with the ether and vanished.

CHAPTER 6

A day or two after visiting Lord Karonin and his family, Otto found himself back at the warehouse. At the rear of the building, Ulf busied himself filling vials with his latest alchemical concoction. Given the lack of stinking, he assumed this one was neither explosive nor flammable.

Otto expected a report from Allen and Sin today, but what he got was Hans, Corina, and the rest of the squad seated around a table playing cards. He didn't bother getting annoyed with them. With nothing to do, it was as good a way to pass the time as any.

They hurried to stand, but Otto motioned them back to their seats. "Where are Sin and Allen? I expected them to be awaiting my arrival."

"Allen's meeting one of the St. Croy serving girls for breakfast," Hans said. "He should be here before long."

"Sin mentioned running down a last-minute lead as well," Corina added. "Do we have time for a lesson?"

"Have you mastered extending all your senses?" Otto asked.

"All but smell. For some reason I can't connect to my nose the way I want to."

"You need to connect to the smell receptors in your brain then create a construct that looks like a nose to collect the scent. No new lessons until you master that."

She pouted but didn't complain.

Otto strode back to Ulf's workbench. "Since we have time, tell me again about the Lords of Alchemy."

"What would you like to know?" Ulf placed the empty flask in front of him and capped the final vial. "I can't tell you much as my own interactions with them amounted to little more than my trial and exile."

"How much influence do they wield?"

"A great deal. They oversee all alchemists in the empire. The head of their order serves as one of the emperor's chief advisors. They also aid both the guards and the army in times of conflict. Not that there's much conflict in the empire. My people tend to obedience. Over a thousand years of reasonably benevolent rule by the same family and no wars worthy of the name make for a calm populace."

"I imagine anyone that complains is dealt with harshly."

"Very. You will have no hope of completing your mission without dealing with the lords. Assuming you can get into the empire in the first place."

Ulf had mentioned before that outsiders weren't welcome. Otto smiled. That would be a problem to worry about after he arrived. "You don't even know what my mission is."

Ulf shook his head. "Doesn't matter. Anything of importance that happens in the empire will involve them. And rest assured, my skills are nothing compared to theirs."

Otto hoped to avoid a fight. He really just wanted to trade for the Heart. Maybe mithril, maybe something else. Within reason, he'd give whatever he had to in order to claim the artifact.

The trapdoor hidden in the warehouse floor swung up and Sin climbed out. She wore her usual skintight black leather. Her long, dark hair was gathered at the nape of her neck and a small patch of dirt clung to her pale cheek.

She closed the door and ambled over to him. "Lord Shenk, I apologize for keeping you waiting. One of my girls contacted me at the last minute."

"I only just arrived. What have you learned?"

"The baron hired three servants for their time in Garen: a cleaning girl, a cook, and a doorman. They also brought one servant with them, a dark-skinned man in his thirties that oversees everything in the household. I learned little of the inner workings of the house. Allen is trying to finagle some information out of the cleaner. She gets the mornings off."

"I'll bet he is. And the other matter?"

"Right, one of the girls I arranged for the emperor's harem contacted me. It seems he hasn't been to see them in over a week. Since his attentions had been quite regular before that, they wanted to let me know."

Otto scratched his cheek. If Wolfric wasn't visiting the harem, the only explanation was the noble girl. Had the fool gone and fallen in love? Otto dearly hoped not. Men in love seldom made good decisions. He needed to meet this noble-woman and try to learn her true intentions. But if Wolfric really had fallen for her, he couldn't do anything drastic. One bad word from the girl could cause him a huge headache.

The warehouse door slammed open and Allen burst in. "Am I late? I am, sorry. It took longer than I expected to get anything useful out of her."

Otto gestured and the door shut behind Allen, cutting off the chill breeze. "So you did learn something useful?"

"Well…"

Otto offered a silent prayer for patience. "Just spit it out."

"Okay, as far as the cleaning girl knows, there's nothing happening. The only weird thing she noticed was that the servant they brought with them, a Mr. Ahmed, speaks a strange language from time to time."

"Strange language?" Otto frowned. For the last thousand-plus years, everyone had spoken the same language. Outside of Lord Karonin's older books, he'd never seen or heard another language. "Who, exactly, does he speak this strange language with?"

"The niece, Jade. She only overheard them a couple times, but whatever they were saying, it wasn't something she understood."

"Interesting. Thank you both."

It seemed the only way Otto would solve this mystery was to speak with the woman herself. He'd have to ask Wolfric to arrange it.

CHAPTER 7

Wolfric took deep breaths to calm his racing heart. He'd never felt this way before meeting a woman before. Jade brought out all sorts of emotions in him. Powerful ones, he thought. Dangerous ones, according to Otto. His dear friend wanted to meet Jade and the idea appealed to and frightened him in equal measure.

Emperor or not, Wolfric held no illusions about the fate of the empire if Otto withdrew his support. He also knew he loved Jade and wouldn't give her up. Not even at Otto's suggestion.

Tonight, he and Jade were meeting in his private dining room and without her uncle as a chaperone. It would be his first time alone with her and just thinking about it made his hands sweat.

He smiled and shook his head. Look at him. Anyone that saw him so out of sorts would think this was his first encounter with a woman. It wasn't, by any means, but it might have been the first time he had ever been alone with a woman that actually meant more to him than a quick tumble.

He reached down and adjusted a fork that didn't perfectly line up with the spoon. Before he could find anything else to fiddle with, the dining room door opened and Jade walked in.

Wolfric's breath caught in his throat. Tonight she wore a gown of deep crimson cut in a far more revealing style than anything she'd worn before. He tried to think of something to say and failed.

Jade smiled at his reaction. "You like the dress? I bought it today on a shopping trip to your Gold Ward. There were many beautiful things there, far more than we have back home."

"The dress is very nice, but you make it beautiful. Please sit. The first course will be along shortly."

He pulled out her chair and she sat, smoothing her skirt under her.

Wolfric took his seat across from her. Better to get it out of the way, then he'd be free to enjoy himself. "My friend and advisor has asked to meet you. I thought we might have lunch together one day soon."

She chewed her lip and looked away. "I've heard stories, mostly told by people of Rolan coming to trade in the barony. They say he's done awful things. That your friend is an evil wizard bent on destroying the world."

Wolfric couldn't stop himself from laughing. When Jade's eyes flashed with anger he realized his mistake. "Forgive me. I didn't mean to make light of your concern, but anyone calling Otto evil has never met him. The only reason we have an empire, and you and your uncle aren't living under Rolan's rule, is because of his tireless efforts. Everyone in Garenland owes him a debt for all he's done."

"I would have thought he owed you the debt," she said. "He serves at your pleasure, not the other way around."

Wolfric wondered sometimes how true that was, but now

was not the time to point out his insecurities. "Be that as it may, if we are to have a life together, you will need to meet Otto. And in this case, I believe sooner is better. You can see he's not a monster and he can see you're not a grifter."

Her frown twisted her lovely features in unpleasant ways. "Grifter? Is that what he thinks, that I want money?"

Wolfric sighed. He was really making a mess of this. "Otto mentioned that it was a possibility. I assured him he was wrong. Even in the short time I've known you, I can tell you aren't that sort of person. For the good of the empire, I can't have my best friend and the woman I love mistrustful of each other. So, we will have lunch together, right here, in two days. Just the three of us. Okay?"

She nodded as the door opened and a pair of servants entered carrying salads and a carafe of wine. The food was placed in front of them and the servants withdrew.

When they'd gone Wolfric said, "Let's not talk any more about Otto. Lunch will take care of itself. There are far more pleasant subjects we can discuss."

And so they did. Through three courses they talked about history and art and the future. When the last bite of cake was gone Jade sighed and stretched, giving him an eyeful of her curves.

"Another wonderful meal." Her smile turned sly. "What shall we do now?"

Her subtle suggestion made his heart race. He forced himself to calm down. Just once he wanted to do things right. "Perhaps we should say goodnight."

Jade's eyes widened in surprise. Clearly that wasn't the response she expected.

"I want to wait. Our first time together should be special, not some after-dinner tumble."

"That's very sweet." She leaned over and kissed him on the lips. Heat flooded him and it took everything in him to remember what he'd just said. "Consider that a promise for the future."

He walked her out of the dining room before staggering back to his bed, alone. Maybe waiting hadn't been the right decision after all.

CHAPTER 8

"Where are we going again and why am I coming with you instead of Corina or your actual wife?" Sin walked through Gold Ward beside Otto as they went to visit Baron St. Croy. Instead of her usual skintight leathers or a dress that would make a whore blush, Sin had on a simple but stylish white skirt and blue blouse. She cleaned up nicely, he couldn't deny that.

So nicely, in fact, that more than one head turned as they passed despite the heavy cloak that protected her from the bitter cold. If he had cared what Annamaria thought, he might have worried about word getting back to her. However, that was hardly a concern for either of them now.

For a midmorning this time of year in Gold Ward, the streets had quite a few people out and about. He'd expected to find the streets empty as the rich and powerful hunkered down by their fires. He shrugged and put the locals out of his mind.

"You're with me because Corina is still too young and inexperienced to notice subtle things that might be wrong. As for Annamaria, I prefer not to have backup that would just as soon see me dead. It's usually best to only have one enemy at a time to worry about if at all possible. Remember, you're playing the part of my secretary. Don't speak unless you're asked a question."

"I know. We already went over all this at the warehouse. Don't worry, I've played plenty of parts over the years, though none as boring as a secretary."

Otto could well imagine the parts she'd played. They reached the rented villa and strode up to the front door. The design wasn't all that different from the Crow's Nest, the former home of the thieves guild and current residence of the former king of Lasil. The paint differed, the rental being a bright white instead of dark gray.

"How much do you suppose to rent a place like this?" Sin asked.

"A lot for a commoner and a trifle for a nobleman." Otto knocked. "All depends on your point of view."

The door opened and a broad-shouldered man in a black and white servant's uniform looked them over. Dark, narrow eyes brushed past Otto, took a little longer with Sin, then returned to Otto.

"Do you have an appointment?"

"No. My name is Otto Shenk and I would like a few minutes of the baron's time."

"You should send your servant to make an appointment then. There are many people that wish to speak with Baron St. Croy."

He wasn't seriously going to close the door in Otto's face? No servant could be that stupid.

Then again, as the door started to swing shut, maybe he could. A flick of Otto's ring and a bit of ether bound the door's hinges open.

Otto let his expression grow hard. "I wasn't asking."

The muscles in the servant's shoulders bulged as he tried to force the door shut. He was more likely to break the wood than Otto's spell.

"Ahmed?" a voice called from deeper in the villa. "What's the trouble?"

"We have a visitor that didn't make an appointment, my lord."

A moment later a balding, middle-aged man dressed in a dark silk tunic and matching pants stopped behind the servant's left shoulder. The baron looked his visitors over and asked, "And who might you be, sir?"

"Otto Shenk."

The baron's eyes widened a fraction. "Ah. I've been expecting you. It's alright, Ahmed. This is the emperor's chief advisor. He hardly needs to make an appointment to visit a backwater baron like me. Please, come in."

With a final glare, Ahmed moved aside. The baron guided them to a sitting room furnished with the usual collection of overstuffed leather chairs and a coffee table. He motioned Otto and Sin towards two of the chairs then sat across from them.

Sin crossed her legs to draw his attention, just as she was supposed to. Being a man with a pulse, Baron St. Croy flicked a glance at her smooth calf before turning back to Otto who had used the distraction to prepare himself to watch for lies along with weaving a silence spell around them.

"I imagine you're here to talk about Jade," the baron said.

"Yes. It's just a standard precaution whenever anyone gets close to the emperor. I'm sure you understand."

"I do. As I said, I've been expecting your visit since the gala. They had their first night alone last night, so I assume things

41

are getting more serious." The baron drummed his thin fingers on his knee while his toe tapped at a rapid clip.

"That's my assumption as well. Shall we start with what happened to her parents?"

"My sister and her husband died in a fire five years ago. A horrible accident involving an oil lamp. That's why I prefer to use Lux crystals."

"She came to stay with you after that?"

"Not immediately afterward. At the time, Jade was fourteen and adventurous. That's why she wasn't home when the fire happened."

"And her intentions toward Emperor Wolfric?"

"I believe her intentions are genuine."

So far he hadn't lied, but he was also answering in such a way that made it difficult to tell. His tension and the vagueness put Otto on alert. Something was up, he just needed to figure out what.

Time for a more direct question. "Did you bring her to the gala specifically to meet the emperor in hopes of her seducing him?"

"Yes. His Majesty hasn't taken a wife yet. Having the emperor as an in-law could only be good for my barony."

All true. Otto considered his next question carefully. Maybe just a blunt yes or no would be best. Hard to talk your way around those. On the other hand, he didn't want to do anything that might aggravate Wolfric. These things were so much easier when the emperor wasn't directly involved.

Sin tugged on his sleeve and he spotted the servant entering from a different door. Ahmed bowed. "My lord, you have a meeting with Count Carne in five minutes."

That was a dead lie. Probably an excuse to end the conversation before the baron said anything obviously incriminating.

Otto stood. "That's okay. Thank you for speaking with me. Can't be too careful where the emperor is concerned."

"I understand completely. Stop again anytime."

Otto and Sin saw themselves out. As soon as they were clear of the villa she asked, "What do you think?"

"They're hiding something. Whether simple greed or something more nefarious, I'm not sure yet. What about you?"

"That servant isn't an ordinary servant. The way he moves suggests some military training. He's probably a bodyguard as well."

"Interesting. I barely even looked at him. This is exactly why I brought you along."

They made their way back to the warehouse. Otto's mind raced with the possibilities. Unfortunately, the only way to find out for sure risked angering Wolfric and Otto needed him happy and going with the program.

Maybe when he met Jade in person, she'd reveal herself, one way or another.

CHAPTER 9

Two days passed quickly and Otto found himself on his way to the palace for a much-anticipated lunch with Wolfric and Jade. The air held the sharpest edge so far this winter and even with his magic, the chill reached Otto's bones. Once again he was happy that Franken Manor sat only a short walk from the castle.

Despite their best efforts, neither Allen or Sin had come up with any more information about the baron and his niece. As usual, it fell to Otto to find the truth of the matter. Unlike a proper interrogation, he would have to approach Jade with kid gloves lest he anger Wolfric. It felt like he was wading into a trap-laden battlefield with no map or reinforcements.

The guards nodded as he passed and Otto made his way straight to the emperor's private dining room. The palace guards on duty outside opened the door for him. Inside he found Wolfric pacing and wringing his hands. He wore his finest black and gold tunic and trousers and his boots had been polished to a mirror shine.

Jade, it seemed, had yet to arrive.

"I've seen men awaiting the gallows that looked less nervous than you," Otto said. "Is all well?"

"Yes, no, I'm not sure." Wolfric finally stopped and looked at him. "You and Jade are the most important people in my life now and I want you to get along. When I suggested this lunch, she looked terrified. Like you were going to turn her into the main course."

Otto chuckled, but inside he went cold. If Wolfric already considered her that important, he would need to be even more careful.

"My friend, all I want—all I have ever wanted—was for you to be happy and the empire strong and peaceful. If this woman brings you the former without endangering the latter, I will love her like my own sister."

"Really?"

"I swear by all the angels in Heaven and all the demons in Hell. But just so there are no surprises, I did pay her uncle a visit yesterday." Wolfric blanched and Otto hastened to add, "A simple background check. Rest assured I was perfectly polite and no threats were made. I believe he expected me sooner."

Wolfric sat, poured himself a glass of red wine, and drank it down in one go. "And how did you find the baron?"

"Evasive, but not outright dishonest. He's hiding something, but whether it's a threat or something embarrassing I don't know. His servant claimed he had another meeting, but that was a lie. I think he wanted to end our conversation before I had a chance to learn more."

"What do you propose to do about it?" Wolfric barely forced the words out.

"I would like, with your permission of course, to ask her a few gentle questions. Just to clarify one or two things."

Wolfric chewed his lip then nodded. "She's already terrified of you, so please, don't upset her. The poor woman has already lost both her parents."

"Yes, in a fire. Her uncle mentioned that. Don't worry, it'll be fine."

Ten minutes later the door opened again and Jade entered. She wore a pale-yellow dress and her hair was up in a bun. Two small pieces of silver jewelry, a ring and a necklace, were her only decorations. Not that she needed more. In her own innocent way, Jade could have given Sin a run for her money in the beauty department.

She took one peek at Otto and quickly looked away. Could she possibly be that frightened of him? Most of the things Otto had done that were apt to frighten someone weren't exactly public knowledge.

Wolfric hurried over and helped his fragile flower into a chair. He sat beside her and Otto took the chair directly opposite. He shifted his vision to watch how her brain reacted to his words. He hoped for everyone's sake she was exactly what she said, a noble girl that had fallen in love with an emperor. Based on all he knew about the nobility, Otto seriously doubted that was possible.

"It's a pleasure to meet you at last," Otto said. "Wolfric's told me a great deal about you, though he may have underplayed your beauty."

"Lord Shenk," she said, her voice little more than a whisper. "Your reputation precedes you."

No lie there, so far so good.

"I stopped by to see your uncle the other day, but other business cut our chat short. I was hoping to learn more about St. Croy Barony. I've never visited the southern provinces of Garenland. I assume it's much different from the central district."

"It's much like Rolan. Before the war, we crossed the border all the time. Our neighboring baron was on good terms with Uncle. I even spent an occasional summer in Rolan, at a town called Blue Cove."

"I'm not familiar with it," Otto said. So far she hadn't lied.

"It's a fishing village on the coast. The clearest water you've ever seen. And the food was beyond compare. I should very much like to visit more often."

"You said you spent some time there this summer since the war had ended," Wolfric said. "Had it changed much?"

"Not at all. In fact, it was like the war never touched it."

"I'll have to take a trip there some time," Otto said. "Assuming my work ever permits. One last thing and then I promise I'll trouble you no more. Were you friendly with any Rolan nobles?"

She shook her head. "My parents didn't approve of Uncle getting so close to nobles from another nation."

That was a lie! Why she lied about it he couldn't say, but she clearly just made that last sentence up. Otto forced himself to focus on what came next.

"By the time they died, things had become so tense, even Uncle stopped visiting his neighbors regularly."

"Well," Wolfric said. "Now that we're all one big happy empire, hopefully he can resume his visits. If that's everything, perhaps we should eat."

"Excellent idea," Otto said.

As soon as they were finished, he would have to pay a visit to Rolan. Whatever she was hiding, Otto meant to learn the truth.

After lunch with Wolfric and Otto, Jade made her way back to their rented villa. As she walked through Gold Ward, doing her best to project timidity and fear, she reviewed everything that had happened before and during the meal.

Otto was clearly suspicious of her. Jade's best guess was that he imagined her as some sort of gold digger looking to marry well. Not an unreasonable theory given Wolfric's position. If he had any inkling of her true purpose, Jade had no doubt she would currently be sitting in a dark hole awaiting questioning and execution.

But just because he didn't suspect her true motives now, didn't mean he wouldn't figure it out. They needed to move and move fast.

She pushed the villa door open rather than wait for a servant. Ahmed needed to move his timetable up as well. Killing the wizard would give her a little more time to finish with Wolfric.

Baron St. Croy poked his head out of one of the doors as she stalked by. Jade just glared at him until he pulled back out of sight. The old fool had done his job. As long as he stayed out of the way, he might live through this. After all, no one had paid the Coiled Serpent to kill him.

At the top of the stairs she met Ahmed and led him to one of the unused bedrooms. When they were out of sight she said, "You need to move against Otto soon. He's becoming suspicious of me. If we delay too long, he'll figure out who we really are."

"He was here asking questions earlier," Ahmed said. "I don't think the old man said anything incriminating and I cut them off as quickly as possible given my supposed position. As for moving soon, I still haven't come up with a good plan."

"What about taking the baby and using it as bait? That was what we talked about with our local contacts."

"I know, but it's not really my way. A direct confrontation would suit me better."

Jade grimaced. He had far too many scruples for someone in their line of work. "You don't have to hurt the baby, just use it to lure him out of the city away from all the soldiers. Then you can have your one-on-one fight. After you kill him, take the brat back to a church or something. They'll make sure she gets to her mother."

Ahmed's scowl deepened, but he nodded. "Very well. I shall begin scouting the estate. Two days should be enough."

"Good. I'll try to time my move against Wolfric for the same moment. If the Reaper stands with us, both our targets will be dead and we long gone before anyone knows what happened."

CHAPTER 10

"Where are we going again?" Allen asked as he and Lord Shenk made their way through Gold Ward toward the portal.

His ill-humored employer had roused him at the unholy hour of dawn, ordered him to prepare for a journey, and waited with poorly concealed impatience for him to dress and belt on his sword. An explanation had been offered, but Allen had been too exhausted to follow the whole thing.

"We're going to Rolan. I'll arrange a horse and supplies for you, then you'll ride to a town on the coast called Blue Cove. I want you to find out if Jade spent time there regularly. A noblewoman is bound to stand out, so either way it won't take you long to learn the truth."

"Right." Allen forced his brain to focus. "And I'm doing this why?"

Lord Shenk turned to look at him with those cold eyes. "You mean besides me telling you to?"

Allen swallowed hard. "Uh, yeah, besides that."

"Because I want to know if she lied about it. If she did, she may have lied about other things. The emperor is besotted with this woman. If she's trouble, I need proof that I can show him. One little lie might not be enough, but it is a start. I need to know everything before the love-struck fool proposes."

Allen stared for a moment. He hadn't realized the emperor was so deeply involved with anyone. He'd seen the girls Sin picked out for his private harem. Why in the world would anyone choose to marry when he had those beauties on standby? Of course, being the emperor, he could probably enjoy the wife and whatever side action he wanted.

"Sounds simple enough." Allen resigned himself to days of riding through the tedious plains of Rolan. The serving girls would keep the tavern running. At this point he was seriously considering turning it over to them. It seemed he seldom had time to handle anything anymore.

"I hope you're right," Lord Shenk said.

They reached the fort a few minutes later and received a welcome of such enthusiasm you'd have thought Lord Shenk was their husband returned from two weeks at sea. The reaction experienced soldiers gave a man barely in his twenties never failed to impress Allen. Lord Shenk carried himself with the sort of confidence only the nobility had. It had to be in their blood.

As soon as the portal opened, they stepped through and emerged in a nearly identical fort in Rolan. More smart salutes greeted them. Allen could barely see the soldiers by the light of the quickly dimming portal. Only the crackling magic of the runes illuminated the yard. They were far enough west that the sun hadn't actually risen yet.

"How may we be of service, my lord?" a man Allen took for the fort commander asked.

"Fetch Oskar and have a horse prepared for my man. He'll need a week of supplies and a bit of coin."

"Of course." The commander barked orders and soon one soldier was running towards the stable and a second toward the barracks.

A couple minutes later, a figure emerged from the barracks and jogged toward them. He was fairly young, with short brown hair and gray, civilian clothes. He saluted like a soldier, fist to heart, and said, "Lord Shenk. How may I be of service?"

"What do you know about a fishing village called Blue Cove?"

Oskar frowned and chewed the inside of his lip. Allen knew that expression and a moment later the man said, "I fear I've never heard of it. Is there trouble?"

"I don't know yet, but I hope to get some answers there." Lord Shenk turned to Allen. "Looks like you're going in blind. I don't expect any real trouble, but be careful all the same. Replacing you would be an inconvenience."

"For both of us, my lord," Allen said.

"Would you like me to join him, my lord?" Oskar asked. "Matters in the capital have been quiet and I would like to do something useful."

"Excellent idea, Oskar. Allen will fill you in on the mission as you ride. Oh, I almost forgot." Lord Shenk dug something out of his pocket and handed it to Allen.

It looked like a glass stick about six inches long. A flash like lightning ran the length of it so quickly Allen thought he might have imagined it.

"This is my latest experiment. I haven't tested it yet, so this is the perfect opportunity. As soon as you learn whether or not Jade lied to me, snap that and speak a message up to ten words. They will be carried to me through the ether. There's no need for you to hang around, either. As soon as you complete your investigation, return to Garen. Not you, Oskar. You can resume your duties here."

Oskar saluted again and Allen nodded.

"We won't let you down, never fear," Allen said.

Lord Shenk just gave him a look before stepping back through the portal.

CHAPTER 11

Annamaria watched the snow fall as it added yet another layer over her garden. The cold and snow combined to keep her in the house. She tried going for a walk the other day, but the bitter chill turned her back before she reached the end of the entry path. She hated winters and always had.

She even found she missed Otto's mother. Katharina had been a welcome companion. Though she obviously didn't tell the older woman everything, there was plenty they could talk about. And the advice she'd offered for tending to Abby had been heaven sent. The little one hardly cried at all anymore. Whether she had her mother-in-law to thank for that or Abby just grew out of her fussy spell, Annamaria neither knew nor cared.

Thinking about Katharina naturally brought her back to Otto. Her husband spent little time at the mansion despite the weather. That was probably just as well. They no longer argued, but that was mostly because they seldom spoke. Otto made it perfectly clear he didn't care what she did or who she did it with. For her part, Annamaria no longer hated him with the passion she once did. Maybe it was inevitable that such a powerful emotion would dim with time. Now all she felt was numb resignation.

Her life was what it was. For better or worse, nothing would change that.

She turned from the window and started toward the bookcase. She hadn't read anything in some time. Maybe a nice romance would take her mind off her troubles.

Halfway to the bookcase, a scream rang out. Her stomach dropped and she ran for the door.

Outside, the hall was empty. The next-door bedroom stood wide open. She ran down the hall and looked inside.

Mimi lay on the floor, limp and unmoving. Abby's crib was empty and the bedroom window wide open.

The room spun and it took all her will not to collapse. Two deep breaths steadied her a little.

She hurried toward the crib, stepping over Mimi in her haste. A rolled-up scroll sat on the white satin sheets.

Before she had a chance to read it, pounding footsteps filled the hall. A guard stepped into the doorway. "What happened, Lady Shenk?"

"Abby's been taken. Fetch my brother-in-law. He's a scout, maybe he can track down whoever did this."

The guard said something over his shoulder and more sounds of running filled the air. Annamaria unrolled the scroll and read.

The message was short and to the point. If Otto wanted to see his daughter again, he needed to come to a cabin beyond the city walls at midnight tonight. Fail to comply and Abby would be sent back to him in pieces.

If that was the kidnappers' demand, Abby was doomed.

Otto cared nothing for the child. If her head showed up on the front step, he wouldn't even blink. Certainly there was no chance of him walking into an obvious trap.

She let the note fall from her nerveless fingers and knelt beside Mimi. A light touch of the maid's neck revealed a strong pulse. Seemed she'd only been knocked out. That was a small kindness.

"What happened?"

Annamaria looked up to find Axel standing in the doorway. "Someone took Abby. They want Otto to come tonight or they'll kill her. Can you find whoever did this?"

"My men are searching outside as we speak, but anyone skilled enough to sneak past your father's guards will doubtlessly be long gone by now."

His words snuffed out the tiny flicker of hope she'd been nursing. "Then Abby's doomed. I don't even know where Otto is, much less how to send him a message by tonight."

"I'll find him and tell him. Don't worry, we'll do everything we can to get her back."

She appreciated his kind words, but clearly Otto hadn't told him the truth about Abby's father. Still, maybe he could talk his brother into doing something. She resolved to hang on to that hope until the last possible moment.

"I'm counting on you."

○

Otto stood at a table in the warehouse and studied a map of the world. He had arranged for a scribe to resize one he found in Lord Karonin's books. The woman charged a fortune, but her work was worth every copper. Using Captain Wainwright's course, Otto had drawn a line with their rough course. He'd hoped to find some way to bypass both stops and go straight for the Celestial Empire. Try as he might, there just seemed no way to manage it.

He straightened and worked a kink out of his neck. What time was it? The warehouse had no windows so he couldn't tell. A quick glance at the guys revealed that the card game was still well underway. He needed to find something for them to do, but couldn't think of anything. He didn't want Hans and his squad losing their edge. Or passing their bad habits on to Corina.

The girl seemed to sense his gaze on her and looked up, smiling.

Before Otto had a chance to say anything, the door burst open and Axel strode in looking as upset as Otto had seen him in a long time. Maybe ever.

"What is it?" Otto asked.

Off to his side, the game was forgotten and everyone had stood.

Axel ignored the squad and said, "Your daughter has been kidnapped."

Otto stared for a moment. Who would be stupid enough to kidnap Abby? The answer came a moment later. Someone that assumed he'd care what happened to the girl.

"Aren't you going to say anything?" Axel asked.

"What would you like me to say? Should I wail and tear at my clothes? Would that help? I need to think clearly. Let's head to the mansion and you can tell me everything."

Hans took a step to join them, but Otto held up a hand. "Stay here and guard the armor. If this is a distraction someone might make a move against the warehouse. Corina, come with me. I'll need you at the mansion to keep an eye on Annamaria."

"Yes, Master." She hurried over, pausing only to collect her heavy cloak, before the three of them set out.

It was earlier than Otto thought, middle of the afternoon maybe. Whoever took Abby must have been a brazen fool. Sneaking onto the property in broad daylight. What did that say about their security? Changes would have to be made. He couldn't have these distractions popping up at random.

"Tell me everything," Otto said.

Axel did so, the little he knew. Apparently, the scouts had tracked the kidnapper as far as the edge of the property then lost him in the city. No surprise there. Tracking one person in a city of tens of thousands would be beyond even the scouts' considerable talents.

"Your wife is distraught and when I left the maid had awoken. According to the note, you're to go to a cabin outside the city at midnight. It's obviously a trap."

"Of course it is. I knew that the moment you said they took Abby. Whoever did this is going to wish they chose someone else to threaten. I'm going to rip their guts out while using magic to keep them conscious through the pain. Before I'm done they will beg for death. If I'm feeling generous, I might grant their wish."

"What do you want me to do, Master?"

"Keep an eye on Annamaria. I can't imagine this is an attempt to lure me away to strike at her, but I'm taking no chances. Axel, if you'd deploy your scouts for the same reason, I would be grateful."

"Of course," Axel said. "If you hadn't said anything, I would have suggested that very thing."

The rest of the trip passed without conversation and soon they stood before the gates of Franken Manor. The guards on duty, both of them shivering against the cold, looked away as he got close. At least they had the good sense to be embarrassed. Otto had no idea what Edwyn paid them, but clearly it was more than they were worth.

They went in through the main entrance and Otto shrugged off his cloak. He'd barely taken a step past the entryway when Annamaria said, "Otto."

She stood at the top of the stairs looking down at him. Otto sighed and turned to the others. "Give us a minute."

He went upstairs alone, keeping silent until they were in her room and the door was closed. Annamaria stared at him, her eyes wide and pleading. "You have to get her back. Please. I'll do anything you want; be the wife you've always dreamed of. Just name your price and it's yours if you save Abby."

Otto saw the truth of her offer, but he no longer cared. "You have nothing I want. I will save Abby and deal with the kidnapper. Not because you ask it of me, but because someone dared come into my home and make threats. That they took something of no value to me is irrelevant. It's the unmitigated gall of the act that irritates me. Rest assured, that when I'm done, no one will ever dare threaten Abby again."

Some of the tension went out of Annamaria. "That is enough for me. As to my thanks, you will have them whether you want them or not."

"I'll leave Axel and his men on watch as well as Corina. You'll be safe until I return. There is something I'll need from you."

"Anything."

"A little blood to guide me to Abby."

"I don't understand. Can't you find her yourself?"

"No. You noticed in the note, the kidnapper mentioned a cabin beyond the city. Do you have any idea how many cabins there are? Whoever this person is, he knows enough about wizards to know that I should be able to trace my own daughter wherever she is. The problem, of course, is obvious."

"She's not yours." Annamaria had trouble forcing the words out. That surprised Otto as she'd never had a problem with her cheating before. "You can have all you need, but not until midnight. If you don't follow the rules, he might kill her before you arrive."

Otto shrugged. A few hours more or less made no difference to him. "Axel said Mimi was awake. Did she tell you anything about the kidnapper?"

"No. Whoever did it hit her from behind. She never even saw him."

Not a surprise, but Otto had hoped for some indication of who he was about to kill.

CHAPTER 12

As Allen and Oskar guided their mounts down the
dirt road that led to the village of Blue Cove, Allen
couldn't help smiling. When Lord Shenk gave him
this job, he'd assumed it would be a miserable slog. He'd
forgotten just how much warmer it was in this part of Rolan in
the winter.

Instead of a chore, the trip had become a treat. He hadn't
been this warm in months and beyond the small collection of
stone houses, the sea was smooth and blue. Fishing boats
bobbed in the surf and a dozen tiny figures carried parcels to
and from them. He made a mental note to bring Sin here,
assuming they ever got some time to themselves.

"Is this your first visit to the ocean?" Oskar asked, jogging
him out of his thoughts.

"No. I went to Lux a couple times on business—my business, not Lord Shenk's."

"Do you like serving him?"

Allen shot him a look and Oskar laughed.

"No, he didn't tell me to ask. It's simply my curiosity."

"Do you?" Allen countered.

"Oh, yes. I've had many positions in the military, but serving as Lord Shenk's agent is the most power I've ever enjoyed. Even the local commander treats me with respect. I understand it's not me they respect, but him. Still, it's better than being looked down on and condescended to. Demanding though he is, Lord Shenk has always treated me honorably."

"Well," Allen said, surprised to hear Oskar's enthusiasm for his position, "I serve in a more informal capacity, so I don't get the reflected glory. That said, he's saved my life twice. I believe if he had to, he would save it again. Having a wizard for a patron is no bad thing."

Oskar smiled. "Agreed. Now, let's see if we can learn anything that will make him happy."

Allen grinned back then focused on the task at hand. If a noblewoman stayed here, there had to be an inn of some sort. Allen couldn't picture her bunking with a local fishing family.

The town had only one street and that street had only one building with more than a handful of rooms. If that wasn't their destination, Allen didn't know what was.

The two men pulled up out front, drawing bored looks from a pair of old men seated out front, smoking pipes and eyeing a checkerboard between them. Dirt caked their hands, streaked their faces, and covered their canvas shirts. He'd seen poorer-looking men, but not in a while.

They tied up to the hitching rail, dismounted, and pushed through the swinging doors into a nearly empty common room. A bar at the far end had a modest selection of liquor bottles behind it along with a middle-aged man that appeared to have recently returned from a famine.

The bartender eyed them with a mixture of curiosity and greed. Strangers were probably not a regular occurrence here.

Allen leaned against the bar and said, "I was hoping you could help me. We're trying to determine if a certain noble-woman spent time regularly visiting this town. You couldn't miss her. Late teens, bronze skin, generally beautiful."

The barman tilted his head back and laughed. In fact, he laughed until his face had turned red and Allen feared he might pass out. At last he gathered himself and said, "Does this look like the sort of place a high-class woman would spend her time? We barely even see our lord, much less anyone else, unless you count the tax collectors. Those bastards visit regularly. I fear you've wasted your time."

Allen nodded and glanced at Oskar who nodded. They went outside and Allen put the same question to the old men. One shook his head and the other turned his head and spat a line of tobacco juice into the dirt.

"I think we're on a wild-goose chase," Oskar said. "Should we stay the night and ride back in the morning?"

Allen blew out a sigh. "I suppose we'd better. He's not going to be very happy that she lied to him."

"No, poor girl."

They went back in, negotiated an only moderately obscene price for two rooms, and went upstairs to rest. As soon as the door closed behind him, Allen dug out Lord Shenk's magical toy, composed his thoughts, and snapped it. "The locals have no memory of Jade. She lied."

A little spark ran up his spine and then the tube disintegrated. Whether it worked or not, he couldn't say.

Allen eyed the lumpy, straw-filled mattress and grimaced. Maybe a quick nap, then he'd tend to the horses. His mission here was complete and, cold or not, he was eager to get home.

Some people thought Allen was paranoid. But he didn't mind. When you dealt with violent, dangerous people for a living, precautions weren't only prudent, they were a necessity. So when the stool he'd tucked under the door to reinforce the meager latch came crashing to the floor, he was up and out of bed in an instant.

A good thing too. A crossbow bolt buried itself in the mattress where he'd been lying a moment before.

He freed his sword in time to meet a swing from the dark blur that came charging into the room.

Shouts from outside argued that Oskar was having problems of his own.

Great, no reinforcements would be forthcoming. At least not anytime soon.

Allen shoved his attacker away. His eyes had adjusted enough to the light that he could make out the figure's dark clothes and straight-bladed shortsword. A mask covered the lower part of his face leaving only dark eyes and thin eyebrows visible. Just inside the door, an empty crossbow lay on the floor.

He had the advantage of reach and his opponent had the advantage of being dressed and fully awake. So it should be an even fight.

The killer looked back over his shoulder and Allen lunged.

A quick spin carried his target out of the way. Allen nearly lost his hand to his opponent's counter.

He squared up again, determined not to make another mistake.

The only way out for the assassin was through Allen or over the railing where a long drop to the common room floor waited.

Time was on Allen's side.

Hopefully Oskar would win his fight and come help. If they captured the man in black, Lord Shenk would no doubt be very happy to make his acquaintance.

The assassin seemed to understand his situation as he eyed Allen then the railing.

"Go ahead and jump," Allen said. "You'll be much easier to deal with nursing a broken leg."

The man in black gave a soft growl and attacked.

Allen parried a slash, countered with a thrust that forced the attacker to backpedal. Behind him the battle had gone silent.

A moment later Oskar said, "Allen? Are you okay?"

"For the moment. Any chance you can give me a hand here?"

The sound of boots on wood was followed by Oskar stopping beside him. Lord Shenk's agent had a shallow cut on his left arm that oozed blood, but otherwise he appeared unharmed.

"Do you always sleep with your boots on?" Allen asked.

"I do when I'm on a mission. You never know what might happen."

Allen could hardly argue with that. "You go high, I'll go low. Let's try and take him in one piece."

"You won't take me alive." Allen had just time enough to realize the assassin was a woman before she leapt over the rail.

He looked down. She landed on her sword, driving it all the way through her body and out her back.

Allen and Oskar shared a look. That certainly hadn't been the response Allen expected.

"A fanatic of some sort," Oskar said. "We may have stumbled into something bigger than I first thought. Can you send another message to Lord Shenk? He'll want to know about this."

"No. He only gave me one of those magic things. Let's get ready and search the bodies. I don't know about you, but more sleep seems unlikely to me."

"Agreed. The sooner we're back in Rolan City, the better."

Ten minutes later found Allen and Oskar in the latter's room standing beside a black-clad body with a deep, foot-long slash in its chest. This one was clearly a man. Allen pulled his mask off and tossed it aside. Maybe a boy would be more accurate. He looked about sixteen, if that.

A quick pat-down revealed no pockets in his black garb. They found nothing but his weapons. Downstairs, the woman —she looked a year or two older than her companion—had a similar lack of possessions. They didn't even have a coin between them.

A door slammed and they both spun, swords drawn. The innkeeper glared at them. "What's all the noise? Can't a body get some sleep without you out-of-towners tearing the place up?"

"We were attacked," Oskar said. "Perhaps you'll recognize the people involved. Come take a look."

Oskar's tone brooked no refusal so the old man shuffled over to stare down at the dead woman. "Never seen her before."

The boy upstairs drew the same response. They'd hit a dead end, literally.

CHAPTER 13

Wolfric and Jade sat side by side in his lounge, sipping wine and enjoying the roaring fire. The warm glow made her look even more beautiful in her black dress. She still wore the same simple, silver jewelry as that first night. He'd even offered to buy her something else as a gift and she declined, not wanting anyone to get the wrong idea.

And by anyone he assumed she meant Otto. Jade seemed much more at ease without him around. He supposed he couldn't blame her. Even knowing him as well as Wolfric did, he couldn't deny his friend had moments of... intensity, that some found disconcerting. For a young woman like Jade, meeting him for the first time, he fully understood how she might have been overwhelmed.

Still, all things considered, the luncheon had gone well. Nothing happened that led him to believe there was a problem. And her own behavior had been beyond reproach. Which made what he planned to do tonight even easier.

"I love you," Wolfric said. "You know that, right?"

"I do, but a girl likes to hear it said." She smiled, her lips glistening with wine. "I love you too. You are easily the finest man I've ever met."

He slipped off the sofa and onto one knee. "Then marry me. We'll rule the empire side by side."

Her eyes widened and her hands shook. For a moment he feared she might say no. Then she slipped her trembling hand into his. "Yes."

Wolfric reached into his pocket, pulled out a gold ring, and slipped it over her finger. It had two rubies flanking a large diamond. He'd wondered on occasion if he'd ever find someone to give it to. The moment he saw Jade, he knew he finally had.

"Oh, Wolfric, it's beautiful." She threw herself into his arms.

After a moment of enjoying the feeling of her wrapped around him he said, "It was my mother's. Father gave it to her when he proposed. He always hoped I'd find someone I loved as much as he did Mother to give it to. I wish he was here to meet you."

"I'm sure we would have gotten along, especially if he was anything like you."

Wolfric smiled but didn't point out just how different he and his father had been. There was no need to dredge up bad memories, not tonight. Not now.

He scooped her up into his arms. "I think it's time to celebrate."

"Mmm." She groaned and kissed his neck. "I like that idea."

CHAPTER 14

Half an hour before midnight, his battle gear—which consisted of his mithril sword and a fine dagger—strapped to his belt, Otto went to Annamaria's room. Axel and the scouts were on patrol and would remain so until he returned. If he hadn't returned by morning, they could assume he wasn't coming back and neither was Abby.

Otto shook off the negative thought. No kidnapper, no matter how skilled, had the power to defeat him. He would find whoever perpetuated this insult and deal with him accordingly.

He turned down the hall to Annamaria's room and found Corina in place in front of her door. She straightened at his approach. "I'm keeping close watch, I swear."

He gave her shoulder a squeeze. "Relax. If I didn't trust you to do this job, I would have asked someone else. I doubt there will be any trouble, but better safe than sorry."

Inside, Annamaria was huddled with Mimi. The latter had a swollen face and black eye from where she hit the floor. She started to stand when Otto entered but he gave a little shake of his head. He needed no empty gestures, especially from someone that had been through what she had.

"It's time."

"It's still early," Annamaria said.

"I need time to make the trip. Searching secondhand takes longer than if I could use my own connection. I've been patient, but there's no more room for delay. If you want Abby back, now's the time."

Annamaria stood, grim and determined. She held out her hand.

Otto drew his dagger and looked at her. Once he would have happily driven it into her chest, now he simply didn't care. No doubt his continued use of powerful magic had dulled his emotions further, just as Valtan had warned him it would. Tonight, that would be a good thing, helping him remain in full control.

A quick flick of the blade nicked her palm and a little trickle of blood oozed out. He smeared it on both sides of the blade and nodded. Mimi quickly bound the wound with a clean cloth.

"Bring her back to me," Annamaria said.

Otto refused to make a promise he wasn't certain he could keep. Instead he turned without a word and left the room. He passed Corina and made his way toward the stairs. The lights all burned in the dining room and sure enough he found Edwyn up and busy devouring a whole pie.

"You're off then?" Edwyn said after swallowing.

"Yes. If I'm not back by dawn, send a message to the emperor. The war wizards will be able to find my body."

"You'll be back and with little Abby. I have no doubts."

"I appreciate the vote of confidence." He left Edwyn to his snack and strode through the front door.

The chill wind slapped him and he put a little extra power into his shield, cutting it off. That done, he became one with the ether and focused on the connection between Annamaria's blood and Abby. The link was of course strong and an instant later he emerged in a clearing facing a modest cabin. He sank into the snow up to his shins and grimaced.

An orange glow emerged from the windows and smoke filled the air. He closed his eyes and sent his vision flying into the cabin.

There were only two rooms: a kitchen and living area, and each had an entrance. Abby lay on the dining table, bundled up in the blanket his mother had made for her, seeming none the worse for her adventure.

So far so good.

Now for the kidnapper. The man in question emerged from the kitchen, a tin cup of water in his hand. It was Baron St. Croy's servant, Ahmed. He was dressed in all black and a sword hung at his waist.

Otto wished he was more surprised, but from the beginning he'd feared something was up with them. He flicked his ring and sent a thread in to bind the man. It nearly touched him before vanishing.

Otto frowned. The only thing he'd ever encountered that created such an effect was mirrorshine, the alchemical compound Markane had provided Uther during his brief rebellion. Any doubt Otto harbored about this being a trap for him vanished like his thread.

Lucky for him, since he first learned of the substance, he'd come up with a few tricks on the not-small possibility that he ran into someone using it again. He drew his dagger and worked his way around to the back entrance, conjuring an ethereal path in front of him so every step didn't crunch in the snow.

The cabin door had only a crude, iron lock which yielded to Otto's magic in about two seconds. An ethereal tentacle caught the wine jug balanced just inside before it could shatter. He slipped through and closed the door behind him.

Light from the living area gave him a good view of the kitchen. No one had been here in a long time. Probably why the assassin chose it.

Now for his surprise.

He forged a powerful connection to his dagger, just like he used to when studying with his former master. The weapon flew up and hung in the air.

Leaving it where it was, Otto walked into the living area.

The assassin turned to face him. Ahmed looked very much the same, yet his eyes now held a hard gleam, all signs of the servant long gone. He held Abby in the crook of his left arm and a dagger in his right.

"You're punctual, very good. Since you're not a fool, I assume you know your magic won't affect me." He moved the dagger closer to Abby. "I applied the mirrorshine to my weapon as well. Any attempt to protect your daughter with magic or stop the blade will fail."

Otto moved deeper into the living room, shifting so Ahmed had to adjust his own position to face him. "So what happens now? You know the limits of mirrorshine as well as I do. I can kill you with indirect magic as easily as direct."

"But not without killing the child as well."

"True." Otto moved a little more until Ahmed stood directly in front of the kitchen door. "So I ask again. What now?"

"Now, you're going to stay very still and I'm going to

approach with your daughter in front of me. Do anything I don't like and she dies."

"You understand what I'll do to you if anything happens to her." While keeping Ahmed distracted with talk, Otto brought the dagger through the doorway and positioned it directly above the man's head.

"I lose my life and you lose your daughter." Ahmed took a step closer to Otto. "Which of us ends up hurt worse? Not the dead man certainly."

Otto adjusted the dagger again and smiled. "But there's one thing you didn't know. Something very important. Abby isn't my daughter."

Ahmed froze, stunned for an instant.

That's when Otto struck.

The dagger streaked down with all the force of his magic behind it, crashing into the assassin's skull, and piercing to the hilt.

Otto caught Abby in an ethereal cushion a foot from the floor as the assassin collapsed. She giggled when he picked her up.

"Enjoyed that, did you?" He sniffed and winced. Ahmed hadn't changed her during her captivity and Otto certainly wasn't about to. "Let's bring you back to your mother."

He'd barely taken a step toward the door when a spark of ether hit his brain along with Allen's message. It seemed no one in Blue Cove knew Jade. Had the assassin used her and her uncle as a way into the city or was something more dangerous at work?

He intended to find that out first thing in the morning. Right now, he had a long walk back to the city in front of him.

CHAPTER 15

Wolfric lay in the dark, a huge smile plastered on his face. He felt cocooned in warmth and contentment. The moon's meager light coming through the window outlined Jade's perfect face. Her eyes were closed and her breathing even. He'd never seen anyone so beautiful, so perfect. His future wife would make a fine empress and an even better companion to spend the rest of his life with. He made a mental note to have Otto dismiss the harem. Now that he had Jade, he wouldn't need them anymore.

He sighed and closed his eyes. Even if he couldn't sleep, he needed to rest. Tomorrow they needed to plan the announcement of their engagement. Word would have to go out to all the governors and nobles as well as the leading merchants. A summer wedding would be nice. Otto could serve as his best man. Certainly no one had ever had a better friend.

He needed to plan a private dinner with Otto and Annamaria. As he considered the possibilities, Jade shifted beside him.

Wolfric opened his eyes.

Moonlight glinted off the dagger in her hand. At first his mind refused to comprehend what he saw.

Time slowed as he took in every detail. The slender, needle-sharp, double-edged blade, cold and hard, contrasted with Jade's warm, soft, bronze skin. He even had time to wonder where she hid the weapon. Certainly he would have noticed it when they were getting undressed. Then again, he had been distracted.

Time sped up as she drove the blade down at his chest.

Wolfric caught her wrist.

For someone so small, she had strength.

He put everything he had into controlling her without hurting her. "Guards!"

Jade hissed and slashed at him with the nails of her free hand, drawing blood from his cheek.

The pain surprised him and he lost his grip. Outside, the guards were pounding on the door. Wolfric never locked it, but Jade must have.

He tried to scramble away.

Jade leapt, driving him to the floor and straddling him. Under other circumstances the rough play might have been fun. Today she wasn't playing. Yet he still couldn't bring himself to fight back.

She had both hands on the dagger and was using all her weight to drive it into his chest.

Inch by inch the tip drew closer.

Wolfric stared at her. "Why?"

Behind them the door crashed open and the guards poured in.

"It's not personal, my love," Jade said as she drove the dagger into his flesh. "I'm just doing my job."

There was a dull thud and Jade's weight vanished. Wolfric was only barely aware of that through the burning pain.

"Your Majesty," Borden said. The captain of the palace guard knelt beside him.

Somehow Wolfric gasped out, "Closet. Circle. Otto."

Borden leapt away, leaving Wolfric alone with his pain. Oddly, Jade's betrayal hurt worse than the dagger. He'd loved her and thought she loved him. How had he been so blind?

As the darkness closed in on him there was a flash and he heard Otto's voice saying something.

Then he heard nothing at all.

CHAPTER 16

Otto had barely taken a step away from the cabin when a powerful vibration ran through the ether. He knew that feeling all too well. Someone was pounding on one of his rune marks. An instant of mental effort tracked it back to the royal castle. No one there would have used it unless an emergency had come up. Given that Otto had walked into a trap, Wolfric may well have gotten more than he bargained for with his new girlfriend.

He looked down at Abby, who smiled back at him. It may or may not have been possible to take someone through the ether with him, but either way he had no idea how to go about it.

"You're going to have to wait a little longer." Otto retreated to the cabin, set Abby on the table, and wrapped her in a bubble of ether. That would keep her warm and safe until he returned.

Becoming one with the ether, he shot back to the castle and appeared in Wolfric's closet. Instead of the emperor, he found a pale, trembling Commander Borden waiting for him.

"What happened?"

"The crazy bitch stabbed him."

Otto's guts twisted. "Is he still alive?"

"Barely."

Otto brushed past Borden and found Wolfric lying on the floor, naked as the day he was born, in a pool of blood. The hilt of a dagger jutted from his chest. Otto focused on the wound. The blade missed his heart by less than an inch, and it had nicked some important blood vessels.

Tubes of ether formed at his command, sealing the wounds and repairing, for the moment, the damaged veins. Though his heartbeat was still weak, now blood could flow everywhere it needed to rather than leaking on the floor.

"We need to carry him down to the Chamber," Otto said. "Carefully. Hopefully its magic will be enough to allow me to heal him."

Borden pointed and four guards hurried over to lift Wolfric gently off the floor.

"What about her?" Borden nodded toward the still-unconscious Jade.

Otto hadn't even noticed her limp body lying there, so focused had he been on Wolfric. "Put her in a cell. No one touches her. I need answers and she's the only one still alive to give them to me."

Another pair of guards carried Jade off and Otto and Borden fell in behind the men carrying Wolfric. Otto sent his magic ahead, deactivating the protective spells shielding the Chamber.

The palace guard must have cleared the halls as they encountered no one as they went.

"Is he going to live?" Borden asked.

"That depends. Do we have prisoners?"

Borden shot him a look then nodded. "Six at the moment, not counting the woman."

"Hopefully that will be enough. Have them brought to the Chamber room, bound hand and foot, as quickly as possible."

To his credit, Borden didn't argue. At his command, half a dozen more guards broke off from their group. The dungeon had a separate entrance from the room where he'd housed the Chamber.

As they slipped through the heavy oak door, one of Wolfric's bearers shouted, "He's bleeding again."

Otto grimaced. Something must have broken loose on the way down. A thread of ether outlined the Chamber door and made it dissolve. "Put him inside, pull the dagger out, and get clear."

"He'll bleed out," Borden said.

"No, he won't, not if I have anything to say about it."

The guards manhandled Wolfric inside the glass cylinder. His limp form slumped against the back wall. It had really been designed for someone to stand in, but it didn't matter. They forced his legs inside before one of them yanked the dagger out and leapt clear.

With a thought, Otto sealed the Chamber. Twenty threads arced out into the mithril tripod at the top. Ethereal lightning filled the Chamber with dancing light.

Fully connected to it now, Otto saw all the damage Wolfric had suffered in minute detail. It was a bloody miracle he was still alive.

First Otto strengthened Wolfric's heart and lungs. He still had a little power left so he sent a trickle to the rest of his organs. Ether mingled with blood, enhancing what remained, and allowing it to carry more oxygen than normal. It took everything Otto could spare to keep Wolfric alive. Healing couldn't begin until the prisoners arrived.

Wolfric's body started to spasm as something else broke loose.

Damn it!

"Where are those prisoners?"

"The cells are a fair distance away, Lord Shenk," Borden said.

They had no time. If he didn't start the healing soon, they'd lose Wolfric.

"Are your men willing to die for their emperor?" Otto asked.

"Would it matter if they weren't?"

"No. I need a volunteer. Pick one that doesn't have a family. Quickly."

"Mader! Step forward. Special duty."

A bald man in his late twenties moved away from his comrades. "Sir?"

"What do you need him to do?" Borden asked.

"Just stand right where he is." Otto pierced Mader with five threads then slapped his hands together, linking the guard to the Chamber.

The magic worked with no direction from Otto. Mader collapsed into a pile of fine dust as his life force was used to repair some of Wolfric's injuries. It did little, but it was enough to stabilize him again.

The other guards stared at the dust pile, their eyes wide and their faces pale. What did they think was going to happen? He had asked if they were willing to die.

Minutes ticked by like hours and Otto's strength started to wane. Pain built behind his eyes. Ten more minutes at most and he'd have to release the spell keeping Wolfric alive. Much as he needed the emperor, Otto wasn't remotely willing to die for him.

Luckily, he didn't have to. Two minutes later, six prisoners were paraded into the room, shackled hand and foot as ordered.

Otto didn't even wait. Threads shot out, pierced them, and he clapped his hands again. One after another the men collapsed into dust. The wounds in Wolfric's chest closed a little more with each death until the final prisoner was gone along with the emperor's wounds.

The lights in the Chamber vanished when Otto released the spell. A minor tweak opened the Chamber and Wolfric staggered out.

Borden hurried forward and slung his cloak around the naked emperor. Wolfric touched his chest where not even a scar remained.

He looked at Otto. "You saved me."

"Of course. How are you feeling?"

"Astonished to be alive. In truth, I feel better than I ever have. Like I could take on an entire army by myself."

"That's an aftereffect of the healing process. The feeling will slowly fade over the next hour or so, then you'll crash, probably sleep for many hours, wake up starving, eat everything in sight, and finally return to something like normal."

"And you, my friend? What did my foolishness cost you?"

Otto swallowed a sigh. This was not the time for recriminations. "Nothing a day or two of rest won't cure. I do have a request."

"Anything," Wolfric said.

"Leave Jade alone until I can question her with you. Extracting information from a damaged vessel is far harder than an undamaged one. But do keep her tightly bound. I'd hate for her to bite her tongue off or something before she can answer our questions."

"Borden will see to it. What will you do now?" Wolfric asked.

"I need to muster the strength to retrieve Abby and walk back to the city. Shall we plan to meet up tomorrow for an interrogation?"

"That's fine, but what happened to your daughter?"

"Long story. I'll tell it to you later." Otto straightened and became one with the ether.

～

When Otto returned to the cabin, he found Abby sound asleep exactly where he left her. The fire had burned down to embers and Ahmed's corpse lay untouched on the floor, dagger protruding from the top of his skull. He'd send someone to collect the body tomorrow. Just to be sure, he carved a crude rune on the floor and put the minimum amount of power into it to make it last a couple days. Be a pain if he had to search every damn cabin in the area.

That done, he scooped up Abby and set out at a slow trudge toward the distant city lights. Shin-deep snow hampered him until he reached the main road, which had been tracked down by constant merchant traffic. A good thing too, since his legs felt like iron weights. The bitter cold helped him stay focused, though it also stabbed his lungs with every breath.

He would have liked to warm both the air and his body, but lacked the power. He'd used everything he had getting back and enchanting that rune. If any other assassins remained in the area, they'd have no trouble with him now.

Happily, his six-hour hike passed without incident.

Assuming you didn't count Abby waking up three hours ago screaming for a meal. He had nothing to feed her and no desire to listen to her screeching. A tiny bit of magic put her right back to sleep. Her still-developing mind yielded even easier than an adult's. Good to know, since teething should be starting soon. If he wanted to work in peace, being able to put her to sleep at will would be useful.

The outer gates were opening as he approached and the sun colored the sky behind Garen bright orange. It was a beautiful sight that he would have enjoyed more had he been less exhausted. As it was, putting one foot in front of the other consumed his entire focus. The men stared as he passed, but kindly remained silent.

The guards manning the gate to Gold Ward recognized him so there was no trouble getting in, though given the blood staining his tunic, they probably thought he murdered someone. They weren't wrong, though the blood belonged to Wolfric, not Ahmed.

"Otto!"

He'd been so focused on the cobblestones that he didn't even notice Axel until he spoke. His brother marched at the head of ten scouts, all of them armed with mithril and looking ready for a fight.

"Axel. Coming to rescue me?"

"It is dawn. Where have you been?"

"Walking. The cabin was further from the city than I believed and the fight took a lot out of me so I made poor time." Otto saw no reason to point out Wolfric's near-death experience, for the moment anyway. "I left the kidnapper's body behind. Turns out the man was an assassin using Abby to lure me into a trap. If you'd be so kind as to fetch his body for me, along with anything else you find, I'd appreciate it.

Perhaps we can figure out who he was and more importantly who hired him."

"No problem," Axel said. "Where do we find the cabin?"

Otto was pretty sure he could muster the strength to do what he had to and avoid collapsing in the street. "Someone loan me a dagger."

Axel offered his own and Otto conjured the ether. He pictured the rune he left behind and imprinted that image on the spell before attaching the whole thing to the dagger. A quick test revealed that the blade glowed when he aimed it at the cabin. Satisfied, Otto returned it to Axel.

"Bring the body directly to the warehouse. Someone will be there to let you in."

Axel favored him with one last look of concern then led his men away.

Otto resumed his trudge and ten minutes later arrived at the gate to Franken Manor. A pair of very alert guards leapt to open the gate. Both saluted and the senior man said, "Welcome home, my lord."

Otto nodded and continued on toward the mansion. He barely made it through the door when Corina tackled him. "I was keeping watch over the grounds and saw you coming. We were so worried."

"It was a rough time, but I got her back. Where's Annamaria?"

"She cried herself to sleep a few hours ago. Want me to get her?"

"You'd better. I have a job for you after." When she left, Otto sent one of the always hovering servants to fetch him pen and paper. He set Abby on the dining room table and slumped in one of the chairs. Finally, he removed the spell that had kept her quiet. He had about twenty minutes before the brat came wailing to consciousness.

The servant returned with a quill, ink, and parchment. He'd written half the note before footsteps on the stairs broke his concentration.

He looked up to see Annamaria hurrying his way with Corina trailing along behind.

"You saved her. Is she hurt?" Annamaria was staring at the blood covering Otto's tunic.

"She's fine. Hungry and smelly, but fine. This is neither hers nor mine. The trip must have exhausted her as she hasn't made a peep in hours. Why don't you take her upstairs? Mimi can clean her up, assuming she's strong enough. I'm headed for bed shortly."

Annamaria scooped up Abby, gave Otto one last, long look, and retreated back upstairs.

Otto dismissed her at once, finished his note, let it dry, folded it over, and handed it to Corina. "Give that to Hans and join him when he goes. I need live prisoners, not bodies."

"Don't worry, Master, we'll handle everything. You just rest."

Otto sighed, but couldn't argue with her. Right now, he couldn't defeat a ten-year-old, much less potential assassins equipped with alchemical weapons.

He needed sleep. And when he woke up, he'd get some answers, one way or another.

CHAPTER 17

Corina practically skipped as she hurried away from the mansion through the city. Her master had finally given her a real mission. Granted Hans would be in charge, but still. It showed he trusted her. She hoped it was a real change and not just desperation brought about by exhaustion.

When she remembered how he looked when he got home from rescuing the baby, she shuddered. Some of the corpses she'd seen on the battlefield had looked better than he did. But he was alive, not angry—not at her anyway—and that mattered more than anything. Actually, what mattered more than anything was having the prisoners he wanted to talk to in custody.

All around her the sights and smells of the city coming awake after a long winter night filled the air. After living most of her life in Rolan, going from small community to small community, she still hadn't fully adapted to life in Garen. Staying focused and alert as she moved down the street took a lot of concentration. An attack might come from any direction.

Not that she expected an attack, but her master would say that's when you needed to be especially alert. Either that or always expect an attack. As far as she could tell, that seemed to be his motto.

Fifteen minutes later she reached the warehouse. The small door was locked so she knocked. It opened at once and she found herself nose to nose with Hans. He looked nearly as tired as Lord Shenk.

"Is he back?" Hans asked.

Corina nodded. "Half an hour ago. Not a mark on him, though from the amount of blood on his tunic, someone had a rough night. He has a job for us. Are you game? You look all in."

"I'm fine. It'll take more than one sleepless night to put me out of action. What's the mission?"

Corina handed him the note and Hans unfolded it. She shifted around to read over his shoulder. He wanted them to hold a nobleman named St. Croy for questioning along with everyone on his staff. Apparently Sin knew where to find his villa in Gold Ward.

Corina frowned. Why would her master have taken the admittedly beautiful thief instead of her?

"I'll wake the men," Hans said. "You find Sin."

Corina set aside her speculation and focused on the matter at hand. Whyever he did it, she was certain he had a good reason. Now, where would she find Sin? It wasn't like the thief lived at the warehouse with the guys.

She snapped her fingers. Ulf would know and he did live here.

Corina ran around his workbench and found the man wrapped up in a heavy blanket and sound asleep on a thick mat. He looked so peaceful she hated to wake him, but her master would be most displeased at any avoidable delay.

A light touch brought Ulf instantly awake, his eyes wide and terrified. "Are they here?"

"Relax, it's just me." He calmed at once and actually seemed a bit embarrassed. Corina pretended to notice nothing out of the ordinary. "Where's Sin? My master has a job for her."

"I see. Forgive my outburst. She's made herself up a spot in the tunnels nearby. Though whether she's there or not I can't say. One moment."

He walked to the hatch that gave access to the thieves' tunnels and yanked on a rope running through a hole in the wood. A faint ring barely reached them.

A few seconds later he yanked twice more.

This time there was some noise and shortly after that the hatch swung open. A rumpled and grumpy Sin poked her head out of the opening. She wore only a red tunic that left most of her legs bare, once again reminding Corina just how much developing she had to do.

Sin looked from Corina to Ulf and back. "What?"

"Lord Shenk has a job for us," Corina said. "He said you could lead us to the villa of Baron St. Croy."

"So he decided to move on the baron. Can't say I'm surprised. I knew there was something strange happening at that place. Let me get dressed and I'll be right there."

Ten minutes later, Sin was leading them across the city back toward Gold Ward. As they quick marched down the street, Hans asked, "What sort of defenses are we looking at?"

"None that I'm aware of," Sin said. "The baron had a

handful of servants, his niece, and himself. I'd know if he hired any mercenaries. He might try to run, but a fight seems doubtful."

"That's good," Corina said. "Master wants to question him."

"If Lord Shenk wants to question him," Sin said. "I doubt it will be good for the baron."

No one could argue with that and they made the rest of the walk in silence.

When they reached the villa, the door was wide open.

Hans motioned for everyone to stop before easing up to the door. Corina held her breath while he listened. At last he waved them up.

"Sin, Corina and I will go in the front," Hans said. "Cord, take the rest of the men and watch the back."

Cord nodded and the four of them hurried around out of sight. When half a minute had passed Hans said, "Let's go."

He lunged through the door. Corina followed right behind, ready to bind anyone that tried anything. Their entrance was certainly anti-climactic.

"Please come in," a voice said from deep in the villa. "I won't resist and I've sent the servants away."

"That's St. Croy," Sin said.

"Think he's telling the truth?" Hans asked.

Corina hated being ignored, so she used her magic to send her sight into the living room. An old man she assumed was the baron sat alone in an overstuffed leather chair. No one else was visible and she saw no weapons or traps.

"Looks safe to me," Corina said. "He's just sitting there waiting for us."

Hans and Sin looked at her.

"What? You know he taught me the far sight spell, right?"

Hans shrugged and said to Sin, "Would you let the rest of the men in and search the villa? We'll check on the baron."

"Sure." Sin left for the back door.

Hans and Corina continued on to the living room where the baron sat facing them. He had his hands firmly gripping the arms of his chair. The fine robe he wore was creased and the sleeves dirty. He'd seen better days for sure.

"Don't move," Hans said.

"I assure you I have no intention of resisting. Since Jade didn't return last night, I've been expecting someone to come calling. Frankly, I expected Lord Shenk himself. Are you bringing me to him? I have a great deal to say."

"Lord Shenk will be along to talk to you when he's ready," Hans said. "Until then, we'll be keeping you company."

"Aren't you worried about your niece?" Corina asked.

"She's not my niece. Jade's an assassin. She used me to meet the emperor."

Hans shook his head. "This is not how I imagined our mission ending."

"No," Corina agreed. "But at least we have a safe and cooperative prisoner. That will please him."

"There's that. Do you want to watch him or fix breakfast? I haven't eaten in hours."

"Have you tried my cooking?"

"Yep. You watch him."

Corina couldn't be insulted. Her cooking stunk and she knew it. With nothing else to do, she sat across from the baron.

"Will your master punish me for my part in the deception?"

Corina considered lying, but couldn't see much point. "Maybe. But it won't be as bad if you do whatever he says and don't lie. Those two things really make him angry."

The baron paled. "I'll keep that in mind."

Corina hoped he did. Wittingly or not, the man helped an assassin gain access to the emperor. He'd need all the luck in the world to survive what was coming.

CHAPTER 18

Otto didn't know how long he slept, but since he felt alive again, he assumed for a while. It was dark out, so he must have stayed in bed the whole day. A snarl from his stomach confirmed his theory.

How wonderful it would be when he was an Arcane Lord and no longer had to bother about things like sleep and food. Exhaustion would be a distant memory. But that situation lay well in the future. Right now, more pressing matters required his attention.

Abandoning his pleasant musings, Otto rolled out of bed, dressed, and stepped out into the hall. Other than a dull ache through his entire body, he felt back to normal. The ether responded to his call and no lingering effects from his excess magic use remained. He was as ready to face the day as he'd ever be.

He had barely taken a step when a shrill cry grated on his ears. Clearly Abby was fully recovered from her ordeal as well and ready to complain again. He marched toward the stairs, determined to find something to eat before heading directly to the palace. Wolfric would be eager to begin questioning Jade and he wanted to be there to make sure nothing happened until he'd extracted every drop of information from the woman. After that, Wolfric could do as he pleased with her.

He rounded a corner and found Annamaria pacing in the hall as she bounced the crying baby in her arms. She spotted Otto and instead of disappearing into her room, she walked toward him. Surprised by her reaction, Otto stopped in his tracks.

"I wanted to thank you again for saving her," Annamaria said. As soon as she got close, Abby fell silent and stared at Otto with her big blue eyes. "I know you owe me nothing but whatever happened between us, Abby is an innocent child."

"She is, albeit a rather loud one." Otto let his expression harden. "Let me make one thing clear. I didn't save her for you. I saved her to make an example out of anyone that would think to use my family against me, even a fraudulent family. Just to make sure no distractions like this happen again, I'll have Axel put some of his scouts to work augmenting the guards. Clearly they are not up to protecting the mansion."

Once again her response surprised him. "Thank you for that. Your brother was quite concerned when he learned his supposed niece had been taken. He seems to have a kind heart."

"Yeah, how that happened in the Shenk family is beyond me. He must take after Mother. Excuse me."

He left Annamaria and before he reached the ground floor the wails started up again. Otto failed to restrain a small, vicious smile. It was worth saving her even if only to deprive Annamaria of sleep.

After a quick but filling meal, Otto was out the door. When he reached the castle, the guards on duty opened up for him at once. Halfway across the yard, he spotted Borden walking on patrol. He had mail on under his tabard and a sword belted at his waist. Clearly the commander of the place guard was still on full alert. Probably not a terrible idea all things considered.

Borden paused as Otto approached and offered a salute. "Lord Shenk, good evening."

"Is he awake yet?"

"Not as of fifteen minutes ago. Frankly, I'm surprised to see you up and about. You looked like death warmed over last night."

"I'm much better now. Best let Wolfric rest as long as he needs to. I have several other matters that require my attention. If he does wake up, please tell him I'll join him for breakfast."

"As you wish, my lord."

Otto turned on his heel and marched back the way he'd come. Anxious as he was to interrogate Jade, it would keep until Wolfric woke. Otto seriously doubted his friend would appreciate it if he started on his own.

Since he couldn't work at the palace, the next closest location was the baron's villa. If Hans and Corina followed his orders, they should have a prisoner for him to question.

Otto strode through the street, unconsciously using the ether to keep himself comfortable in the bitter evening air. He thoroughly pitied all those that had to be out on a night like this with no magic. The people of Gold Ward, it seemed, had more sense than he did and were staying inside tonight. That suited him fine as he had no desire for more distractions.

Ten minutes later found him marching up the path to the villa. Cord must have drawn the short straw as he stood outside in front of the door. Bundled up in a heavy cloak and wool mittens, his hood up and covering his face, only puffs of frozen air gave away the fact that he hadn't frozen to death.

"Lord Shenk." Cord saluted. "We weren't sure when to expect you and Hans wanted someone out here to greet you when you arrived."

"Thoughtful of him. Did you do something to make him mad?"

"Maybe won a few too many hands of cards."

Of course, it would be something to do with the card game. "Well, I'm here now so you can come inside. Did the baron give you any trouble?"

"Not a bit. He was expecting us when we arrived and immediately gave himself up. Seemed eager to talk to you."

In Otto's experience, not many people were ever eager to talk to him. "Then let's hear what he has to say about his 'niece.'"

"Master!" As soon as he stepped through the door Corina came running and greeted him with a hug. "Are you okay now?"

"More or less. I see you delivered my message and completed your task. Well done."

"It wasn't very hard. He just gave up."

"So I heard." Hans and the rest of the squad came around the corner and saluted. There was no sign of Sin. "Where did you stash him?"

"The baron is in the living room. He's been reading while we waited for you. The man seems remarkably calm given his circumstances. Do you want me to start a fire so we can heat some irons?"

"I don't think that will be necessary. And if it is, we'll bring him back to the warehouse, so we don't disturb the neighbors."

Otto led the way into the living room. Baron St. Croy looked up from his book with the most hope-filled expression

Otto had ever seen. "Lord Shenk. Thank heaven you're here. They have my family. Please, you must save them."

Otto stared at him for a moment. "Maybe you'd better start from the beginning."

Baron St. Croy did so. Apparently, Jade, Ahmed, and three others showed up at his modest castle in the middle of November. They explained that he was going to help Jade meet with the emperor so she could seduce and murder him. He would also provide a cover for Ahmed who would find some way to deal with Otto. Should he refuse to help or fail in any way, his wife and two children would be killed. With no other choice he agreed and brought them to Garen for the gala.

"I believe you know the rest," the baron said. "Their three confederates are still in my barony, living in my castle." His voice rose as he named each offense. "If word of their comrades' failure reaches them, my family is as good as dead. Please, with your magic, surely you can save them."

Saving them would be easy enough, the question was, did saving them serve him better than letting his enemies think the game was still on? He needed more information.

"I'll consider your request. In the meantime, I want you to work with Hans, make a map of the castle, show me where your family is likely to be as well as the ones holding them hostage. I'll need detailed descriptions as well."

"I am at your service. Anything I can do, I will gladly do."

Otto sensed no lie in the man's words and he seemed genuinely concerned about his family. "Corina, do you want to come with me or stay with Hans?"

"Go with you," she said at once.

"I assumed so. Hans, you know what to do. Have a plan ready for me by midmorning. After I finish with Jade, I'll make my decision."

Hans nodded. "Understood, my lord."

Before Otto and Corina took their leave, he went upstairs. Jade would have had her own room, somewhere to plot and meet with Ahmed away from the servants. He wanted to take a look around. If Ahmed had alchemy to aid him in his mission, Jade might have as well.

They found the room easily enough; it was the only one with a woman's clothes in the closet. "Check for anything magical."

He and Corina spread out. Otto went right to a collection of bottles sitting on the dresser. He found nothing magical, just a collection of makeup and perfume. Completing the search took ten minutes and turned up nothing of interest. He pocketed an atomizer that smelled of the perfume she wore during their lunch meeting. He might be able to use it to help Wolfric feel less stupid and more angry.

Otto led the way downstairs and out the front door. As soon as they were outside Corina asked, "What are we going to do now?"

"Assuming Axel's back with the assassin's body, an autopsy."

⟳

B ack at the warehouse, there was no sign of Axel, but he had left the assassin's body in a wagon that held two more corpses. Otto frowned as he considered the bonus bodies. They had the same bronze skin tone as Jade and Ahmed. That couldn't be a coincidence.

Corina had her gaze locked on the bodies, but she didn't seem especially troubled. That was a relief. She was toughening up nicely. Whether that was a good thing in the long run or not, he couldn't say. All Otto knew for sure was that it was necessary.

"Lord Shenk." Allen stepped out from behind one of the giant suits of armor. "Have I got a story to tell you. Oh, your brother dropped off a body for you and said he'd be at the barracks if you needed him."

Otto nodded. "I assume you're the source of the extra corpses?"

"Yeah, those two tried to kill Oskar and me in Blue Cove. Lucky I'm a light sleeper and your spy's paranoid. Anyway, no one ever heard of Jade. I think she fed you a line of bullshit."

"Indeed, I've recently come to that conclusion. Thank you for confirming it." Otto saw no need to tell him the woman had nearly succeeded in killing the emperor. "Did you learn anything else from your would-be assassins?"

"Afraid not. Their pockets were empty and the weapons they used locally purchased. If there's nothing else, I need to get back to the tavern before my serving girls quit."

"There's nothing at the moment. And well done. You've reminded me again why I kept you alive."

Allen hurried off, leaving Otto and Corina alone with the bodies. The back of the wagon was as good a place as any to do his work. Otto climbed up and went first to Ahmed. His body had relaxed enough to be easily moved. Otto turned his clothes inside out and checked his skin for marks, but found little beyond a bunch of old scars. He'd seen plenty of battles, that was certain.

Otto yanked his dagger free of the man's skull, grimaced, and tossed it in the wagon bed. He'd grab a new one from the armory, the blade was just ordinary steel, nothing special.

"We didn't learn much," Corina said.

"No, but I didn't have especially high hopes. People in their line of work aren't apt to carry incriminating information on their persons."

"You don't seem as upset as I imagined you'd be," Corina said.

Otto considered that for a moment. He was certainly upset at this pointless interruption to his preparations, but he didn't feel any emotion that strongly anymore. People and situations were now divided between things that advanced his plans and things that held them back. The former would be used and the latter removed. It was that simple.

"Anger has its uses, but it can also cloud your judgement. Wolfric will be angry enough for both of us. If I'm to resolve this crisis with the minimum of damage to the empire, I must keep a clear head. Let's head back to the mansion. A few more hours' sleep wouldn't do me any harm, especially with an early morning interrogation to oversee. I'll be trusting you to keep an eye on things until morning."

She brightened at the prospect then frowned. "Are you expecting more trouble?"

"Until I'm sure Jade and Ahmed were on their own in the city, I don't plan to relax my guard. I didn't survive one assassin only to get overconfident and fall to a second."

◌

As Otto hoped, the night passed without incident. After lending Corina a guest room to sleep in, he left for his breakfast with Wolfric. The bitter air slashed at him as he made the short walk to the palace. The guards at the gate looked especially miserable as they huddled around their charcoal brazier, its feeble heat barely enough to cut the chill. Not that they would ever voice a word of complaint where either he or Borden could hear it.

He smiled to himself. If he ever needed a distraction, eavesdropping on the guards' barracks might be entertaining.

Just inside the main keep, he found Borden waiting for him. The captain of the palace guard looked tense, well, tenser than usual. Otto had never actually seen the man relax, though he assumed he did so in private.

"Everything alright, Borden? You're looking more tightly wound than usual."

"It's the emperor. He's been up for hours."

Otto nodded. "And?"

"And as soon as he woke up he went to the dungeon. He's been sitting there staring at Jade for three hours. He said nothing, either to me or to her. He's just sitting there. I'm worried."

Otto understood both Borden's worry and Wolfric's obsession. After what happened, it would take some time for Wolfric to get over it, assuming he ever fully did. Otto had hoped that he might wake up and pay a visit to his harem, burn off some of the excess energy the Chamber would have given him.

"I'll talk to him. Have everyone pull back. What might be said needs to be heard by no one but the two of us."

Borden saluted. "Yes, Lord Shenk. And thank you."

Otto waved off his thanks. What he did, he did for the good of the empire. They walked together through the cool halls to the door to the dungeon. Borden dismissed the two guards at the top of the stairs.

"I'll make sure you're not disturbed."

"No," Otto said. "I'll make sure we're not disturbed. You need to go away as well. When we've finished, I'll let you know."

Borden didn't argue, hurrying away with almost unseemly haste.

Otto watched until he was out of sight, opened the door to the dungeon, and stepped through. After closing the door behind him, he wove a simple bar of ether that would stop anyone from following behind.

The darkness was eerily silent as he strode through the dungeon. Usually there would be small sounds from the prisoners, but since Otto had sacrificed them all to save Wolfric, the cells were empty. Just as well considering the conversations that were about to happen.

He found Wolfric sitting on a simple wooden stool just a stride from the bars of the final cell in the row. He wore a black and gold soldier's uniform and had his sword belted at his waist. As Borden said, his gaze was fixed on the prisoner.

Jade was bound to a frame attached to the wall; her arms stretched to either side. She was still as naked as when they captured her. Someone had added a ball gag that kept her from biting her tongue off.

Otto stopped beside his friend and looked down. "Borden tells me you decided to skip breakfast this morning. Shame, I was looking forward to your cook's fine pancakes."

Wolfric finally tore his gaze from Jade. "I've been sitting here trying to figure out how I could have ever believed she loved me. There was never a moment of doubt in my mind. She twisted me around her finger so easily. If I can be manipulated by her, how can I be trusted to rule an empire?"

"Consider this a learning opportunity," Otto said, speaking as the voice of experience. "All the mistakes you made with Jade, you can avoid when the next woman comes strolling into your life."

"How can I ever trust another woman? How can I even trust the women in my harem?"

"As to the women in your harem, you can trust them because one of my agents procured them and I interviewed them myself to make certain they had no hidden agendas. I assure you, given where they came from, living a life of luxury in the palace is a huge improvement. When the next noble lass catches your eye, let me talk to her before you grow too attached. At the very least I can find out if she secretly wants to kill you."

Wolfric barked a humorless laugh, breaking some of the grim mood. "Fair enough. Now, shall we see what this treacherous witch has to say for herself?"

"Splendid idea." Otto wove a dome of silence then bound Jade so she didn't try anything foolish when he removed her gag.

As soon as she finished coughing, Otto set the colored wheel to spinning in front of her. Like any normal woman without magic to protect her mind, Jade succumbed in short order.

When she was fully under, he asked, "Who sent you?"

"The Coiled Serpent," she said in a dull monotone.

Wolfric looked at Otto and asked, "Who the hell are they?"

Otto shrugged. He'd never heard the name before today. "And who is that?"

"The assassins guild I serve."

"Who hired you?"

"Eddred of Markane."

Wolfric's fist slammed into the cell door, rattling it in its frame. "I swear, if I ever get my hands on him…"

Otto shared that sentiment, though he'd be just as happy to

have Eddred knifed in a back alley somewhere, anywhere, as long as he was removed.

"Tell me about the Coiled Serpent," Otto said when Wolfric had gotten himself under control.

"We contract most of our jobs in the City of Coins. Our agents are all over the world, though most aren't assassins, just spies and information gatherers. Our leader sets the price of a target and an assassin or team of assassins are dispatched to eliminate that target."

More out of curiosity than anything Otto asked, "How much were we worth?"

"Two hundred pounds of gold each."

Wolfric grinned. "At least we weren't cheap."

"Indeed." Otto returned his attention to Jade. "Now that you've failed, what will happen?"

"Another team will be dispatched as soon as it becomes clear that we've failed."

"How long do we have?"

"Impossible to say."

"Having to worry about assassins for the rest of my life holds no appeal," Wolfric said.

"For me either. I may have to go to the City of Coins and deal with the assassins permanently. If I need to burn the whole city down in the process, I can live with that."

"I'll be joining you on the journey," Wolfric said. Before Otto could argue he continued. "It will be safer than staying here where an assassin might jump out at me at any moment."

He had a point and Otto didn't feel like arguing. "Fair enough. I'll gather the war wizards and we'll head to Rolan to commandeer a ship. From there it's less than a week to sail to the city. When we're finished, they'll wish they'd never accepted that contract."

Otto turned his focus back to Jade. "How do you recognize each other?"

"We have marks, serpents, tattooed on the inside of our lower lips."

"All your agents or just the assassins?"

"Just the assassins. Most of our agents are simple mercenaries. They care only for our gold."

"Interesting." He scratched his cheek before turning to Wolfric. "Do you have any more questions for her?"

"No. Before we go, I want to see her publicly hung."

"That might not be the best idea," Otto said.

Wolfric glared at him. "Surely you don't think we should let her go."

"Of course not. I think we should kill her and toss her body in one of the foundries. We don't need everyone knowing what happened here. The baron wants his family saved and will do anything to make that happen. Convincing him to say Jade met with an accident on their way home to collect some family heirloom for the wedding will be simple enough. You can play the grieving lover and make the people love you all the more."

"We turn her betrayal into something of value for us." Wolfric rubbed his face. "I wonder if I shall ever come to think as clearly as you. I'll leave the arrangements in your care. The sight of her sickens me."

"As you wish." While he forced reluctance into his tone, having Wolfric out from underfoot would only make completing the many tasks ahead of him simpler.

That said, he didn't want Wolfric losing all his confidence. Otto reached into his pocket and pulled out the atomizer he'd taken earlier. "I took this from her room at the villa. It's an alchemical solution designed to weaken your mind and make you more susceptible to suggestion. Don't be too hard on yourself, my friend. No one could have recognized what she was doing."

Wolfric grunted, seeming less than reassured.

Probably best to move on. He pocketed the perfume and said, "When I've found the ships we need, we'll leave for Rolan and set sail for the City of Coins and revenge."

CHAPTER 19

Otto and Wolfric rode into Port Palomino on the Rolan coast at the head of a column of fifty war wizards, along with Corina, Hans and his squad, and a company of royal guards. The city had an actual wall, a rarity in Rolan given the sparse forests. The warmth and fresh sea air did wonders for everyone's mood. Even Wolfric had relaxed a fraction, though he still scowled far more than he smiled.

Six days had passed since their discussion with Jade. She and all her co-conspirators were now so much ash thanks to a convenient foundry that did some side work for Sin and her guild. Otto had also rescued Baron St. Croy's family. The grateful baron had eagerly agreed to spread the word of Jade's tragic accident. Before setting out through the portal, Otto had ordered Sin and Allen to try and track down anyone associated with the Coiled Serpent.

"Your Majesty, Lord Shenk!" Oskar came marching their way. The spy must have been waiting just inside the gate.

"Who is this again?" Wolfric asked.

"One of our agents. He placed the patch on Rolan's portal and has been keeping an eye on the province for us." Otto waved him over and the royal guards made a path. "You found ships for us?"

"I did. Not the most awe-inspiring vessels, but both are seaworthy and will carry you safely to your destination. Given the time crunch, I couldn't afford to be fussy."

"Don't worry, Oskar," Otto said. "The war wizards will make up for any deficiencies the ships might suffer. Show us the way."

The column marched behind Oskar to the docks, where a pair of double-masted sailing ships were tied up at the farthest-out piers. The spy hadn't lied about their rough condition. Neither looked like it had seen a drop of paint in years. Despite living on the water, the sailors watching them dismount didn't look overly familiar with a bath.

"There's still time to remain behind," Otto said to Wolfric.

The emperor just shook his head. "I will see this through if I have to sail with the Reaper himself."

Arguing with him would be pointless so the group divided itself up and climbed aboard. Otto hung back with Oskar and said, "I assume you vetted these men?"

"As well as I could in the few days I had. Both are merchant men and neither has any dealing with the city as far as I can determine. They care nothing for politics, only my promise of gold. Besides, how stupid would they have to be to betray a ship full of wizards?"

"Fair point. Look after our horses. With any luck we should have this wrapped up in a couple weeks."

"Count on me, my lord."

Otto clapped him on the shoulder and hurried up the gangplank where an impatient Wolfric stood tapping his toe. "I assume we can leave now?"

"As far as I'm concerned. Oskar will take care of things here."

Ready though they were, the ships stayed in dock for another hour before the tide and wind were correct for launch. As soon as they were, the ships set sail.

Otto stood beside Corina near the rail and out of the sailors' way. He wasn't going to pretend to be happy about going to sea again so soon, but the assassin threat wouldn't wait. He swallowed a sigh. Things had been going so well up until now.

While he might find torture distasteful, if he ever got his hands on Eddred of Markane, he might just make an exception.

CHAPTER 20

"I had always heard that the walls of the City of Coins were impressive," Wolfric said. "It seems that was no exaggeration. How will we get inside?"

Otto and Wolfric stood in the front of the first ship and studied the distant city. Even from several miles away, the walls looked massive in the midday sun. Otto guessed their height at several hundred feet and probably another hundred thick. The only way in was the port. When they were raised, the walls were built solid without gate. They ran from the ocean's edge in a semicircle back to the shore again. Even worse, enchantments had been woven into the stone to protect it from magical attack.

The harbor didn't look any easier to approach. A pair of massive towers held a chain that could rise to block any ships from entering and they were protected by the same magic as the walls.

"We don't necessarily have to get inside," Otto said. "We can just burn it down from a distance, assuming they refuse to give us what we want. After all, the city isn't our enemy, the assassins are."

"If the city's rulers are giving shelter to the assassins, then they are our enemy as well." Wolfric crossed his arms and his face settled into that hard, stubborn scowl Otto had come to know and dislike.

"I'm confident that once we explain their situation, whoever's in charge of the city will do the right thing. They may need a bit of coaxing, but that's what we brought the war wizards for."

"Sail off the starboard bow!" the lookout called from above.

Otto sent his sight out over the water and quickly spotted the small sloop headed their way. It held a dozen sailors and one wizard. Not an attack force then, probably someone coming to ask their intentions and decide if they could be trusted to enter the harbor.

He blinked his sight back and said, "The welcoming committee. They can carry our message back to their masters."

"They won't try something foolish, will they?" Wolfric asked. Otto couldn't decide if he was hoping they'd attack or concerned that they might.

"Not with the tiny force they've sent, assuming they're not suicidal. I suspect it's a formality for visiting merchants. Either way, we'll know soon enough. Captain, slow us down and prepare to receive guests."

There was a shout of acknowledgement followed by orders to do things with the sails. Otto still didn't fully understand the processes aboard ship and he didn't especially care to. As long as the sailors knew their business and got him where he wanted to go, that was enough.

Ten minutes later even those on deck could see the

approaching ship. They were lowering their own sails and slowing as they came closer.

"Do you want to do the talking or shall I?" Otto asked.

"You start and I'll jump in if I want to add anything," Wolfric said.

Otto nodded and a few minutes later a rope ladder was lowered to the smaller sloop. The wizard climbed up first. She wore a crisp sailor's uniform in white and gold with polished black boots. A shield of modest power surrounded her. If that was the extent of her power, then she represented no threat.

When she stepped aside, an older man Otto assumed commanded the ship joined her on deck. He wore an identical uniform, though his stretched tight across a massive chest. Tattoos covered his bare arms and a brass-hilted arming sword dangled from his hip.

"Welcome to the City of Coins," the man said with a bright, warm smile that seemed totally out of place on his blocky, scarred face. "I'm Captain Hotic of the city navy. What have you come to trade?"

"My name is Otto Shenk of the New Garen Empire. We are here because a group of assassins called the Coiled Serpent attempted to kill the emperor and myself. Your leaders allow them to operate openly in the city. We require that all members of that group be turned over to us for punishment."

A much more appropriate scowl replaced the captain's smile. "We don't take kindly to demands. All are welcome to do business here. What happens outside our walls does not concern us. If you have a problem with assassins in your empire, that is hardly our concern. I suggest that if you have nothing to trade, you turn your ships around and sail back where you came from before we send you to the bottom of the sea."

Wolfric stepped in front of Otto. "And I suggest that you tell whoever's in charge that they'd best hand over the people I want or we'll burn the city down, assassins and all. You have until sunrise tomorrow."

The female wizard started a spell.

The moment she did, Otto crushed her shield, wrapped a tentacle of ether around her neck, and drove her to her knees. "None of that, now. We only need your captain to deliver our message. Behave, or he can take your body back as a warning."

Her magic clawed at his tentacle, but her feeble power didn't come close to breaking his grip.

The captain went for his sword.

He only drew it halfway before Borden and Hans both had their own weapons at his throat.

"I suggest you calm down," Otto said. "Before you make us do something you'll regret."

Captain Hotic eased his half-drawn sword back into its sheath and Otto released his grip on the wizard.

"That's better," Otto said. "Now, tell whoever's in charge of your city what we said. I assure you it's no idle threat. We've brought enough war wizards to do the job with some to spare. Your wizard can confirm that's the truth. Now run along."

The pair climbed back into the sloop and Otto shoved the ships apart. He doubted the city fathers would see reason right away. Some people needed a slap in the face from reality. They'd have to keep a close watch tonight lest the enemy try something foolish.

CHAPTER 21

Captain Hotic stood outside the door to the city
council chamber. The cool, stone room at the heart
of the government building served as the seat of the
city government. The lords of the city decided everything here.
He clasped his hands behind his back, less for protocol than to
keep them from shaking. He considered himself a brave man.
In theory, anyway. The truth was, he'd never seen combat.

People came to the city to trade. None of them wanted
trouble, only gold. And the undead infesting the desert hadn't
found a way into the city since before his grandfather was
born. They had known peace for centuries. Who would have
believed foreigners from the north would be the ones to
change that?

Not him, certainly. He spoke with merchants from many
kingdoms on a weekly basis. He'd heard news of the empire's
formation, but didn't imagine it would change anything for
them. How wrong he'd been.

Now he found himself in the great stone building at the

center of the city where the lords decided everything from taxes to who to bar from the harbor. He didn't want to be here. No one in their right mind sought the attention of the lords. But his duty was clear. As the senior officer of his ship, he had to report the threat.

"Captain?"

He'd been so focused on his worries that he hadn't noticed the beautiful aide that had emerged from the council chamber. Thin, nearly sheer blue fabric covered her mahogany skin and lush curves. One of the benefits of being a lord of the city was having the most beautiful servants to wait on your every whim.

"Yes, ma'am."

"They'll see you now."

"Yes, ma'am."

She smiled, flashing perfect white teeth. "Try to calm down. Despite their fierce reputation, our masters are not the sort to punish someone out of hand. They value loyalty and you have been a loyal servant, have you not?"

"Yes, ma'am."

She shook her head and led him into the council chamber. The inside was dark and it took a moment for his eyes to adjust. When they did, he saw the six masked lords of the city. They wore billowing robes in addition to the masks to disguise their identities. Each oversaw a single aspect of the government and they worked together to ensure business went on as it should.

"Captain, your message sounded urgent," Lord of the Watch said. "Please, tell us what has happened."

He did so, detailing his brief encounter with the imperials. When he finished, he said, "According to my ship's wizard, they have over two score wizards on their ships led by the most powerful wizard she has ever encountered. They want the Coiled Serpent assassins turned over to them by morning or they threaten to burn the city to the ground."

"Of all the arrogance," Lord of the Watch said. "The City of Coins has stood since the fall of the Arcane Lords. If these northern fools think we will fall so easily, they had best think again."

"How many wizards can we field?" Lord of the Scale asked.

Lord of the Staff grimaced. "Twenty, twenty-five if we send the apprentices as well. But they need only defend. That is a far easier task than attacking. We'll let the invaders exhaust their wizards then our harbor fleet will sail out to sink them."

Lord of the Watch nodded eagerly. "My soldiers are the finest anywhere. They train to fight undead horrors that would turn an ordinary man's guts to water. Mere humans will pose no challenge."

Hotic's throat tightened. They wanted him and his fellow captains to sail out and attack the imperials? If they held anything back, his people would be sitting ducks. And even if they made it to the ships, he'd seen the skill with which their warriors moved. Mortal men or not, this would be no easy fight.

Despite his concerns, Hotic remained stoically silent. He knew his duty even if it terrified him.

"Captain," Lord of the Watch said. "Alert your fellows to the threat. When we give the signal, you will all sail out to defeat the invaders. Rest and prepare yourselves. Harbor patrols are suspended until this matter is resolved."

"As you command, Lord." Captain Hotic bowed and left the council chamber.

Outside he took deep breaths to calm his racing heart. He knew and accepted his duty. Come what may, he would not shirk this task.

That he may die in the doing changed nothing.

CHAPTER 22

Dawn was just tinging the sky red when Otto gathered the squad leaders of his war wizards for their pre-battle meeting. To a person they looked at him with a mixture of fear and eagerness. The group had gathered belowdecks on the ship Otto and Wolfric called home, for the moment anyway.

The war wizards had had little enough to do since the war with Straken ended. Not that guarding the empire wasn't important, but with no external threat, it did become tedious. Otto only avoided the boredom because he had his own goals to accomplish. He thanked all the angels that this madness happened now and not when he was halfway around the world in the Celestial Empire.

"We learned a lot about assaulting a walled city during the battle with Straken," Otto said. "One advantage we have today is that we don't care about seizing the territory. We just want to do as much damage as we can to force the city's leaders to give in to our commands."

"We'll be using large-scale attack spells then?" one of the leaders said.

"That's right. I assume they have a force of wizards that will oppose us. You need to launch your spells on a high arc, force the enemy wizards to build a shield over their heads. With luck, that will leave their legs exposed."

The war wizards looked around at each other then one finally asked, "Why would we want to leave their legs exposed?"

"So I can cut them off at the knees." Otto's smile was cold and humorless. "While you keep them occupied defending the city, I'm going to attack the wizards themselves. If I can kill or maim a sizable portion of them, it will make the second stage of the battle much more effective, assuming they don't give in at once. Are there any other questions?"

No one spoke, so Otto said, "If our plans change during the battle, Corina will relay my orders. Go and ready your people. We attack on my command."

A pair of rowboats ferried the wizards back to the second ship. As Otto and Corina watched them she asked, "Why do you want me to relay the orders?"

"Simple. I'll be focusing my magic on the wall. Extending my voice to the other ship will break my concentration. That could be the difference between victory and defeat. If you're not certain you're up to the task—"

"No! No, I can do it. I just didn't understand why. Thank you for explaining, Master."

He nodded and turned his gaze back to the city walls. The sun had risen enough to reveal figures moving around on the battlements. He debated extending his sight, but any wizard watching would destroy his construct instantly. Better to wait until the battle started.

He'd convinced Wolfric to remain belowdecks until the fight ended. Otto had enchanted his cabin to keep enemy threads out and Wolfric safe. The last thing they needed was to lose him now after he survived an assassination attempt.

Otto glanced over at the second ship. Looked like everyone was in place. "Tell them to attack."

Corina lips moved but no sound emerged. Across the water, two score targeting threads arced up and out towards the city. One squad held back to act as a reserve in case the enemy counterattacked.

Fireballs shot out, glowing orange spheres of destruction aimed at the heart of the city.

Otto sent his vision along behind them, low over the water where the enemy wizards would be less likely to notice.

Just as he expected, the first fireballs exploded against an ethereal barrier. With so many spells coming all at once, it was too hard for the outnumbered wizards to smash them one at a time. Sweat poured down their faces as they withstood the first barrage and every eye focused on the sky.

They'd never know what hit them.

Otto conjured an ethereal blade made from twenty compressed threads. None of the weaklings on the wall had any hope of stopping it on their own.

"Second barrage, fire," he said.

The fireballs screamed in again.

The instant the first one struck the barrier, Otto made his move.

His ethereal blade hit the nearest wizard right above the knees and sliced both her legs off like they were nothing.

The woman's screams of agony distracted her allies enough that two of the fireballs snuck through, exploding in the city and setting a dockside warehouse alight.

The remaining wizards redoubled their focus, restoring the barrier to full strength.

Otto struck again.

He slashed three more in a span of ten seconds, leaving them legless.

Someone finally noticed his construct and attacked it, trying to rip the threads apart. The enemy wizard's construct had only five threads and couldn't begin to scratch Otto's.

He killed the man with a slash to the chest that left him in two pieces.

"Third barrage," Otto said.

More fireballs smashed their way through this time as the wizards divided their focus between Otto's sword and their barrier.

Even with their modest attempt at defense, he killed three more before the last fireball burst.

Otto let the construct vanish and returned his awareness to his body. Three shots was all the war wizards were good for, assuming he didn't want to exhaust them. And he didn't. This siege might last a while and he needed to preserve his wizards' power.

"Tell the assault team to rest and have the reserves take defensive positions. We'll hit them again this evening."

"Done," Corina said. "Did we win? I saw some fireballs slip through."

"Round one certainly went to us, but we won't win until the assassins have been eliminated. Burning the city is only a means to an end. Keep an eye on things here. I have to update the emperor."

Otto left a beaming Corina on deck and descended to Wolfric's cabin. Ideally the assault would convince those in charge to give in. But if there was one thing Otto had discovered, it was that nothing ever went in the direction he considered ideal.

CHAPTER 23

When the final fireball had faded to embers, Captain Hotic left his sloop and ran for the battlements. Even from the docks he could hear the wizards screaming. Whatever Lord of the Watch had expected to happen, this surely wasn't it.

He dodged a ten-man bucket brigade running for a warehouse ablaze near the water. Deeper in the city more fires sent plumes of smoke into the sky. Given the number of fireballs the invaders sent against them, it was a miracle anything remained intact.

Hotic coughed as a gust of wind carried acrid smoke from the city into his path. At the base of the wall, litter bearers carried a wizard on a stretcher toward the city center where divine healers would try their best to save the man. Before they left, he caught a glimpse of the man's legs, gone from the knee down, the cut perfectly smooth.

At the top of the wall he found Commander Baileon kneeing beside another wizard that had been cut perfectly in half. His tan uniform was spotted with blood; even his bald head was splattered. Finally he raised his head and spotted Hotic.

The commander nodded toward a spot away from the wounded and Hotic joined him.

"I don't think this is how Lord of the Watch thought our battle would go," Hotic said.

Baileon grimaced and smudged some blood off his cheek. "None of us expected this. I've never encountered wizards of such power. And so many of them. I counted nearly forty targeting threads. The only reason the city still stands is that they stopped when they did. I'm going to have to completely rethink our defense."

"Is there anything the harbor patrol can do?"

"No. If you sail out there without wizards to protect your boats, you'll be sunk in seconds. And I can't spare a single wizard if we want to have any chance of protecting the city."

"Perhaps the lords will give in to the invaders' demand," Hotic said. "I mean, we owe the assassins nothing. Is protecting them really worth having the city burn down around our ears?"

"It's not about the assassins," Baileon said. "It's about not letting some foreigners sail into our port and tell us what we have to do and who we're allowed to do business with. If we give in this time, we'll have to give in every time anyone shows up and threatens us."

Hotic scratched his chin. That didn't really follow in his mind. When a more powerful force showed up, giving in made sense. And it certainly didn't oblige anyone to give in to anyone else. It seemed more like the lords' ego wouldn't let them surrender. That struck Hotic as a stupid reason for the city to burn down.

What the hell good was principle to the dead?

CHAPTER 24

"They're not idiots, unfortunately." Otto sat on the iron footlocker in Wolfric's cabin and wiped the sweat from his brow. The small room felt stuffy and the air close. Heat combined with a lack of ventilation made it hard to breathe. Not that Wolfric seemed overly discomforted.

The second bombardment had just ended with considerably poorer results than the first. He'd only killed one wizard this time, but the war wizards had slipped more fireballs through the defensive wall. It wasn't a horrible effort, but it was less overwhelming a win than he wanted.

"I didn't suppose they survived here for so long by being weaklings." Wolfric had grown a beard during their time at sea and he gave it an absentminded scratch. "Will you try again tomorrow?"

"I think moving on to the second phase of the assault would be prudent. It would also reserve the wizards' strength."

Wolfric frowned. "Are you certain about this? Can you control the creatures?"

"I don't need to control them, just force them into the city.

Once inside they'll do what they do with no prompting from me. Trust me, if anything will rattle the city's leaders, this will."

"Very well. Go ahead with phase two. Hopefully it will convince the fools to do the right thing and spare us another day of pounding them with fireballs."

"Yes, hopefully." Otto stood. "If you'll excuse me."

Otto quickly left the stifling cabin and went up on deck. The slightly less stifling evening air came as a bit of a relief. He glanced at the sky. It would be twilight soon, the perfect time to find what he sought.

He sent his sight flying toward the desert beyond the city. About a mile from the walls, he marked a spot and blinked his vision back to his body. His heart lurched when he found Corina standing right next to him.

"Make some noise when I'm scouting. Are you trying to give me a heart attack?"

"Sorry, Master. Can I come with you tonight?"

"No. I'm traveling through the ether and even if I wasn't, my task is far too dangerous to have you along. Stay here and pay attention. Wolfric's safety is in your hands while I'm gone."

She smiled. "I'm not sure Hans and Commander Borden would agree."

"Both of them have their uses, but they can't see everything a wizard can." He looked dead into her eyes. "I'm trusting you with the emperor's safety. Take nothing for granted."

"I won't let you down, Master."

He nodded and became one with the ether.

An instant later he appeared in the sands outside the city where he'd left his marker. There were supposed to be undead all over the place, yet he sensed nothing beyond the endless dunes. If he had to go hunting for the creatures, this might be a long night.

With a shrug, Otto set out across the sand away from the city. At least the walking was easy. There wasn't so much as a stone bigger than his head visible in any direction.

About half a mile from his point of origin, the ether swirled to his right. He'd never sensed anything like it. Hopefully this was what he sought. Adjusting his course slightly to his right, he marched on, every muscle tense, and a powerful ethereal barrier surrounding him.

The power he sensed grew ever closer, but he still saw nothing. Had he made a mistake? Perhaps the creatures lurked elsewhere.

Directly ahead of him the sand exploded upward as ten humanoid figures rose from under the sand. That made sense. There was nowhere else for them to hide and it wasn't like the undead had to breathe.

The creatures moved closer, giving him a better view of their misshapen forms. They had certainly been human once, but now, twisted by magic, they were monsters. Hunched over with elongated limbs and oversized jaws filled with three rows of teeth like steak knives. Their bodies were emaciated, the ribcages poking out of skin like leather. The creatures stared at him with glowing red eyes.

"Why doesn't the meat run?" one of them asked.

"Yes, we like the taste of fear," another said.

Just as Otto hoped, they retained at least some awareness. A deep philosophical conversation was probably too much to ask, but he could talk to them.

"I have a proposal for you," Otto said. "How would you like to sneak into the city and slaughter a bunch of humans?"

"Meat doesn't talk," said the biggest of the group, a near-seven-foot creature that stood more upright than the rest. "It bleeds."

Perhaps it led this pack? Otto wasn't certain. Did the concept of leadership even enter into their thinking?

When the giant ghoul took a step toward him, Otto pointed. An ethereal lance made up of twenty compressed threads smashed into its head, blowing the twisted appendage apart in a burst of brains and blood.

"As I was saying," Otto continued. "I'm not meat. But I am offering you a chance to kill and devour as many humans as you can."

"You are one of the masters," the first ghoul that spoke said. "Forgive us, great one, we did not recognize you."

The nine remaining members of the pack fell to their knees and touched their heads to the sand. Otto smiled. It seemed he would get what he needed after all.

"I take it you're interested in my offer?"

One of the ghouls looked up at him. "We'll be killed if we go into the city."

"You're already dead," Otto pointed out. "How long has it been since you've fed? Since you've killed and rent flesh? Half the city's wizards are dead and the other half exhausted. You'll never have a better chance to slaughter all the humans you want. Eventually their superior numbers will overcome you, but isn't that better than rotting out here, starving, in the vain hope someone's stupid enough to leave the safety of the walls?"

The one ghoul seemed to have taken up the role of spokesman for the group. "Why do you ask us and not command? You are a master. We couldn't resist your orders if we wanted to."

Otto had no doubt that Amet Sur and the other Arcane Lords had some way to control the undead, but he hadn't learned it yet. Not that he had any intention of telling these creatures that.

"I ask, because in my experience, willing fighters are more motivated than slaves. I'll compel you if I must, but I prefer to secure your willing aid."

"Want to kill!" one of the other ghouls growled, and bared its fangs.

The others snarled their eagerness as well.

"It seems we have an understanding. Follow me."

Otto turned his back on them, a move of supreme confidence calculated to show just how little of a threat he considered them. When, after twenty paces, none of them had attacked, he let out the breath he'd been holding.

The sun had fully set when they reached the base of the wall. Using his magic, Otto enhanced his vision, rendering the world in shades of gray. On the battlements, a guard passed by, never looking down, completely ignorant of what would soon happen to the city he was supposed to protect.

"How will we climb up?" the ghoul spokesman asked.

"I'll lift you. Gather together in a tight group."

The undead did as he asked and Otto conjured a disk beneath them. He needed twenty-five threads to do it, but soon the monsters rose into the darkness. When they reached the top of the wall, he felt them leap off.

His construct had barely dissolved when the screaming started.

Satisfied with his work, Otto followed the base of the wall to the ocean. Once there, he conjured an ethereal walkway and strode across the water toward their ship, extending it as he went.

By the time he reached the side of the ship, he had nearly exhausted himself. Happily, a rope ladder fell from above followed by Hans's worried face peering down at him. "Are you well, my lord?"

"Perfectly, though I'm in serious need of sleep."

Otto climbed the ladder and at the top Hans pulled him aboard.

"Do you think there will be trouble tonight?" Hans asked.

Otto smiled and looked back at the city. "No, I do believe they'll be too busy to trouble us tonight."

CHAPTER 25

E ddred of Markane stood on the balcony of his rented room in the City of Coins. The air had cooled since the sun went down, but it never really got cool. He couldn't wait to get home. Even in the middle of winter, Markane had its charm. The white plumes when you exhaled, icicles hanging from the eaves, snow covering everything and making the land look clean and pure...

He sighed. Happy memories to distract him from his current predicament only took him away from reality for so long. Then he'd catch a whiff of smoke or see the orange glow of flames and reality would come crashing back.

When ships bearing Garenland wizards sailed within sight of the harbor, Eddred hardly believed what he was seeing. He'd thought by now that both Wolfric and Otto would be dead at the hands of the assassins he'd hired. Apparently he'd been overly optimistic. Now the enemy was here and he could only think of one reason why.

They'd learned where the assassins came from.

The fireballs that eventually started flying made the truth of the situation quickly clear. Eddred blamed himself. If he'd just let it all go instead of looking for revenge, none of this would have happened.

He shook his head. If he hadn't contacted the assassins, Lord Valtan would have found someone else to do it. The Arcane Lord was even more determined than Eddred to kill Wolfric and Otto.

Well, Otto anyway. Whatever the young wizard found in Colt's Land had really put a scare into Valtan. And a frightened Valtan was something Eddred never wanted to see again.

A scream shattered the darkness.

Below him, figures moved in the night. A woman came running out of an alley into the light, a gray-skinned, misshapen figure galloping after her.

Eddred had never seen one of the undead that infested the deserts beyond the city's walls, but he'd heard tales enough to recognize one of them. How did the creature get inside?

The obvious answer came to him a moment later. Otto Shenk had let them in. More repayment for the assassins that had tried to claim his life. After the battering they'd taken during the bombardment, he doubted the city's wizards would be in any shape to fend off an attack by undead. And damned if Eddred was going to have any more lives on his conscience.

He darted back into his room, buckled on his sword, and shot out into the hall. Eddred paused long enough to slam his fist on the door across from him. It opened a moment later.

"Your Majesty?" said Adam, one of his two wizard bodyguards.

"Wake Lilly, there are undead in the city and I mean to hunt them down. I'll fetch Uther while you two are getting ready."

"Is that wise?" Adam asked. "Neither I nor Lilly have any experience fighting undead. Lord Valtan never instructed us how. We don't even know any offensive spells."

"Then we'll learn together. My actions brought this mess on the city, and I have to do something to make it right. In two minutes, I'm going out there, with or without you two."

Adam ran to wake his partner. Eddred left him to it and went down another door. He had barely knocked when the door opened, revealing the scruffy face of Uther of Straken. His chest was bare and it looked like he had just gotten out of bed.

"What's going on now?" Uther asked. "I heard enough screams outside to do a torture chamber proud."

"Undead in the city. I'm going out to fight them. Will you help?"

Uther snorted a laugh. "I've seen your bladework. All you're going to do is get yourself killed. Let the city guards handle it. That's what they're paid for."

He had a point about Eddred's sword skills, but that didn't matter, not tonight. "This is all my fault. I have to do something to help."

"Then I'd best go with you. It's not like I have the coin to pay for this room on my own."

A little over two minutes later the four of them strode out of the inn into the now-silent street. Three bodies lay in pools of blood a little ways away. Chunks had been taken out of them, bitten out most likely.

"Where are they?" Eddred asked.

Adam and Lilly closed their eyes and a faint glow surrounded them as they wove the ether.

"I sense eight," Adam said at last. "They're spread out all over the city."

"The nearest is four blocks north," Lilly added.

That was enough for Eddred. He drew his sword and marched north.

The streets remained quiet for three blocks. The only people they encountered were those that dared peek out from behind their closed curtains. All he got was the impression of terrified, pale faces that sagged with relief when they saw Eddred and his companions instead of an undead horror.

They rounded a corner onto the fourth block and there it was. The gray-skinned creature stood in the center of the street, an arm dangling limp and half eaten in its right hand. Judging from the ragged strips of flesh dangling from its shoulder, Eddred guessed it had been ripped off its former owner. He shuddered at the strength that must have taken.

"We'll try to slow it down," Adam said. "What little I know indicates that you have to cut its head off to kill it."

Eddred tightened his grip on his sword and glanced at Uther who nodded.

The two men separated and came at it from opposite directions. The monster watched them with its glowing red eyes, seeming untroubled by a pair of armed warriors stalking toward it.

Ether streaked past them and wrapped around the undead's arms, legs, and chest.

It finally snarled and thrashed, tossing the arm away in its fury to escape.

"Hurry, Your Majesty," Lilly said, her voice strained. "We can't hold it for long."

Eddred charged and swung with all his might towards the creature's neck.

Despite the magic binding it, the monster raised an arm in time to intercept his strike.

The keen edge of Eddred's sword slammed into the withered limb and barely cut it. He'd hit softer oak logs.

Uther hacked at it from the opposite side, carving a groove in its side, but doing no real damage.

The beast roared and swung its clawed hand at Eddred.

He leapt back, avoiding the blow.

Uther took up the assault, actually landing a slash to its neck that barely made a crease.

How in heaven's name were they going to kill the monster when their weapons barely scratched it?

Eddred looked back at Adam and Lilly. "Can you two make our weapons more effective? We're never going to stop it like this."

"We can, Majesty, but not while binding the monster," Lilly said.

"Then let it go. Uther! Fall back!"

Uther gave the undead beast a final, ineffective whack before disengaging and backing away to join Eddred. "Do we have a plan?"

"Adam and Lilly are going to release the creature and enhance our weapons instead."

Uther winced. "I'm not sure that's a good plan. Didn't you feel how strong that thing is? One solid blow is apt to break bone if not kill us outright."

"It's the only way. Once they're exhausted it'll be free and we won't have them to increase the potency of our blades."

"Ah, hell. Fine, let's go for it."

"On three, Majesty," Adam said.

The wizard counted down. On three, the ethereal flow shifted.

The instant it was free, the undead charged them.

It was faster than Eddred expected.

Uther stepped in front and swung his sword.

The monster raised its arm to defend. The bright steel struck home, slicing its arm off at the elbow.

No blood spurted and the beast didn't even slow.

Taken off guard by its lack of reaction, Uther was too slow to defend.

A clawed hand sliced him across the chest. Twisted magic exploded out of the undead's fingertips into Uther. The prince's body went rigid as he collapsed.

The undead raised its hand to finish him off.

Eddred charged in and swung.

His blade bit deep into its neck, sending its head falling to the earth with a plop. The body collapsed a moment later.

Adam and Lilly hurried over.

"Are you well, Majesty?" Lilly asked.

"Well enough. Check on Uther."

Adam did so. After a moment he said, "The wounds are shallow. We just have to wait for the paralysis to wear off."

"Where's the next one?" Eddred asked.

Lilly shook her head. "I'm not sure. That battle drained me. I doubt I have strength enough to enhance your blade again, much less bind one of those things. I think our night is over."

"But there are more of them," Eddred said.

"And there are others to deal with them," Adam said. "Dying tonight will do nothing to help the people of this city."

Eddred slumped to the stone street. Adam was right of course. Dying might assuage his guilt, but it would help no one. And taking his companions with him was hardly the honorable thing.

"So be it," Eddred said at last. "We tried anyway."

His smile was bitter, humorless, and directed mostly at himself.

We tried anyway. That should be their motto.

All he ever did was try and fail.

CHAPTER 26

C aptain Hotic once more found himself summoned to the lords' council. This time the messenger came for him before the sun had risen. Not that he'd been asleep. Reports of the undead attacks throughout the city had reached the docks and all the captains and crews were on full alert lest the ships be threatened.

None of the ghouls had come their way, thank heaven, but from what he'd heard, the rest of the city watch had been decimated trying to kill the creatures.

So he couldn't claim the summons had surprised him. Now, he stood in a dark corner and tried to go unnoticed. Lord of the Watch had only just taken his seat and the others were staring at him.

"Explain yourself," Lord of the Scales said, at last breaking the fragile silence. "What happened to your boasting about training to fight monsters and that human warriors would be no trouble?"

"Our training is based on manuals from the ancient times," Lord of the Watch said, all traces of his former confidence long gone. "We followed it to the letter, but the creatures proved stronger than we ever imagined. After the bombardment, our wizards were in no shape to help. The reality of fighting undead proved far worse than I ever imagined."

"And our losses?" Lord of the Scale asked.

"Sixty-three watchmen and over four hundred citizens. I don't have the final number yet. As best we can tell, only nine ghouls made it into the city."

This brought murmurs of concern from the other lords. Hotic shared that concern. If only nine of them did this much damage, what would happen if ten times that many made it into the city? He shuddered to think.

"I won't ask how they got over the wall," Lord of the Scale said. "I think we can all guess who the responsibility lies with. Ladies and gentlemen, I fear we must face the harsh reality. Another day and night of fighting the invaders may well be the end of our city. Though it pains me to suggest this, I fear there is no choice but to give in to their demands."

"That will ruin our reputation," Lord of the Earth said. "No one will trust us to do business again."

"May I make a suggestion?"

Hotic snapped his head around at the unexpected voice. An ancient man with a thin white mustache hanging down his chest stepped out of the shadows. So still and silent had he been that Hotic hadn't even known he was there.

"Grandfather Edge," Lord of the Scale said. "Please, if you have anything to offer don't hesitate to speak up. That's why I asked you here."

Hotic swallowed the lump in his throat. This was Grandfather Edge, the leader of the assassins guild and, some said, most favored of the Reaper himself.

"Let me go to the outlanders. I will offer to rescind the

contract and never take another on them. They will be safe from my followers, which, I assume, is what they really want."

"I have no objection," Lord of the Scale said. He looked around at the other lords, but no one spoke. Finally, he turned to Hotic. "You will transport Grandfather to the invaders' ship. They are familiar with you and will recognize you as a messenger."

Hotic hoped the lord was right. He figured there was a better than fifty percent chance that they sunk his boat on sight.

CHAPTER 27

"Sail ho!" the lookout called from his post far above the deck.

Otto had only been up for a few minutes when the cry rang out. He tossed his half-eaten breakfast aside and sprang to his feet. His vision shot out over the water towards the sloop headed their way. It was the one that had approached them when they arrived, only this time lacking a wizard. She had probably been reassigned to the wall.

He let his vision drift over to the captain then added his voice and hearing. "State your purpose."

The poor man nearly leapt out of his skin. When he'd recovered a modicum of composure he said, "I have a proposal from the city lords. May my ship approach so we can talk?"

Otto saw no harm in that though if they offered anything less than total capitulation, he doubted Wolfric would accept. "Very well, but behave yourself. I have no particular desire to kill you, but I won't hesitate to do so."

"Understood. You'll find that none of my crew is armed."

Otto glanced at the rest of the men on board. None of them

carried so much as a belt knife. A prudent decision. Far better for everyone if there were no misunderstandings.

"Bring your ship along our right side. I'll have someone waiting with a ladder."

Otto returned his senses to his body. "Captain, we're about to have visitors. Have men standing by to help them aboard."

Once he received an affirmative reply, Otto went back below deck to fetch Wolfric.

Ten minutes later, Otto, Wolfric, Hans, Borden and a force of soldiers had gathered on deck. The messenger sloop was tied up and the captain as well as an older man climbed on board. Hotic wore a white and gold uniform that was already plastered to him with sweat. The second man dressed in all black and looked perfectly at ease surrounded by armed men. His face was a mass of wrinkles and he wore a mustache that hung down past his chin.

"You don't think they're going to try and negotiate again, do you?" Wolfric asked.

Otto shrugged. He had no idea what the purpose of this meeting was and didn't care to guess. An ethereal barrier surrounded him and Wolfric just in case they tried something desperate and stupid.

Their guests stopped ten feet from Otto's group. The captain bowed and said, "Thank you for allowing us aboard. Let me introduce Grandfather Edge, the leader of the Coiled Serpent assassins guild."

Beside him, Wolfric stiffened. "You sent Jade to kill me."

Edge nodded. "I deemed her the most likely to succeed. Jade has a way with men."

"Had," Otto said before a shouting match broke out. "Whatever you have to say, say it."

"Here is my offer," Edge said. "I will cancel the contract on the two of you and offer my promise that no one will take it up again. I will further guarantee the lives of your families and friends. In exchange you will leave the harbor and never return."

Wolfric's scowl was so deep Otto feared his face might break. "What's to keep us from killing you and the rest of your people? We'll be just as safe then."

"No, you won't," Edge said. "You think all my assassins are here? Even if you killed all of us in the city, others would take up the contract. My guild has members all over the world. We won't stop until both of you are dead or all of us are. You got lucky once. You might get lucky twice. But four times? Ten times? How long do you think you can hold out?"

He had a point, but Otto hated giving in to threats. On the other hand, he had enough to worry about without looking over his shoulder every five seconds for assassins.

"We'll consider your offer," Otto said.

Wolfric took a step forward but Otto laid a restraining hand on his arm.

Edge seemed satisfied with Otto's answer. "If your ships have set sail by noon, we will consider that an agreement."

Without another word, the leader of the assassins guild turned on his heel and climbed back down to the sloop. Otto was a fairly confident person, but he doubted he had the confidence to turn his back on so many enemies without a moment's hesitation. The old man clearly didn't fear death. Perhaps dealing it out for a living made you immune.

When the messengers had gone Wolfric said, "Are you really considering accepting his offer? We have the city on the ropes. One more day and we'll have everything we want."

Otto shook his head. "No, we won't. You heard what Edge said and I believe him. Dealing with the assassins here, while satisfying, doesn't solve the problem. We take his deal and we remove one of Valtan's most lethal weapons from play. Make no mistake, my friend. The assassins are only a tool. Without them, it will take our real enemy considerable time to find a replacement."

"I don't like letting them get away with threatening us."

"I'm not thrilled about it either, but we need to consider the big picture. Destroying the City of Coins gains us little and costs our merchants a lucrative market. It's time to cut our losses and go home."

Wolfric slumped a fraction. "Fine. Give the order. I'll be in my cabin."

"Did we win?" Corina asked as they walked toward the helm to talk with the captain.

"More or less. With the assassins out of the picture, we can focus on the journey to the Celestial Empire. Spring will be here before you know it and much work remains to be done."

CHAPTER 28

The battle with the undead left Eddred exhausted and he slept until well past sunrise. When he finally woke, he groaned and sat up. His body ached from shoulders to calves. He had been far too lax in his training. That would have to be remedied.

"Good morning, King Eddred."

He nearly fell out of bed when the soft, feminine voice spoke. In the shadowy corner of the room, the lovely figure of Naja sat in the only chair. She rose and bowed to him. She wore the same billowing black dress and veil which left only her eyes visible.

"Is that one of your assassination techniques?" he asked. "Scaring someone to death?"

"I've used it before. But frightening you wasn't my intention. I am here with bad news."

Of course she was. How come no one ever brought him good news? "Let's have it."

"The guild master has rescinded the contract on Wolfric and Otto. Your gold will be returned to your ship by the end of the day." She shook her head. "I am sorry, but it was the only way to save the city. We will not accept another contract on either of them or their families. This is the bargain we struck."

Relief flooded through Eddred. The whole assassination business had always sat badly with him, especially after what happened to the city. Having the matter closed for good took a weight off his mind. True, they still needed to find a way to stop Otto and Wolfric, but now they could focus on finding a more honorable way to go about it.

"Thank you for coming to tell me. We'll be taking our leave in the next day or so. While I hope to return some time, if that doesn't come to pass, it was a pleasure to meet you."

"You are a good man, Eddred of Markane. Whatever happens in the future, I wish you all the best."

Eddred sighed as she slipped silently out the door. He needed to talk to Lord Valtan. He doubted the Arcane Lord would take the news well.

☾

The voyage back to South Barrier Island seemed to Eddred the longest of his life. The hours ticked by like days and every minute he couldn't stop thinking about the death and destruction his quest for revenge had caused. Lord Valtan claimed they were trying to save the world, but from Eddred's perspective, it seemed they were only making things worse.

"Land ho!" the lookout in the crow's nest called.

From his place by the helm, Eddred could barely make out the narrow strip of green that was the island.

Another six hours passed before they finally tied up to the longest dock. The moment the gangplank hit into the wharf, he hurried down; for some reason Eddred, who normally loved being out to sea, felt an overwhelming need to feel the earth beneath his feet. Uther and the rest of the crew followed at a more sedate pace.

Eddred sighed. "It's good to be home."

Beside him, Uther snorted. "This little patch of dirt is no more your home than it is mine. Where is your master? We need to plan our next move. You know that bastard Shenk isn't going to be sitting still for long."

As if summoned by Uther's words, an ethereal projection of Lord Valtan appeared a short distance away. Everyone but Uther bowed.

"What happened?" Valtan asked.

"The assassins lost their nerve!" Uther said before Eddred had a chance.

"Two Garenland ships loaded with wizards showed up in the City of Coins's harbor," Eddred said. "Wolfric demanded the assassins be handed over or they'd burn the city to the ground. Otto's war wizards made a credible start the first day. And that night he set a bunch of ghouls loose in the streets. They killed more people than the fire."

Valtan shook his head. "Is there no depth the man won't sink to?"

"The city lords decided to make a deal," Eddred continued. "The leader of the assassins promised not to accept a contract on Otto, Wolfric, or their loved ones in exchange for the city being spared. I have our payment on the ship."

"So what do we do now?" Uther demanded. "It's been nearly a year since I arrived and we've accomplished exactly nothing."

Valtan turned his glowing gaze on Uther. "You are not a

prisoner here. If you wish to take your chances elsewhere, by all means, go. A boat can be arranged by the end of the day."

"I don't know how to sail a boat," Uther growled. "I just want to save my father and free my people. Killing Otto Shenk would be a nice bonus."

"I share your frustration," Valtan said. "But this was never an enemy that would fall quickly or easily. Though I had high hopes for the assassins."

"I've had enough." Eddred spoke so softly the others didn't seem to hear him. "I said, I've had enough."

Every gaze focused on him and his throat went dry.

"What are you saying?" Valtan asked.

"I'm saying, all we're doing is making things worse. How many more people have died because of our efforts? If we'd just minded our own business, Garenland would have left us alone and our families would still be alive. Hiring the assassins only caused more people to suffer in the City of Coins. Worst of all, we've accomplished nothing to even slow Otto's efforts. It's time to let it go."

Uther took a step towards him and for a moment Eddred feared the angry prince might strike him. "Let it go? You mean forget that my land has been conquered and my father made a slave?"

"Your father started this mess." Eddred didn't care what Uther did. He wouldn't let the younger man pretend his precious father didn't play a major part in the chaos that had infected the continent. "If Straken had curbed its ambition, none of this would have happened."

"Enough!" The force of Valtan's roar nearly put Eddred on his backside. "If Otto Shenk succeeds in his quest, what has happened up until now will seem a pleasant memory. Arcane Lords consume and destroy. It is what we are. Only by the narrowest of margins did I escape that fate and only then after seeing the horrors the others committed. Power and lack of experience will cause Otto to overreach, probably killing thousands in the process. He. Must. Be. Stopped!"

Eddred swallowed a sigh. That was exactly the response he'd expected. "Do you have a new plan? If it seems feasible, I will continue the fight. But not at the expense of more innocent lives."

"Thank you, Eddred. Unfortunately, I don't, as of yet, have a new plan. Take some time. Rest here. When I think of something, I'll return." So saying, Valtan vanished.

There was a modest, seemingly deserted village not far from the dock. Maybe they could find some fresh food and a clean bed. For now, that was the best Eddred dared hope for.

CHAPTER 29

As Otto stepped out of the portal into Lux, a warm spring breeze washed over him. After the madness with the assassins and the City of Coins, the rest of the winter passed without issue. Otto focused his time on researching the Celestial Empire, both with Ulf and on his own using the library in Lord Karonin's armory.

His master had very little to say about the empire. It seemed she and Lord Xi Cheng didn't like one another and avoided each other as much as possible. The way she said this made it clear that further questions wouldn't be welcome. It seemed that, despite there only being six of them, the Arcane Lords didn't all especially like one another. Too many big personalities, Otto suspected. No doubt only Amet Sur's overwhelming power kept them from going to war against each other. That and the distance between their various empires.

He shook his head at the pointless speculation and stepped aside to make room for the rest of his team. Axel was coming, along with ten scouts, and Hans and his squad rounded out the combat portion of the group. Corina would be joining of course. If he left his apprentice behind, he'd never hear the end of it. Besides, he found her company pleasant and sometimes even insightful. On a journey of over ten thousand miles, having another wizard to talk to would be welcome and he didn't want to bring any of the war wizards on the off chance more trouble sprang up in his absence.

When the last member of the team emerged, Otto deactivated the portal and led the way toward the dock. Henry, his agent in Lux, fell in beside them.

"I trust everything is ready," Otto said.

"Yes, my lord. All the supplies I could fit on board your ship, plus the special trade goods. If you don't mind my saying so, the improvements make her a lovely vessel."

"They had better make her comfortable. The last trip was bad enough. Damned if I'm going to spend every night for three or four months in a bloody hammock. Anyway, well done arranging everything."

"Of course. Is there anything else I can do before you depart?" Henry asked.

"No, we're as ready as we'll ever be."

"Then I bid you fair wind and smooth seas."

Otto frowned. "Isn't that a Lux expression? Going native on me?"

"Perish the thought, but it's difficult not to pick up a few things when you live somewhere long enough."

Otto didn't especially care what sayings Henry picked up and dismissed the matter at once. As long as his loyalty remained in the right place, he could talk however he wanted.

At the docks, Captain Wainwright stood at the bottom of the gangplank to greet them. He looked as happy as Otto had ever seen him, his blue and white uniform crisp, his beard trimmed, and a big smile creasing his face.

"Lord Shenk, welcome. All the work is done and the *Star* is as fit as she's ever been. I can't tell you how excited I am to begin the trip."

Otto shook the man's hand. "However excited you are, it's not half as excited as I am. I want to be out of here as soon as possible."

"You're in luck. The tide will turn in half an hour. As soon as it does, we'll throw lines and set sail. We're going to make history, my lord."

Otto doubted Wainwright knew just how right he was. He led the way up the gangplank. Time to see what all his gold bought.

It turned out that what his gold bought was a modest room at the best inn he'd ever visited. There was a single-person feather bed, a soft leather reading chair, a writing desk with bolted-down supplies, and a chest of drawers, also bolted to the floor, with locking drawers. It wasn't Franken Manor, but it was a massive improvement over what he had last trip.

He'd barely settled into the chair when someone knocked on his door. "Enter."

Captain Wainwright poked his head in. "Is everything to your liking?"

"It's sufficient. I assume you've settled on our final course."

"Aye, I have. I don't expect any issues until we reach the Frozen Narrows. Assuming we can thread the needle, it should be smooth sailing until we reach the island. Heaven knows what we'll have to deal with there."

"Let's just worry about getting there. We have two months to plan that little adventure."

"Right you are. If you'll excuse me."

Wainwright closed the door and Otto sighed. Now for the boring part. Weeks on end of tedium. Though if this trip was anything like the first, he'd be wishing for boredom before it ended.

CHAPTER 30

Otto's breath puffed white as he stood beside the ship's rail. His magic, combined with a heavy wool cloak, kept him from freezing, if not exactly comfortable. They'd been sailing for nearly five weeks with no issues.

In fact, Captain Wainwright kept the ship well away from land lest they draw the attention of something nasty in the Dead Lands. While it might have extended the journey by a day or two, that was a price Otto would gladly pay if it avoided a fight with some undead monster. Otto didn't know what sort of creature might think a ship full of men would make a tasty snack and he had no desire to find out.

He'd spent much of the trip studying the undead and how best to control them. If an emergency happened and they were forced to land, it seemed a prudent precaution. Not that he was all that confident in his newfound skills.

Unfortunately, the moment of reckoning might be coming sooner than he wanted. Directly ahead, a spit of blackened land jutted out into the ocean on the left side. On the right, thick chunks of ice bobbed in the waves. Thankfully small waves at the moment, though that would change once they reached the Narrows.

At the helm, Captain Wainwright gripped the wheel, a grim look of determination on his face. Though certainly fearful of the risks, the handful of times they'd spoken about the passage the captain's eyes lit up with excitement for the challenge. Otto knew just how he felt. Every time he attempted a new spell, the same excitement filled him. Granted, failing to learn a spell wasn't apt to end up with them all dead, but still it was exciting in its own way.

"Master?" Corina came towards him, her slight figure wrapped in a heavy, fur-lined cloak. "I thought you said it got warmer when you went south?"

"It does, for a while. If you go far enough south, it grows cold again."

"That makes no sense."

Otto smiled. "Much of life doesn't. Help me keep watch."

"For what, ice floes?"

"No, the lookouts can spot them easily enough, we need to watch for anything magical coming from the Dead Lands." Otto pointed at the rapidly closing mass of blackened earth. "We'll be within a quarter mile of land when we pass through the narrowest part. If anything's going to happen, it will happen there."

Corina shivered. "Just looking at the blackened earth gives me the chills. What happened to it?"

"According to the books I've read, when the undead plague destroyed Amet Sur's former empire, something happened to the land. So many beasts of corruption striding across the ground killed it in a way fire or any other natural force couldn't. I doubt anything will ever grow there again. It is literally a land of the dead."

"That's horrible." The wind howled, blowing her hood off.

"Focus now. We're approaching the Narrows."

The wind continued to pick up, propelling them forward at a furious pace. The masts creaked and the canvas cracked like whips.

"Reef those sails before the mast snaps!" Captain Wainwright shouted.

Sailors hurried into the rigging. Every second Otto expected one of them to go tumbling into the sea.

But the sure-footed men never hesitated and soon they had half the canvas down. That brought the ship's speed to something manageable.

Or so Otto thought. The sailors had barely finished their work when something bumped their hull.

"Report!" the captain shouted.

"We hit a floe!" one of the sailors said. "Just a small one. No damage."

Wainwright's curse was carried away by the wind. "I need two men in the forecastle! Signal me if we're going toward another one."

A pair of sailors ran to the front of the ship. Otto would have volunteered to keep watch with magic, but he needed all his attention elsewhere.

The right-hand sailor waved and pointed.

Wainwright adjusted their course closer to the Dead Lands.

Otto liked that decision not in the least, but he liked sinking even less and held his tongue.

Even with half their sails down it felt like the ship continued to pick up speed. When Otto glanced back, another sailor had joined Wainwright at the wheel and it looked like it was taking everything both men had to hold their course.

At least they hadn't bumped into anything else, due in large part to the frantic signaling of the men at the front of the ship.

A shiver of dread ran down Otto's spine.

"Master?" The quaver in Corina's voice made it clear she sensed it as well.

The source of the darkness became clear a moment later. A black cloud was approaching from the Dead Lands. Somehow it moved north to south despite the west-to-east wind.

"A Black Wind," Otto muttered. He'd read about them, but his books indicated that they were rare. Clearly not rare enough.

"Master, what should we do?"

There was nothing to do except ride it out and hope they survived. "Stay alert. Anything gets past me, you'll need to deal with it."

He left Corina and ran toward the helm. As soon as Captain Wainwright saw him Otto said, "We need more speed. Everything you can muster."

"I'm barely holding her steady as it is. We put on one more yard of canvas and we risk the masts."

Otto pointed at the Black Wind. "If we don't get through that before my power runs out, it will scour the life out of everyone aboard. Every second matters."

"I'll go three-quarters sail, but not full. We break the masts and we'll be stuck here."

Otto nodded and left the sailors to their work. There was one more thing he needed to do.

He raced to the stairs leading to the lower decks and shouted. "Axel, Hans, bring your men up on deck and make sure they have their mithril weapons. Now!"

A minute later the cloud was less than a mile away and all the soldiers were on deck. The ship thrashed through the heaving seas with such force it was all Otto could do to stay on his feet.

"Spread out along the rail," Otto said. "Draw your weapons and hold them aloft. Whatever you do, don't lose them."

"Heaven's mercy, what is that?" Axel stared out over the water at the Black Wind.

"That is what I'm trying to stop. Now move your men into position before it arrives or we're all dead."

Happily there were no further arguments and the soldiers quickly dispersed around the ship. As soon as they did, Otto ran ether through their mithril weapons, strengthening a barrier that quickly encompassed the entire ship. Even with the mithril enhancing his magic, it took thirty threads' worth of ether to enclose them.

And not a moment too soon. He had barely finished the barrier when the Black Wind hit it. The power of the corruption nearly drove him to his knees. He could feel the darkness and its desire to consume their lives. It was evil on a scale he'd never encountered. Even the ghouls, for all their vileness, were understandable as predators. But this had no mind, just an emptiness that wanted to consume everything.

The seconds dragged on as the darkness waged a relentless assault on the ethereal barrier. Each tiny blow would have been nothing on its own, but thousands of them every minute nearly drove him mad.

Sometime through the passage, he finally realized what they were dealing with and why it didn't obey the gale. The Black Wind was actually a huge swarm of undead insects. It had never occurred to him that bugs might become undead, though anything living could, so why not bugs?

At some point Otto's mind went blank, overwhelmed by the nonstop assault. His only focus was on maintaining the barrier.

The pain vanished into a pocket in the back of his mind.

The rolling deck became a vague background presence.

Keep the barrier up, damn it! Nothing else mattered.

That mantra ran through his mind over and over.

Some time passed. He couldn't begin to guess how much. Until finally there was something else.

A voice. He knew that voice.

"Master!"

Otto blinked and found Corina standing directly in front of him.

"Master, it's okay. We're past the Narrows and we've left the Black Wind behind. You can release the barrier."

Release the barrier? It took him a moment to process that.

They were safe then.

He took a deep breath and let the magic slowly unwind. When it was finished, he asked, "Is everyone okay?"

"Yes. You didn't let a single one through."

"Good." Otto fell flat on his face and darkness claimed him.

○

Otto sat up in bed and groaned. He'd fainted again. This was getting to be a habit. Judging from the sound of rushing water outside the hull, they were still making progress. And from the darkness outside his window, he assumed he'd slept the entire day.

A light appeared and he turned to see Corina sitting in his leather chair. She had shed her heavy cloak and judging from the bloodshot eyes and dark circles, she hadn't slept in a while.

"How long this time?" Otto asked.

"It's a little after midnight, so I'd say sixteen hours. Not as bad as last time you wore yourself out. I don't know how you do it. Just maintaining the five threads' worth of ether I kept at the ready nearly killed me. You used about five times as much."

"I did what was necessary, nothing more. How is the ship?"

"According to the captain, three of the timbers cracked, but we're in no danger of sinking and we're not taking on water. They braced the hull to reinforce it, he said. I didn't actually watch the process. Figured I'd be more in the way than a help. Besides, I didn't want to leave you alone."

Otto grunted and swung his legs over the side. "Did any of the men get hurt by the magic?"

"No, though they did complain of tingling in their hands for a few hours afterward." Corina shook her head. "Given the alternative, that didn't seem so bad."

Otto shuddered to think what would have happened had the Black Wind gotten in. Those insects would have eaten them down to the bone in seconds. "Is there anything to eat? I'm starving."

"I figured you would be." Corina handed him a plate covered with a white linen napkin. "I'll let you eat in peace. Hans is probably still up waiting for news. He worries like a mother hen. We would both appreciate it if you stopped giving us fits."

"You sound like my mother. Go on. I'm going to eat and sleep again. I should be fine in the morning."

Corina gave him one last, long, searching look before ducking out into the hall. Otto tossed the napkin aside and looked with distaste on the cured ham, biscuit, and apple on the plate. Unappetizing or not, he ate it all and washed it down with tepid water from the pitcher beside his bed.

The next two weeks were as peaceful as the passage through the Narrows was harrowing. The weather warmed as they turned back northeast and everyone was glad not to have to wear their heavy cloaks anymore.

Otto's strength quickly returned, more quickly, in fact, than he expected. Perhaps constantly pushing himself to the point of exhaustion was building his stamina a little more each time. He liked to think there was at least some benefit to be had beyond survival.

The only downside to the whole event was the men looked at him even more warily now. Before they had hid their nerves whenever he was around, but now they didn't bother. Even Hans stiffened when he walked by. Hopefully they'd get over it sooner rather than later.

Only Axel and Corina still treated him the same. He doubted Axel would ever really hold him in awe. His brother had beaten him up too many times when they were kids to really consider him a danger. He did show respect now, and that was enough for Otto.

Respect was all he'd ever wanted. If he had to frighten people into giving it, well, that was a price he was willing to pay.

CHAPTER 31

"Land ho!" The lookout's shout made Otto flinch.

He and pretty much everyone else was out on deck trying to escape the stifling heat below. They had reached the tropics again and with it came intense heat and humidity. Sweat plastered Otto's tunic to his back and soaked his hair.

Was that better or worse than the cold? He couldn't decide. Otto hated both extremes with a passion.

Fifteen days had passed since the passage through the Narrows and nearly two months since they left Lux. To say everyone was eager for some time on solid ground would be putting it mildly. They had also been going through their water at a rapid clip, so refilling the casks would be a relief.

Despite the island—or at least the mountain jutting up out of the center of it—being visible for hours, it took the rest of the day and night to reach it. Otto stood beside Captain Wainwright as he brought them into a natural harbor, took down the sails, and lowered the anchor. They ended up about a half mile offshore, a reasonable enough trip for the ship's two dinghies.

"I've never seen anything like this place," Captain Wainwright said. "It's like this harbor was made for ships to anchor in."

"Perhaps it was," Otto said. "One of the Arcane Lords might have built it for some reason we can't even imagine. All that matters today is that it makes our task that much easier."

Axel approached from the lower deck. "We're here. How do you want to handle this, little brother?"

"I'll take Hans and his squad to collect the water. You and your scouts can handle the hunting. We'll meet back on the beach before sunset. Sound good?"

Axel nodded then grinned. "Do you know how long it's been since I went hunting for beasts instead of men? I suppose we're not apt to find boar or deer here, but anything will be welcome. I'm so sick of jerky I can't even put it into words."

"The crew and I will reinforce the hull where we hit that ice floe. It's not serious, but I'll feel better when we've put some two-inch-thick oak planks across it."

"I'll leave that in your hands, Captain," Otto said. "As soon as we've refilled our supplies, I want to be on our way. We still have, what, a month to go before we reach our destination?"

"Thereabout," Wainwright said. "Don't worry, we'll have the patch in place by noon and be ready to go when you are."

That was exactly what Otto wanted to hear. He and Axel went down on deck and set about collecting their various team members.

"Do you think we'll see any monsters?" Corina asked.

"I certainly hope not. Besides, I need you to stay on the ship."

"But—"

"No buts. If anything attacks the ship while I'm gone, your lightning will be the best way to chase it off quickly. I have no desire to end up marooned on a jungle island."

She frowned but didn't argue. That pleased Otto as he had no intention of changing his mind. Despite her complaints, he didn't make these decisions to annoy her. If Otto said he needed someone somewhere, then he had a good reason for it.

Half an hour later, Otto climbed into the dinghy with Hans and his squad as well as ten empty water casks. The heavy wooden barrels had slots for poles that would allow two men to carry them. He didn't know how much they weighed full, but whoever got stuck ferrying them wasn't going to be happy.

The crew lowered them down and they set out for the island. Axel's boat was already nearing the beach. Hopefully they'd find something edible. Just the thought of fresh, roasted meat set Otto's mouth to watering.

While the men pulled for shore, Otto sent his sight soaring out ahead of them. If he found a source of fresh water before they landed, that would speed things up considerably.

The beach extended about twenty yards to the edge of the jungle. Under the thick canopy, it was nearly as dark as evening with dappled shadows making it hard to pick out anything that might be lurking in ambush. It was a predator's paradise and if they didn't want to end up on the menu, they'd have to be cautious.

He flew up above the treetops and looked down. Soon enough he found a gap in the leaves. Flying over, he saw exactly what he wanted, a clear lagoon. That would be the perfect place to fill the casks. Otto tagged the water's edge with a thread and returned his sight to his body. They only had a few hundred yards to go to reach shore. Axel and his scouts had already vanished into the jungle.

The front of the dinghy hit the sand and everyone jumped out. Three of the guys pulled the boat further up on the beach then they anchored it in place with a grappling hook and rope.

"So where do we find water?" Hans asked.

"I did some scouting as we approached. There's a lagoon about half a mile inland. You and I will take point, four others will carry a pair of casks, and the last man will handle the rear. Sound good?"

"Sounds better than wandering at random looking for a puddle," Cord said. "I volunteer for rear guard duty."

Hans clapped him on the shoulder. "Good man. That's the most dangerous position."

Cord shot him a pained look.

"You weren't just hoping to avoid hauling water, hmm?" Hans asked.

"Of course not!" His indignant reply rang hollow.

Otto shook his head. "You two can bicker over your card game. I'd like to finish up before something hungry comes looking for us. Did you forget what they call this island?"

"Right, giant beasts." Hans turned to the men who were lugging a pair of casks out of the boat. "You heard Lord Shenk. Let's get a move on."

Two minute later they were on their way through the jungle. The shade made it cooler, but if anything, Otto would have sworn the humidity increased. In fact, if it increased any more it would be raining. A little ways into the jungle they hit a game trail that headed in the right general direction. Despite the risks of running into a predator, they followed it.

Hans had his sword out and his head on a swivel. With just his magical vision, Otto hadn't noticed how noisy the jungle was. Birds called overhead, some other creature howled in the distance. Insects buzzed and tried to drain his blood. Without success, thanks to the ethereal barrier protecting his exposed skin. From the curses behind him, it sounded like the others were less fortunate.

They had rounded a bend not far from the lagoon when the jungle went silent.

"Lord Shenk." Hans stopped in his tracks.

The rest of the men set their burdens down and drew their weapons.

"I noticed it too," Otto said. He sent threads of ether out in every direction in search of whatever had scared the birds into silence.

He found it a moment later. A huge beast crouched behind a wall of low shrubs. It probably waited in ambush on the game trail for whatever came to the lagoon to drink. Like Otto and his companions, for example. Unfortunately for the hunter, they weren't prey.

Otto wrapped a thread around the beast's heart and sent lightning crackling down it.

It roared and lunged out of hiding only to die at Otto's feet.

"What the hell is that?" Hans poked the black-furred creature with his toe.

Otto didn't know what it was. It looked vaguely catlike, with smooth black fur, six-inch fangs, and a thick tail. That was where the similarities ended. This thing was easily twenty feet long not counting the tail, had six legs ending in long claws, and milky, white eyes.

Whatever it was, hopefully it didn't have friends.

"Let's go," Otto said. "The lagoon is just ahead."

Five more minutes of walking brought them to the bank of a lagoon that looked like something out of a story. At the far end a waterfall roared as it poured into the pool. Even the air felt cooler here. A long rest would have been nice, but heaven only knew what might show up. Best if they did what they had to do and returned to the ship where the monsters couldn't reach them.

It took a while to fill the casks and while they were doing it Otto sent Cord back to skin the beast and collect its head, claws, and fangs. Something so rare and exotic might make a good trade item and he wasn't willing to leave it behind to rot.

Soon they were slogging their way back through the jungle. This time Otto kept threads out all around them just to be safe. With most of the team stuck lugging the now much heavier casks, he didn't want to take any chances.

The trip back to the beach took nearly three times as long as the walk in. Otto gave the guys a fifteen-minute rest before they set out again with two more empty casks. Nothing troubled them this time. It would probably take some time for another predator to realize the cat thing was dead and move in to claim its territory.

It was a hot, sweaty, exhausted group that made the final trip to the lagoon. Otto hadn't done much in the way of physical labor, but the constant need to be on alert drained him mentally. They hadn't even encountered another creature and the birds seemed content to fill the air with a cacophony of calls that would have even drowned out Abby.

When they reached the shore of the lagoon, everyone slumped to the sand. Otto didn't have the heart to rush them. Sunset was still hours away, so they had time. A little rest would hurt nothing. Just to be sure, Otto kept his focus outward toward the jungle. Damned if he had come this far only to let some beast sneak up on them now.

There was a splash and Cord said, "I swear I'm going to sleep for a week when we're done."

Most splashes prompted Otto to turn. The squad was gathered at the water's edge, each of them busy pouring handfuls of water over their face and backs. He scowled at the noise, but didn't reprimand them. They had worked hard today, hard enough to have earned—

A shadow moved through the water.

Otto never had a chance to call out a warning or summon his magic, so fast did the huge reptile burst out of the water and snap down on Cord. It dragged him into the water and out of sight before Otto fully processed what was happening.

Everyone was at a loss for words. Everyone but Hans. "Back to the ship! Forget the casks. Move it!"

Otto just gave him a look.

"With your permission, my lord?"

Otto sent threads out into the water and quickly found the creature that had killed Cord. It was swimming toward the far end of the pool, the unfortunate soldier's body in its mouth. A moment later it dove into a cave and Otto let his threads dissolve.

"It's gone. Fill the casks and we'll head back. Be sure to clean the blood off first." He motioned Hans off to one side. "Did he have a family?"

Hans shook his head. "None of us do, not to speak of anyway. The squad is our family."

"Then I'm doubly sorry, for the loss of a good soldier and a brother of sorts."

"Cord knew the risks that come with this job, we all do. Don't trouble yourself on our account. This is the most important thing any of us has ever been involved in. I speak for everyone when I say we have no regrets."

Otto wondered if Hans really spoke for his comrades, but said nothing. Done was done and they still had a long ways to go.

CHAPTER 32

The jungle shade made a welcome change from the blinding heat of the sun beating down on them. Axel had no idea what sort of game they might find, but judging from the constant stream of squawks and hoots coming from the canopy, there was no shortage of life. He slapped the back of his neck and came away with a splattered bug and some of his own blood.

Yeah, there was plenty of life and little of it friendly.

He sliced a vine in half and pressed on. Colten had gone ahead of the main group to look for tracks. The youthful scout vanished into the jungle with the same skill he showed back home. The techniques were the same even if the plants were different.

"What are we hunting for exactly?" Cobb asked.

"Meat. I don't care what it looks like as long as we can eat it. There must be something around here."

"Yeah, I just hope whatever we find doesn't consider us a meal instead."

Axel seconded that idea. He hacked a frond out of the way.

Beyond it he found Colten crouched on a game trail examining the ground. A thick carpet of fallen leaves covered the dirt, but he trusted Colten to make sense of the seemingly random patterns in the litter.

"What did you find?" Axel asked.

"I'm not sure, sir," Colten said. "Something passed through here not that long ago, something big, with four legs and a long tail. I've never seen tracks like it. Truth is I'm not sure if it's a predator or prey."

"It's prey now," Axel said. "Archers, ready your bows. I assume everyone swapped their mithril arrows for regular steel."

Everyone had which was good since he doubted Otto would be very pleased if they wasted the nearly priceless weapons hunting for dinner.

They set out behind Colten, everyone now on full alert, their movements nearly silent. A moment of pride washed over him at how quickly his men switched from relaxed to alert. There was a reason they were the best and this just reminded him why.

A quarter mile down the trail, a deep roar followed by a heavy thud filled the air.

Everyone froze and Colten looked back for instruction. Using hand gestures Axel told him to move up and take a look. Colten gave him a thumbs-up, snuck off the trail, and vanished into the jungle.

More bellows filled the air along with the heavy thuds. What in heaven's name was going on? Axel had never heard anything like those noises.

"I don't like this," Cobb muttered.

Axel shot him a glare and he fell silent.

Long minutes later, Colten emerged from the jungle and waved them up. Axel hurried over and said, "Report."

"Damnedest thing I ever seen, sir. There're two lizards fighting in a clearing about a hundred yards ahead. They've got to be at least forty feet long. If you want to take a look, I doubt they'll even notice us."

Axel wasn't sure he wanted a closer look, but he'd read that reptile meat was high quality and tasted similar to chicken. If they killed the two lizards, that might yield enough meat to last the rest of the trip.

"Show me."

"Are you kidding?" Cobb asked. "How are we supposed to kill two forty-foot-long lizards?"

"We have mithril swords. We'll cut their heads off. Now come on."

They followed Colten through the jungle to the edge of a large dirt clearing. Just as he said, a pair of huge lizards were brawling in the dirt. As he watched, they hissed at each other from about fifteen feet away, rose up on their back legs, and slammed into each other chest first. They grappled back and forth for a few seconds before breaking apart again and roaring.

"They just keep doing the same thing over and over again," Colten said. "No idea why."

Axel didn't know why either and he didn't care. All that mattered was they were exhausting themselves which would make them easier to kill. The trick would be to attack while the lizards were in the clinch. They should have enough time to close before they separated.

"Okay, here's the plan." He laid it out and Cobb wasn't the only one that looked less than thrilled. "It's called the Island of

Giant Beasts for a reason. What did you think we were going to find?"

"Slightly less giant beasts," Cobb said. "But we're here now. If we're going to do this, let's do it."

Axel grinned. Cobb might like to bitch, but when the time came there was no one Axel would rather have at his back.

The scouts drew their swords or nocked arrows.

Out in the clearing, the lizards bellowed and flicked their tongues.

They reared up and charged each other.

"Now!" Axel led their own charge.

Arrows arced over his head and clattered uselessly against the lizards' thick hide.

Damn it! Maybe they should have brought the mithril arrows.

One of the lizards spotted them and opened its mouth.

Axel hurled his sword with all his might.

The tip pierced the roof of the lizard's mouth and came out the top of its skull.

It collapsed, killed instantly.

Axel slowed and let his men charge past. With no sword, he'd be a liability.

They hit the second lizard from the side, their weapons slicing through its hide like butter.

The beast roared and thrashed. Its tail caught a scout and sent him flying fifteen feet across the clearing.

It was a final act of defiance. Cobb slashed its head half off and took a blood shower in the process. He staggered away, a crimson mess. The lizard collapsed to the dirt, unmoving.

Axel hurried over to the injured scout and sighed with relief when he saw the man still moving. "Stay still. Where are you hurt?"

"My ribs and back. Don't think anything's broken though. Remind me to thank Lord Shenk for this armor."

Axel grinned and offered his hand. Once he was on his feet, Axel walked over to the dead lizards. Even dead they were an impressive sight.

Cobb glared at them, hands on hips. "I need a bath."

"Yes, you do, but first why don't you crawl in that other one's mouth and retrieve my sword."

Cobb shot him a rude gesture which broadened Axel's grin into a full-fledged smile. "Let's cut them up. I want to be back on the ship before dark."

The scouts needed their mithril blades to slice the thick hide, but the meat underneath seemed tender enough. The light, tight-grained flesh did indeed remind Axel of chicken, or maybe pork. Either way it looked very tasty. The trick would be getting it smoked before it spoiled

They had the first lizard processed and were working on the second when the ground shook.

"What was that?" Cobb asked.

Axel had no answer. An earthquake maybe? "I don't know, but it's another reason to hurry up the hell out of here."

There was another tremor moments later, then another and another. Axel left the men to their work and walked a few yards away from them. Those felt less like earthquakes than the footsteps of something really big.

He turned his gaze from the ground to the treetops. Sure enough they were shaking and the shaking was getting closer all the time.

"Wrap it up," Axel said. "Gather what we have and let's go."

"Sir?" Colten asked.

"Something's coming, something big. Whether scavenger or

something worse I don't know and I don't want to be here when it arrives."

"No argument here." Cobb started wrapping the meat nearest him in the canvas they'd brought for exactly that purpose.

The others followed suit, spurred on by the increasing power of the tremors.

Seconds later trees crashed into the clearing, toppled by a lizard easily ten times as big as the ones they'd killed. Its tongue flicked out and its head swung toward the partially butchered corpses.

Axel didn't wait for it to think. "Move!"

The scouts ran for the trail pursued by a roar that shook the air and made Axel's ears hurt.

As they sprinted down the trail Cobb asked, "Think that's their mother?"

"Less talking, more running."

Axel gasped for breath, ducked vines, and leapt roots. Instinct as much as vision kept him on his feet. His men staggered beside him, stumbling over rocks and generally struggling to make time on a trail that had been hard without a giant lizard chasing them.

Speaking of the lizard...

He risked a glance back. The beast was only ten yards behind them and gaining. It didn't have to worry about tripping. Instead it simply stomped flat anything that got in the way. Trees shattered as its tail whipped from side to side.

"How much further?" Axel demanded of anyone that might answer. From his position at the rear of the column, only the heads of his men and the mass of trees behind them were visible.

"I can see the beach!" Colten shouted back.

Thank heaven. Now they just needed to reach the boat and make it out to sea before the lizard caught up to them. He shook his head. How, exactly, they were going to do that was another matter altogether.

They raced out of the jungle but didn't slow. Otto and his group were loading the casks into their dinghy.

"Get out of here!" Axel shouted and waved his hands.

Otto looked his way just as the lizard smashed through the tree line and onto the beach.

No way were they going to make it to the boat. That thing was going to eat them before they got off the beach.

Otto ignored Axel's frantic gesture and strode toward them, raising his hands as he went.

A moment later lightning arced out over the scouts' heads.

The lizard roared again, this time in pain.

Another burst of lightning was followed by a huge crash.

Axel skidded to a stop beside his brother.

"It's dead," Otto said. "You can relax now."

"Dead. How?" Axel forced the words out between gulps of air.

"It's just a beast. A big one to be sure, but still an animal. My lightning exploded its heart as easily as it would a human's. Besides, no way was I losing another man."

Axel straightened, his heartrate back to a normal, and studied Otto's team, now one short. "What happened?"

"Even I can't kill something if I don't see it coming. We were taken by surprise. Another lizard, smaller than yours, but still big, came out of the water and snatched Cord. I was focused on the jungle and missed it. Not a mistake I'll make again."

"Well, it looks like you found the water and we've got the meat. Shall we head back?"

Otto nodded. "The sooner we're off this wretched island, the happier I'll be."

"Lord Shenk!" Cobb said. "The ship."

Axel and Otto both whipped around. Five winged creatures circled the *Sea Star*. Axel guessed their wingspan measured fifty feet minimum.

A bolt of lightning shot out, singeing one of the giant birds and sending it flying off.

"Corina can't hold that many off by herself for long," Otto said. "We need to hurry."

CHAPTER 33

Corina paced on deck and watched the beach. How could he have left her behind again? She was supposed to be his apprentice. She couldn't learn anything if her master left her on the ship every time they arrived somewhere. She swallowed a curse, not that Corina imagined the sailors would be offended, not after she heard them in the galley when they thought she wasn't around.

The pounding stopped and she turned to look at the side of the ship. They'd put the final plank in place and were smearing tar all over it. A single whiff of the stuff when they first brought it on deck had sent her as far from the job as the ship allowed. Whoever had to make that stuff surely earned their coin.

A gust of wind blew her hair across her eyes. She brushed it aside and looked up.

The biggest damn bird she'd ever seen flew across the ship, its shadow blocking out the sun as it passed. The beast flew low enough that she could count individual gray feathers. It opened its beak and let out a squawk that hurt her ears.

Another cry prompted her to turn around. Two more birds of the same sort were winging their way toward the ship. More squawks from the opposite direction made a total of five giant birds.

Panicked shouts from the crew mingled with the birds' calls. The combination of noise and fear made her pulse pound in her ears.

Why was it every time she complained about her master leaving her behind, something horrible happened? First bandits in Colt's Land and now giant birds. Assuming she lived through this, Corina swore she'd never complain again.

Captain Wainwright ran over beside her. "You can stop them, right?"

"I can try. Have everyone go below deck. We don't want one of the sailors getting turned into bird food."

"Right." The captain hurried away, shooing his men ahead of him like a shepherd with his flock.

Now Corina needed to avoid becoming bird food herself while figuring out how to drive off the beasts. Lightning would probably be best, but she didn't know if she had power enough to kill them. Another shadow passed over the ship. Not to mention what might happen if one of them crashed into the ship. Visions of broken masts, shredded canvas, and snapped rigging filled her imagination with her furious master laid over it all.

No, caution would definitely be the order of the day.

Corina put her back to the main mast and sent out a targeting thread. It passed through the bird easily enough. When she felt its heart, she loosed a bolt of lightning.

It took only moments, but by the time she released her spell, the target had moved and she ended up only singeing its tail feathers. The bird squawked and banked away from the ship, soaring back to the island.

Not what she had in mind, but it was gone, so she'd take it.

The ship lurched about thirty degrees toward the front. Corina staggered, caught herself on the mast, and peeked around it.

One of the birds had landed in the forecastle. It cocked its head and met her gaze before letting out a weird squawking growl.

Corina ducked back out of sight. She needed to deal with that one before it—

The ship shuddered and thrashed.

Corina looked again. The bird was trying to force its way around the front mast.

Something cracked.

So not good.

Her targeting thread shot out. As soon as it passed through the bird's flesh, she fired a second lightning bolt.

This one hammered home and the smell of burnt feathers mingled with pained squawking. The bird staggered back and splashed into the ocean.

That was two down.

There was a rush of air. The remaining three birds dove out of the sky and splashed down beside the one she killed. The sound of tearing flesh filled the air as they fed on their former companion.

Corina shuddered, but better they eat their friend than attack the ship. All at once the feeding frenzy went silent. She should really take a look and find out what was happening. Corina told herself that three times before the message reached her feet.

She had barely taken a step when the sound of boots on the

deck prompted her to turn back. Her master stood beside the rail. Hans was busy climbing up behind him. Relief such as she had never known flooded through her. She ran over and hugged him.

A gentle hand on her head wiped away the rest of the fear. "You did well."

Corina smiled and stepped back. That was the best praise possible. "Thank you, Master. When those birds showed up, I feared for our safety, but my magic worked on them fine."

He nodded. "They're just beasts. Oversized ones to be sure, but beasts nonetheless. Where's the crew? We need to load our supplies and get out of here before anything else shows up."

"I second that plan," Hans said.

The rest of the squad had made it up on deck, but someone was missing.

"Where's Cord?" Corina asked.

Hans shook his head. "Didn't make it. Some damn lizard-looking thing came out of nowhere and ate him. Bloody miracle we didn't lose anyone else."

Corina could hardly believe what he just said. One of the guys had been killed, when her master was with them? It seemed impossible, yet the truth was undeniable. Cord was gone.

"The crew," her master said. "Quickly."

"Right, sorry." Corina hurried for the door to the lower decks and shouted the all clear.

Sailors came boiling up from below. While the men started pulling casks of water over the side, Captain Wainwright joined her master and Hans near the main mast.

"I heard a crack when I was below," the captain said.

"One of the birds landed in the forecastle," Corina said. "I think it damaged the front mast trying to reach me."

Captain Wainwright hurried toward the front of the ship and examined the mast. He ran his hands along it, muttering and shaking his head. "This is no good. If we put up so much as a single sheet, she'll snap right off. It needs replacing."

"Can we sail without it?" her master asked.

"Yes, but you'll lose a third of our speed and if we need to make a getaway, not having that mast will be a serious problem."

"What about the Land of the Demon Binders?" her master asked. "Can we make it there?"

Captain Wainwright grimaced. "Yeah, it's only two weeks or so northeast, but we might be better off taking our chances without the mast."

"No. As you said, if we need to flee in a hurry, a distinct possibility if things go wrong in the Celestial Empire, I want to have every bit of speed we can muster. Take us to the demon binders as soon as the supplies are loaded. I'll be in my cabin trying to figure out what we can trade for a new mast."

Corina debated following him, but from his stony expression decided to wait on deck for a while.

"He'll be alright," Hans said. "I think losing Cord bothered him."

Corina watched her master's retreating back. Hans was probably right, but not in the way he thought. Lord Shenk no doubt considered losing Cord a personal failure. That would certainly bother him more than the death of a single soldier.

She tried to think of something that would cheer him up, but nothing came to mind. Her master wasn't the sort of person that a joke or kind word would affect. Corina would just have to be patient and be ready if he needed anything. That was part of an apprentice's job after all.

CHAPTER 34

T he chill that ran down Otto's spine had nothing to do with the temperature. They were still in the tropics and sweat plastered his tunic to his back. No, this chill was entirely magical in nature. The ship eased its way through a thick fog that rose off the water as they moved toward the Land of the Demon Binders. At least, according to the charts Otto had found in his master's library, they were headed toward that fabled land. He seriously doubted anyone living had ever visited the place.

"Master, why do I feel like I want to throw up even though my stomach is fine?" Corina had come to join him on deck the moment the strange fog appeared and with it the magical dread.

"Look closely at the ether. You can see the tiny threads of darkness running through it. That's corruption, a sign that demons, undead, or something equally nasty is nearby. I've never seen it diffused like this. It must be some sort of barrier to dissuade those less determined than us. Wrap yourself in an ethereal barrier. That will block most of the effect."

One of the sailors vomited noisily over the side. For those with no magic to protect them, the effect of the fog must have been far worse.

"My lord, should we turn back?" Captain Wainwright asked from the helm. The good captain, as stalwart a fellow as Otto had ever met, trembled when he spoke.

"Have you thought of another way to fix our forward mast?"

"No."

"Then sail on. It can't be much further."

Less than a minute later, a rhythmic splashing sounded deeper in the fog. He couldn't tell exactly where it was coming from. The sound was muffled and indistinct.

Corina clutched his arm. "What is that?"

"Sounds like paddles. If there's trouble, I'm going to need that arm. Why don't you go fetch Hans and the guys? Tell Axel to stay below but to keep his ears open for sounds of trouble."

"Yes, Master." She hurried belowdecks.

Once he was alone, Otto allowed himself a single, deep, steadying breath. Looking terrified would do nothing to improve morale, but if he was honest, this whole situation scared the hell out of him. They had no idea what they were sailing into, no idea how the locals viewed uninvited visitors, no idea about anything really beyond the fact that they needed a port to do repairs.

"My lord?" Hans and the remaining four members of his squad emerged from below deck, swords drawn.

"Put those away," Otto said. "I think we're about to have visitors and we don't want them thinking we're spoiling for a fight."

Hans hesitated, one of the few times he'd failed to obey an

order instantly. "Having the blades out helps with the sickness."

Otto frowned and studied the ether around Hans's sword. Whenever one of the wisps of corruption touched the mithril, it went up in a puff of invisible smoke. Just the presence of mithril purified the corruption. How interesting.

"You can keep them drawn for now, but as soon as whoever's coming gets here, put them away."

"Yes, my lord." After a moment Hans asked, "Are you certain it's a who and not a what?"

"Unless the local monsters travel by boat, I'm pretty sure it's a who."

"It is." Corina's voice held a brittle note Otto hadn't heard before. "But I'm not sure what sort of a who he is."

Otto waved at Hans who reluctantly sheathed his sword then went to join Corina at the ship's rail. From out of the murk, a canoe made of bone came toward them. What he had first taken for oars turned out to be fins attached to the side of the canoe that propelled it forward. A single man stood in the front. He wore an odd headdress made of some kind of leather stretched over a frame. The skull of a small animal stared out from just above the brim. His clothes were no less odd. He wore a black robe woven with barbed wire that dug into his flesh in places.

Just when Otto thought things couldn't get any stranger, he spoke. "What is your purpose here?"

The stranger's voice sounded like a multitude of voices all speaking slightly out of time. Just listening to it made Otto's stomach churn.

"We're travelers on our way to the Celestial Empire," Otto said. "Our ship has been damaged and we need a port to make repairs. Yours was the nearest."

The odd fellow stared at Otto without seeming to see him. At last he said, "You have goods to trade for your repairs?"

"We do."

"Very well. The Cult of Astaroth agrees to sponsor your visit. You will restrict yourselves to their enclave. Anyone caught outside of that district will be sacrificed. Follow me."

The canoe turned and headed back toward the fog. A path opened as it passed, making a tunnel through the mist for them to follow.

"Was that a person?" Corina asked.

"I wish I knew," Otto said. If it was, he couldn't help wondering what sort of person wore a robe woven with barbed wire. If that was the local fashion trend, Otto had no desire to follow it.

Something bumped the underside of the hull.

From his place at the helm Captain Wainwright said, "Something has us, Lord Shenk. I'm no longer in control of the ship."

Otto refused to let the captain's panic infect him. The moment that happened, he was doomed. Since discovering the corruption in the local ether, he'd been reluctant to extend his senses, but now he needed to know what they were dealing with. Whether he could do anything about it was another matter.

Resting a hand on his mithril sword, Otto sent his gaze out down toward the water. Pain stabbed his eyes, but he ignored it. Under the hull, a... creature had the *Star* in its grasp. It looked a bit like a whale, only with frills and tentacles coming out of its back. The tentacles looked purpose built for grasping ships. He guessed they measured a good foot in diameter and were probably strong enough to crush the hull should the beast be so inclined.

Otto released the spell and the pain vanished. His cheeks felt wet and when he went to brush the tears away his hand came back bloody.

"Corina, don't touch the ether here unless it's life or death." Turning to the captain Otto said, "Everything's okay. Have the sailors lower all sails. We'll be taken to the dock automatically."

Otto silently hoped he was right about that. Since meeting Lord Karonin, he'd been out of his depth plenty of times, but right now he felt like he was in the deepest, darkest hole ever.

◌

Just as Otto predicted, the bizarre creature controlling the ship guided them right to a dock. So gently it barely made a sound, it eased the ship into place. At least the dock itself looked normal enough. Made of wood treated with tar for preservation, it wouldn't have looked out of place in Lux.

The dock quickly disappeared into the fog. The city itself, assuming there was a city, remained hidden behind a vail of mist and corruption.

In the water beside them, their odd guide glared at Otto. "A representative of Astaroth's cult will be here shortly. Do not leave your berth until they arrive."

With an extravagant flourish of his leather headdress, the man and his canoe paddled off into the fog. A pair of sailors put the gangplank down and hurried to tie the ship up before scurrying back aboard.

"What should we expect, my lord?" Hans asked.

Otto had no idea. "The Cult of Astaroth worship the demon lord of disease and undeath, so a hale and hearty fellow with rosy cheeks and a big smile are unlikely. What little I know

185

comes from a book nearly a thousand years old. We'll have to keep our wits about us and remain calm."

Corina's laugh came out as a high-pitched giggle. "Keep calm? I can barely keep from leaping over the side and swimming away from this place. It's wrong in ways I can't begin to describe."

"Given what I saw guiding the ship, I recommend staying out of the water. If you'd feel better, you can go below and stay with Axel. There's no shame in being afraid, especially here. I'll negotiate with whoever shows up and try to get us out of here as quickly as possible."

She bit her lip and straightened. "I'm your apprentice. My place is at your side. I'll be okay."

Otto squeezed her shoulder. Corina's courage and determination made him proud. "Good. You may notice something I miss."

The conversation ended when the sound of hard boots on wood came echoing out of the fog. The mist parted, revealing the last thing Otto expected: a woman, and a beautiful one at that.

She dressed in a black robe that hung down to midcalf, but was slit in such a way that with every step her pale, smooth thighs appeared for a second before being obscured again by the cloth. A black metal chain served as a belt, cinching the robe tight to her narrow waist. It didn't have barbs, which made him feel a little better about her sanity.

A cutout in the shape of a jagged symbol Otto didn't recognize revealed the tops of her impressive breasts. Her eyes glimmered with crimson fire against skin so pale her black veins were visible underneath.

She stopped at the foot of the gangplank and smiled up at them, bloodred lips parting just enough to reveal slightly elongated eyeteeth. "Welcome to the Land of the Demon Binders. You should be honored to know that you are the first guests we have welcomed in a hundred years."

Otto wasn't certain what he felt, but honored wasn't it. "Thank you. Please, won't you come aboard?"

She climbed the gangplank, looking perfectly at ease on the swaying board.

"No need to beat around the bush," she said. "You told The Voice that you had trade goods. Of what sort and how much?"

"We have mithril—"

She hissed and scowled. "You will find no one interested in the vile metal here. In fact, it will be better for all of you if you take none of it off this ship. Continue, please."

Otto couldn't have been more shocked by her reaction. Everyone valued mithril, or so he'd believed. "We have some fine liqueurs and high-quality weapons. Perhaps if I knew what you valued…"

Her smile returned. "Why don't you just show me what you have and I'll tell you what I want. Fair enough?"

He didn't think it was fair at all, but they were desperate, so he nodded. "Follow me. All our trade goods are in the hold."

They descended into the ship's interior. Axel and the scouts must have retreated into their quarters as there was no sign of them. Otto led their guest to the modest hold and opened the door.

The mithril was locked inside wooden chests—a precaution that seemed especially prudent now. Swords, armor, and other items made by Garen's finest smiths gleamed in the light of two Lux crystals.

She ignored them all and went straight to the giant feline hide they'd collected on the island. "Where did you get this? An intact skull with full cape of a six-legged leopard is very rare."

"On the Island of Giant Beasts," Otto said. "That's also where the mast was broken."

"I'll trade you this pelt for a new mast, whatever help you need with repairs, and three months' worth of rations."

Otto stared at the woman but saw no sign she was joking. "I accept your offer. How soon can work begin?"

"An hour? I need only give the order." She finally stood. "You are a wizard. Would you like to join me tonight for the summoning ritual? I'll show you exactly why that pelt is so valuable."

Never one to pass up the chance to learn new magic, Otto said, "I'd be delighted. May I ask your name?"

"Names have power. Only Lord Astaroth knows my true name now, but you may call me Lady White."

"I'm Otto, it's a pleasure to meet you."

Her laugh was rich with darkness and malice. "No one has been pleased to meet me in a very long time. The work crew will arrive within the hour and I will send a palanquin for you after dark. Be sure to leave your mithril behind."

Otto nodded, led her back upstairs, and blew out a long breath after she'd gone.

"Are you sure going with her is a good idea, Master?" He'd nearly forgotten Corina was even there so distracted had he been by Lady White's presence.

"Never let fear hold you back from learning something new. You'll never advance like that. Besides, if she wanted us dead, I suspect we'd already be feeding the creatures of the deep."

᧐

E ven after sunset the fog showed no sign of thinning. Otto stood on deck examining the new forward mast. The workers Lady White had sent seemed human, albeit thin and poorly dressed. His first thought had been slaves, but they wore no irons and bore no brands. Nor did they speak, either to each other or to the crew. In the end, Captain Wainwright had ordered his people to stay out of the way and let the workers do their thing.

That proved to be a good decision and soon enough the new mast was in place. The captain, though troubled by the workers' behavior, deemed their efforts acceptable. He assured Otto that they would be able to sail in the morning with no trouble.

Otto liked the sound of that. Though they had been treated hospitably enough, he had no desire to linger. On the other hand, he couldn't deny his excitement at the prospect of learning a new form of magic. Whatever Lady White had planned, it was bound to be interesting.

The sound of loud, clattering footsteps approaching through the fog drew his attention. That must be his transport.

Hans and Corina waited beside the gangplank to see him off. Neither Axel or his scouts had set foot out from below deck since they arrived. He doubted his brother was scared, but maybe the corruption was proving too much for them. Otto couldn't blame them if it was.

"Be careful, my lord," Hans said.

"Yeah, that Lady White seems a little off," Corina added.

"Both of you calm down. Everything's going to be fine. Besides, I engraved a rune at the base of the gangplank in case I need to flee quickly. Getting out of the harbor in this fog and with the monsters guarding the water is another matter, but I have taken precautions."

From out of the fog, a palanquin born by four creatures from your worst nightmare appeared. They had humanoid bodies, but that was where the resemblance ended. Each one had the head of a vulture; black, rotten wings; hands that ended in talons; and skeletal feet that should have crumbled under the weight of their burden.

The palanquin itself appeared to be an ordinary wooden box about six feet by eight and seven feet tall. Perfectly comfortable for a single passenger, as long as you didn't dwell on what was carrying you.

With more confidence than he felt, Otto strode down the gangplank, never looking back lest he give Hans and Corina something else to worry about. One of the vulture creatures opened the door for Otto, who climbed inside. He felt naked without his mithril sword, but still had plenty of power at his disposal. If this was a trap, his enemies wouldn't find him easy prey.

As soon as he was settled, the bearers picked the palanquin up and they set off at a brisk, but smooth, trot. Otto brushed the curtain back, but saw nothing but fog. It seemed like they traveled in a bubble surrounded by endless mist. Clearly his hosts were paranoid about him getting even a tiny look at their city, assuming there was a city. He could have been in the middle of nowhere for all he knew.

At last they stopped again and the bearers lowed him to the ground and opened the door. Otto stepped out in front of a black tower about five stories high. Gargoyles in the shape of vultures jutted from scores of ledges. When Otto looked closely, he would have sworn their eyes glowed red.

The tower's front door opened and Lady White stepped out. The warm glow of firelight gave her pale skin a healthier appearance. She had changed from the black robe she'd worn earlier into something more formal. Calling it a gown seemed wrong. No one had ever worn such an outfit to a gala. It was all black of course, with red highlights. A high, stiff collar framed her face and tapered down to merge with a tight bodice and short skirt that left her legs bare from midthigh down to black leather shoes with four-inch dagger heels. A black cape that ended just above her ankles made a perfect frame for her.

"Welcome, Otto." She bowed and smiled without it reaching her eyes. "I'm so pleased you decided to join me tonight. I believe you will gain a great deal from our ritual. It will certainly enhance my own power. If my superiors in the cult had any clue of the wondrous pelt you'd brought, they never would have put me in charge of greeting you."

Again with the pelt. He still couldn't understand how the skin of a dead animal was worth everything she claimed. "I'm looking forward to observing. Any sort of new magic is of great interest to me."

"Please." She beckoned him in and Otto stepped through the door which closed behind him with a rather final-sounding thud. "This way."

She led him through empty passages that looked more like tunnels than the inside of a manmade structure. They encountered no one else, but more than once Otto would have sworn he sensed eyes on him.

From behind him came a powerful, burning rage. Otto spun but found only emptiness.

"Don't mind my familiars," Lady White said. "They're jealous of anyone I bring for a visit. The poor things have never been good at sharing me. They're harmless, unless I wish it otherwise."

The subtle threat made Otto smile. Lady White was clearly a woman after his own heart. The featureless stone passage continued, along with the subtle flashes of malice, for another minute or so until they finally reached a door. She pushed it open revealing a round chamber with a symbol carved in the center. It wasn't one Otto had seen before.

Wait. Yes, he had. It was the same design as the opening in Lady White's dress from that morning. It must have some significance in the Cult of Astaroth. He made a point of memorizing it for future research.

She closed the door and spoke a word in a language unknown to Otto. The ether surged around them, forming a barrier.

"There, now we can begin. This is my private summoning chamber. It's warded so that even my superiors can't see what I'm doing. A girl needs her privacy now and then."

"Especially when binding demons," Otto said.

"You recognize its purpose? I'm impressed. I had assumed you knew nothing about our magic."

"I don't," Otto said. "The name of this country is the Land of the Demon Binders. It didn't take a genius to guess the purpose of your most secure room."

She laughed and clapped her hands together, a rather girlish gesture considering what was about to happen. "True enough. Now, on with the demonstration. To bind a demon, you need something to bind it to. Your litter bearers, for instance, were stitched together from dead slaves and parts of giant vultures, a bird we have in great quantities. The power of the demon you can bind is directly related to the strength of the body you bind it to."

"Do beasts make better hosts than humans?"

"Depends. If I want to create a warbeast, for example, an animal, specifically a powerful predator, is ideal. Echoes of its savagery linger in the remains, calling to a more powerful demon. If you want a subtle servant, humans tend to be better."

Otto nodded. The explanation made sense, though he'd never heard that a corpse was anything more than an empty shell of flesh. "Is there anything I can do to assist you?"

"No. I must do this alone. Remain still and silent and whatever you do, don't manipulate the ether. The slightest uncontrolled vibration will ruin the ritual and set free an insane warbeast."

Otto appreciated the level of trust it must have taken for her to allow him to watch. Of course, it wasn't like he wanted to fight a demonic warbeast. He didn't even know what one was, much less what it could do.

Lady White moved to stand in the circle directly in front of the pelt. She threw her hands up and crimson light flowed from her fingertips into the magic circle. The light didn't stop until every inch glowed.

In the ether, only the corrupt flecks responded to her magic. The pure ether acted only as a conduit for the corruption. He'd never seen anything like it.

The ritual continued.

Next she made a circle, combining the thumbs and forefingers of both hands. Inky blackness filled that circle then slowly oozed down into the pelt. The darkness was pure corruption. Looking at it made Otto nauseous. He couldn't imagine actually touching it the way Lady White did.

When the darkness had fully engulfed the pelt, she lowered her hands. For the first time Otto saw something like strain on her beautiful features. Wrinkles creased her forehead and her lips were compressed in a tight line. Clearly the ritual took its toll.

The pelt now bobbed on top of the darkness. Slowly the two merged as the darkness gave the pelt dimension, restoring it to a semblance of life, though one far from natural.

When the ether calmed at last, a dark caricature of the six-legged leopard stood in the center of the circle, its eyes glowing red.

Lady White clapped once and the ominous aura that had filled the room vanished. "The summoning is complete."

She pointed at her new warbeast, then at the floor. It sat on its haunches and looked up at her like a loyal pet; only the lolling tongue was missing.

"Congratulations. I've never witnessed anything like what you just accomplished."

"The summoning is simple enough, the hard part is subjugating the demon to your will. Even an instant of doubt will result in you turned into a bloody lump of meat. Happily, I left my doubts behind long ago. Still, it's thirsty work. Would you join me for a glass of wine?"

Otto nodded, his own mouth feeling as dry as a desert.

They left the warbeast in the summoning chamber and Lady White led him down a passage he hadn't even noticed when they passed it earlier. It ended at a salon decorated in high style, the furniture all done in black leather, and a table carved from bone and ebony. She gestured to one of the tables then sat opposite him.

A bottle of wine and two glasses appeared out of nowhere, poured, and landed on the table. Lady White took the glass in front of her and drank deeply. Otto took a sip from his own glass and smiled at the high quality of the vintage. They should export it, such fine wine would bring an excellent price in Garen.

"I suppose this is where you try and recruit me to your cult," Otto said.

Lady White set her glass down and the bottle topped her off. "Hardly. Your soul is of no interest to Astaroth. What little of your mortality remains is too mingled with the ether to be of use. No, I have another proposal for you."

Otto took another sip to cover his surprise. He'd felt certain she would try and convince him to become a demon binder. "I'm happy to consider any proposal you'd like to make."

"The Cult of Astaroth is currently in a poor position here. To increase our power, we have sought to expand outside of our homeland."

Otto nodded, his expression neutral. If she imagined him welcoming demon worshippers into the empire, she was crazy. "Go on."

"To that end, we've sent agents to the Celestial Empire. A small cell has established itself in their capital city. While they've gained some followers and created a modest force of undead warriors, the empire is too organized for us to truly thrive. I don't directly oversee that operation and reports from my subordinate have been slow in coming. Hardly ideal, but far from a surprise given the forces opposing us. I know little of the details beyond what I've told you, but I believe we can help each other."

"My interest in the empire is narrow. Getting deeply involved in local politics doesn't concern me."

"Exactly, that's why you're useful. The last message I received indicated that they want someone that can kill a high-ranking official thus clearing the way for someone allied with us to assume the post."

"So you need an assassin. I have no problem taking on that role. But what can you do for me?"

"We can provide you with a way in." She leaned forward so their faces were only inches apart. Up close she smelled of grave earth and decay. The lovely Lady White might be a bit less alive than he'd first thought. "You must understand, the empire is a sealed nation. They have only a single point of contact with the outside world and no foreigners are allowed in. Our agents can smuggle you across the border and into the capital. I assume that's where you want to go."

Otto didn't know exactly where he wanted to go. Perhaps she could tell him. "I'm looking for the lab or workshop of their Arcane Lord. I don't know where that is exactly."

"Then you need our help even more. Kill the official, and we will help you complete whatever mission you're on. I swear it in Lord Astaroth's name."

Was an oath sworn in the name of a demon lord worth anything? He didn't know, but doubted he'd find a better offer.

"Agreed."

"Excellent. One of our agents will meet you in the port city of Han. He or she, I can't say which, will be dressed in all black with a single red flower somewhere visible." She stood and held out her hand. "I believe Lord Astaroth guided you to us. Perhaps one day we will meet again."

Otto gently grasped her hand. It felt cold, like the hand of a corpse. "Indeed, this has been an illuminating experience."

They parted and soon enough he was on his way back to the ship, once again carried by the demon bearers. Illuminating or not, he'd had his fill of the Land of the Demon Binders.

✿

After the rather harrowing events in the Land of the Demon Binders, Otto was glad to be back at sea. Their exit from the harbor had been accomplished by the same means as their entrance, the bizarre sea beast and the odd being Lady White called The Voice.

Now two days away from the fog-shrouded land and standing on deck in the bright, warm sun, Otto took a moment to consider the deal he'd made. At the time, accepting Lady White's offer of help had seemed like the prudent move. But now he wondered.

Putting his fate in the hands of demon worshipers he wasn't even sure were still alive seemed like pushing his luck. On the other hand, if the empire was as sealed off as she claimed, there might not be any other option. Once he'd had a look around the city and spoken with their agent, he'd make up his mind for sure.

Feeling a little better about his decision, Otto turned to find Corina staring at him. "Did you need something?"

"No, it's just that you've seemed on edge since we left that awful place. Are you sure you don't want to talk about what happened?"

Otto had remained silent about his conversation with Lady White for the very simple reason that he didn't feel like explaining his decisions. And there was no question in his mind that his apprentice and his bodyguards, not to mention his brother, would all disapprove of him doing business with the Cult of Astaroth. Which was fine, he didn't especially care what they thought. Otto just didn't want to have a debate.

"They offered me a way into the empire in exchange for

helping them remove a local magistrate that's causing them problems. It's a last resort, so don't worry about it."

"They only offered you a way in? What about the rest of us?"

He'd been thinking about that. After what happened in Audin, he would actually prefer to leave them behind this time. Worrying about Hans and Corina getting into trouble was a distraction he didn't need. If the price was having no one to watch his back, then so be it.

"You all will remain behind and prepare for the voyage home. The ship will need a full refit and maintenance. That's plenty to keep you busy."

"But you could get into trouble without us," Corina said.

Otto shook his head. He appreciated the concern, but on this his mind was made up. "Not this time. Once I secure the Heart, I'm coming straight back here via the ether. I can't take you or the guys with me. If it all falls apart, I can escape on my own more easily. It'll be safer for all of us."

She looked like she wanted to argue some more but he held up a hand. "I know you want to help. And I appreciate it, but this time, the best thing you can do is watch over the ship and make sure everything is ready for my return. Depending on how things go, we may need to leave in a hurry."

"Hans isn't going to like it," she said.

"Of that I have no doubt."

CHAPTER 35

Port Han wasn't actually part of the Celestial Empire. It was the largest city on a peninsula that jutted out into the ocean to the south. It wasn't a particularly large area and Otto couldn't imagine why the empire didn't simply conquer it and claim the port for their own, but for whatever reason, they hadn't.

He stretched and yawned, enjoying the early morning air from his place in the ship's forecastle. Since leaving the Land of the Demon Binders, Otto had gotten rested and his magic was now at full strength. If this mission was anything like what he had to deal with in Colt's Workshop, he was going to need every bit of power he could muster. Especially since he wouldn't have any backup.

Neither Axel nor Hans had been thrilled when he told them he was going in alone, but in the end, they really had little to say about it. Considering how tightly controlled the empire was, a dozen foreigners would stick out too much to be useful. They'd be caught and executed in hours at best. Otto wasn't exactly happy about the situation either, but it was what it was.

Ahead of them, the city grew larger by the minute. After the City of Coins, Port Han's wall wasn't terribly impressive, but it no doubt served its purpose. The buildings consisted of large warehouses near the dock, and smaller buildings further inland. All pretty typical.

Four hours later they sailed into the port without so much as a greeting from anyone in charge. No ships patrolled the harbor or surrounding water. Ships of every size were tied up seemingly at random.

Axel joined him as the sailors finished their work. "This can't be normal."

"It might be normal for here," Otto said. "The business district in Garen used to let people come and go as they pleased before we changed the rules. This might be something similar. Either way, we need to have a look around. Leave six men to guard the ship. The rest of us will go exploring."

Axel nodded and went to issue orders. Otto made his way to the helm where Captain Wainwright stood with his arms crossed as he gazed out over the city.

"Not what you were expecting, Captain?" Otto asked.

"Not exactly. Aside from the style of the buildings, this could be any of a dozen ports I've visited. I thought things might be more exotic."

"I'm taking a party to look around. Would you like to join us? I'm sure you need supplies to prepare the ship for the journey home."

"I'll take you up on that. We have room enough for ten more casks. If I can find some kind of preserved food that will last long enough, maybe we can avoid any stops on the way home."

"That would suit me very well. I'll leave it in your hands as I fear logistics are outside my area of expertise."

The shore party set out down the dock toward the city. With every step Otto expected some sort of official to show up and ask for money, either a bribe or tax or whatever. But they reached the city proper without issue.

"At least there's no fog," Corina said.

Otto smiled and turned the group away from the warehouses and towards an open-air market. "The ether is pure here as well. We should be able to use our magic safely."

The sounds of the market reached them before the sights. Merchants shouted about the quality of their wares. Others cried out with offers of food and drink. Everyone spoke the same language as Otto and his companions only with a dozen different accents.

As they walked through the market, Otto kept his eyes peeled for someone in black and red. This would be the most natural place for Lady White's agent to try and spot them, especially if he didn't want to attract attention.

"What are we looking for exactly?" Hans asked. The good sergeant kept a constant watch on the crowds and sounded nervous. He probably expected an attack at any moment.

"We aren't looking for anything in particular," Otto said. "We're just getting a feel for the lay of the land."

"It's crowded, loud, smelly, and an attack might come from any direction," Hans said. "What more do you need to know?"

Otto chuckled but said nothing. Hans would worry. It was his nature and part of his job as a bodyguard. No doubt losing Cord made him even more vigilant. Speaking of vigilant... "Has anyone seen any guards?"

"Plenty," Axel said. "I think every stall had at least one."

"Not them, I mean a city guard. People in uniform making sure no one gets murdered or robbed."

"Oh, then no, I haven't."

"No officials, no guards, it's like this city has no authority." Otto frowned. There had to be someone in charge. The walls and docks didn't maintain themselves. "Let's find a tavern. There's bound to be someone that can tell us what's going on here."

"We passed a stand selling maritime supplies a little ways back," Wainwright said. "I want to go back and see what they have."

"Take a couple scouts with you," Axel said. "Cobb, pick a man and keep him safe."

"Sure, send me when we're on our way to a tavern." Cobb grabbed the youngest looking of the bunch and set out behind Captain Wainwright.

Leaving the open-air market behind and moving into the city proper, Otto couldn't help noticing the buildings. There was no cohesive style. People just built whatever they wanted. Single-story buildings, multistory buildings, shops, residences, and taverns all mingled at random.

"There's a place." Hans pointed across the street at a two-story building with a frothing mug on the sign. It looked reasonably maintained so they wouldn't have to worry about it collapsing on their heads.

Otto led the way across the street and pushed through the swinging doors. As he expected at this time of day, the common room was nearly empty. A single table held five men that, judging by their weapons and scars, worked as mercenaries. The sole other occupant was the bartender, a slender, almost gaunt woman around forty wearing a simple tan dress.

He went to the bar while the others found them two tables.

"What can I get you, stranger?" the woman asked.

"A round of drinks and some information."

She looked over his head, her dry, cracked lips moving as

she counted the members of his party. "Drinks will be half an ounce of silver. Information is more costly."

Otto placed a silver coin on the bar and she dug out a scale. A little weight went on one side and the coin on the other. When both sides stabilized, she shrugged and said, "Close enough," and pocketed the coin. "I'll bring your drinks then we can discuss your questions."

"That's fine, thank you." Otto returned to the others and took a chair beside Corina.

"Learn anything?" she asked.

"I learned this city doesn't mint its own coins. They sell by weight of metal. Probably wise given the different nationalities I saw in the market."

A few minutes later, the bartender arrived carrying an overloaded tray that looked far too heavy for her skinny arms. She set the tray in the middle of the table and everyone helped themselves to a mug. Otto took one sniff, grimaced, and set his mug back down. He'd have to be considerably thirstier to drink that swill.

"Will you join us?" Otto asked. "I have many questions."

"Do you have gold to pay for the answers?" she asked.

Otto placed a double eagle on the table. "I believe that should purchase anything I want to know."

She licked her lips and nodded. "Yes, it will."

When the bartender had dragged a chair over Otto said, "When we docked, there was no sign of a port authority or guards as we strolled through the market. Does this city have an organized government?"

"Not as such. The five most powerful merchant companies act as a city council of sorts, overseeing the docks and making sure the city doesn't fall apart. But for the most part, people are expected to look after themselves. We all pay a small fee every month for collective maintenance, but that's it."

"So you could walk outside and murder someone and no one would arrest you?" Axel asked. "Sounds like chaos."

She shrugged. "It is to an extent. And we like it that way. Who needs a bunch of smug nobles telling you what you can and can't do? We have collectives that provide security. If you killed me, for example, the other members of the collective would hunt you down and kill you. Everyone knows the rules, except new arrivals, who learn quick or die quicker."

"What about the Celestial Empire?" Otto asked. "They don't mind having chaos on their southern border?"

"They don't care about us. Their merchants come here with a small army to trade before crossing back over the wall. Our fate doesn't interest them in the least."

Otto perked up at the mention of a wall. "So their border is fortified?"

"Ha! That's putting it mildly. Only registered merchants can cross and only with native guards. The wall is patrolled at all times and stretches from ocean to ocean. Magical guard beasts swim in the waters offshore, devouring anyone stupid enough to try and swim. No, trying to get into the empire uninvited is a death sentence."

That was an unfortunate bit of news. His hopes of sneaking in without the help of Astaroth's cult dimmed to nothing. Still, at least he wouldn't be wondering.

"Are there safe places to rent rooms in the city?" Otto asked.

"Do you have any more gold?" she asked. "Places that provide security are expensive. Most merchants simply stay on their ships or camp outside the walls surrounded by guards."

"Assuming the price isn't totally unreasonable," Otto said. "I believe I can manage."

The others were looking a bit woozy as they wobbled in their seats. After one drink even Corina should have remained clearheaded.

A scraping drew his attention to the rough-looking men at the other table. They had all gotten to their feet and drew an assortment of weapons.

He turned back to the bartender who shrugged. "Robbing foreigners pays considerably better than selling drinks and information. Especially since no one will come to avenge you."

"You think you're going to rob me?" Otto asked.

"Considering I've got five guys, all of whom are alert and not drugged and all your guards are nearly unconscious, I'd say yes."

"Then you are an idiot." Otto flicked his iron ring and sent binding threads into all six people, freezing them in place. "Trying to rob a wizard without one of your own is unwise."

He smiled at the fear in her eyes as he stood and unsheathed his mithril sword. Drawing fire from a hanging lantern, he wrapped it around his blade. Swift, hard strokes cut the mercenaries' hands off at the wrist and seared the wounds shut.

Bound as they were, the mercenaries couldn't even scream.

Otto kicked them over onto the floor and repeated the process on their feet at the ankles. With them dealt with, he returned his attention to the bartender. A small adjustment to the binding spell allowed her to speak. "Please. I didn't know you were a wizard."

"Obviously. Do you think that makes me any happier? Is the poison you gave my companions fatal?"

"No! No, they're just knockout drops. Lethal poisons are

too expensive."

"Of course. Once the unlucky people are unconscious, a dagger to the throat is cheap." Otto rested his still-flaming sword on her shoulder, drawing a pained screech. "Tell me, what's the job market like for a bartender with no hands?"

Tears streamed down her face. "What do you want?"

"Are there any other ways into the empire? Surely there are smugglers."

"No. I swear, the imperials have cut off every means across the border. Unless you can fly, it's the gate or nothing."

Otto saw nothing to indicate she was lying. "Very well. I'm going to spare your worthless life and in exchange, you're going to tell your friends we are not to be messed with. Spread the word far and wide. If I have any more trouble during my time here, I'm coming for you. Do you understand?"

"Perfectly. Thank you."

Otto nodded and collected his double eagle from the table. Now he just needed to wait for everyone to wake up so they could find an inn. Preferably one that didn't poison their drinks or try to murder the clientele.

〇

The knockout drug only lasted an hour. One by one the others came around, groaning and rubbing their faces. The bartender was long gone with orders not to return until Otto and his companions had left. Her thugs lay where he'd left them. Most of them had passed out from shock, but one unfortunate fellow remained conscious, whimpering in the fetal position. Otto had no pity for the would-be murderer. When you lived by the sword, you best be ready to die by it.

"What happened?" Corina asked.

"Our charming hostess drugged your ale," Otto said. "Lucky for all of us that I prefer wine. It seems poisoning and robbing patrons from outside of the city is a sideline for them. It was nothing I couldn't handle. How are you feeling?"

"Like I swallowed a rat's nest and termites crawled into my brain." Corina groaned and laid her face on the table.

"Try channeling ether through your body. That should help purge any toxins."

"What about the rest of us?" Axel asked in a pained voice.

Otto took a breath and sent a fine mist of ether through his brother's body. Axel's eyes popped open and he stared at Otto. The spell lasted only seconds, but hopefully it wiped out any poison in Axel's system.

"Better?"

"Much." Axel chuckled. "Where were you when I used to go out on a bender in Castle Town?"

"Probably sound asleep in my bed like you should have been."

Otto repeated the spell for Hans, then the rest of the soldiers. When he had everyone back in fighting form he stood and said, "If the bartender can be believed, there are inns that offer protection as part of their services. I want to rent a room where I can leave a rune in case I need to flee quickly. Hans, you and your squad will be in charge of security."

Hans nodded and Axel asked, "What about me and the scouts?"

"Having seen the state of this city, you will focus on protecting the ship and Wainwright as he handles our resupply. Corina, you'll help out wherever you're needed. If we find a reliable inn, I suggest eating there as a group just in case."

No one argued and they quickly set out from the tavern. Otto led the way deeper into the city toward some of the bigger buildings. He assumed some of them would be inns. Out of the corner of his eye he spotted a figure in black, but as he turned for a closer look, whoever it was slipped into an alley and out of sight.

Cursing his luck, Otto focused on the task at hand. If that had been his contact, he or she would try again later. Right now, finding a secure base of operations was most important.

The first inn they found had a red tile roof, three stories, and half a dozen guards dressed in leather armor and carrying crossbows and short swords patrolling the outside. It looked promising, but Otto didn't want to raise his hopes too high.

As they neared, four of the guards raised their weapons while the remaining two stepped off the porch to greet them. Not wanting to risk getting shot, Otto bound their triggers. The guards wouldn't notice anything amiss unless they tried to fire and if they did that, he'd kill them all before they had a chance to complain.

"What's your business here?" the right-hand guard asked.

"We need a room for six guests," Otto said. "My other companions will be coming and going from time to time. Having seen a bit of this city, security is paramount for our needs."

"That is an expensive list of requirements," the guard said. "I assume you have gold to pay for it."

"Payment isn't an issue, but the last time I showed my gold, I was nearly killed and robbed, so you'll understand my reluctance."

The guard's stony expression finally cracked into a faint smile. "If you weren't completely correct in everything you just said, I'd be offended on behalf of my city. As it is, I need some proof of payment before I can let you in to negotiate with the overseer."

"Fine. I killed the last group of thieves. If I have to, I can kill a second." Otto reached into his pocket and pulled out the same double eagle he'd shown the bartender.

"Now that's a coin. Okay, weapons down, boys. We have a new guest. Follow me to the overseer."

The other guards lowered their crossbows but continued to watch with narrow, suspicious eyes. He didn't blame them. In fact, if he was going to stay here, he'd prefer suspicious guards. By the same token, Otto waited until they were inside to remove his spell.

"Wow." Corina gaped at the inside of the inn.

Otto agreed with the sentiment even if he controlled his expression better than his apprentice. The common room was decorated with white silk tablecloths. Red lanterns hung from the ceiling casting a warm glow over the room. Attractive female servants in skimpy red dresses carried drinks to the handful of occupied tables. The guests were dressed in fine robes and tunics. At least three different nationalities were represented among the guests.

Everyone looked up when Otto and his companions entered. Apparently a large, armed group wasn't that strange and they quickly went back to their meals. Their guide led them to a small desk off to one side of the room where a portly man with a long gray beard and expensive silk robe stood waiting.

He eyed them with the same narrow, suspicious eyes as the guards outside. "Samhain, what have you brought me?"

"Guests, sir," the guard said. "They have gold."

The portly man's face brightened at once. "Well now, that's fine. Run along, Sam, I have matters to discuss with our newest guests."

"Yes, sir." Sam took his leave, hurrying through the common room and out the door.

"So, what can I do for you fine people? But where are my manors? I am Clarendon, the owner of this establishment."

"We need a room," Otto said. "Members of my group will be coming and going and I'm not certain how long I'll need the room, so I'd like to pay for a month in advance."

"No problem at all, sir. We have several rooms available. A monthly rental will cost you six ounces of gold. Food and drink are extra."

Otto placed two double eagles on the table and Clarendon pulled out a scale. He weighed the coins against a lead disk. "Looks like about seven ounces. Shall we call it five weeks?"

"That's fine. Can you show us the room now?"

Clarendon gave a pained expression and snapped his fingers. One of the scantily clad serving girls hurried over and bowed. "Show our new guests to room seven."

Otto accepted an iron key and followed the girl upstairs to a room marked with a golden seven. "Here you are, sir."

She bowed again and hurried away. Otto pushed the door open. The room itself was quite large, with a living area and two bedrooms. More of a small apartment than an inn room.

"For what that thief charged, I expected more," Axel said.

"It is sufficient." Otto went to the left-hand bedroom.

There was plenty of clear space between the bed and the wall. A few deft slashes carved a rough symbol. Next he poured ether into it until it glowed in his magical vision. That should last at least a year or until he erased it.

He stepped back out of the room and said, "We're all set here. Hans, no one sets foot in that room until I'm back. Understood?"

"Yes, my lord."

"Axel, let's return to the ship. Hopefully Captain Wainwright has completed his shopping without getting his throat cut."

Axel chuckled though Otto hadn't really been joking. They left Hans and his squad in the room and started toward steps.

Corina started to join them, but Otto said, "Stay here until we're sure we weren't followed."

She pouted but turned back. Satisfied that she wouldn't abandon her post, Otto went downstairs. At the foot of the steps his gaze was immediately drawn to a woman dressed in an all-black dress with a slit running to the hip standing beside an empty table. Their gazes met and she shifted, revealing a rose tattoo on her right thigh.

No question about it then, this was his contact. "Go on ahead of me. I'll catch up."

Axel looked from Otto to the woman and back. "Careful, little brother. She might be more than you can handle."

Otto snorted. "We have a mutual friend. She's supposed to be my way into the empire."

"All the same, be careful." Axel waved and led his scouts out of the inn.

Otto angled over to the woman. As he approached, he looked her over closer. Judging from her skin tone and black hair, she hailed from the Celestial Empire. In fact, she could have been Ulf's younger, more attractive, sister.

He stopped across the table from her. "You're Lady White's associate?"

"And you are Otto. She told me a great deal about you." Her voice held a warm, melodic tone like that of a singer. "My name is Jet and I have great confidence we will accomplish our mutual goals. Shall we sit and talk?"

Otto moved around the table and pulled her chair out for

her before seating himself. With a thought, a bubble of ether surrounded them preventing anyone from listening in.

"So, from what I've heard, getting into the empire is a daunting proposition. How can you accomplish it?"

She smiled, revealing perfect white teeth. "Simple. I'm a registered merchant. I can come and go pretty much as I please. When we reach the wall, you'll have to hide in a special compartment. Once we're across, you'll be in danger of execution every moment should you be found. As will I and all those with us."

"Risky. What did the Cult of Astaroth have to offer a beautiful, obviously rich woman to convince you to put everything you have in danger?"

"I am all those things, but time will eventually claim everything that I have. Astaroth offers eternal life to all those that serve him. You spent time with Lady White?"

"Some."

"She is beautiful as well."

"Very," Otto agreed.

"She is also over two centuries old. Her heart hasn't beat for most of that time. Her demonic servants grant her immense power." A hungry look came over her. "I want that power for myself. Rich as I am, I'm still weak compared to imperial officers. If I say or do the wrong thing, it could all be taken away. If we succeed, my place in the Immortal Circle is assured. I will gamble everything on that."

Otto didn't know what the Immortal Circle was, but he assumed it was some high office in the Cult of Astaroth. He also didn't doubt Jet's sincerity. The woman was as determined as Otto himself.

That made him feel considerably better about putting his fate in her hands.

CHAPTER 36

After their meeting, Otto set out with Jet's caravan the next day. He traveled light, carrying only the clothes on his back, his mithril sword, and a modest sum of gold. Everything else he left on the ship under Axel's supervision. There was enough wealth in the hold to resupply them several times over, so he had no fear that the others would have problems on that front. Surviving the madness that was Port Han was another matter altogether.

Given their considerable skills, he felt certain Hans and Axel would manage. Should worst come to worst, Corina's magic would be an important asset as well. He said a silent prayer to any angel that might be listening that they avoided serious trouble.

"You look lost in thought," Jet said.

They were seated side by side on the bench of the center wagon of her modest caravan. The journey to the border took three days so he wouldn't have to hide for a while. Having seen the tiny smuggling compartment, he was happy to avoid it for as long as possible.

"Just worried about my people in Port Han. That is a city unlike any I have ever visited."

She offered a bright smile. "There are certainly none like it in the Celestial Empire. The lords and ministers all desire order and control. Anything that interferes with that gets dealt with. Harshly."

"When you say lords, you mean the Lords of Alchemy?"

She blinked in surprise. "You've heard of them? I'm surprised. Few outside of the empire would recognize their name. Yes, the lords are the true power in the empire since Lord Xi Cheng died. The emperor, may he rule for a thousand—"

Jet stopped in midsentence and spat over the side of the wagon. "Excuse me. I hate myself every time I repeat that stupid expression. He may sit on the throne, but that's all he's in charge of."

Replacing a minister made more sense now, especially if they were the ones that wielded real power. "Are there many others who feel as you do?"

"Not that many. The empire has run this way for thousands of years. The majority are content with the current system and those who aren't have already been either executed or driven out. Only those able to hide their true feelings and work within to undermine the system remain. But with your help, we will finally make our first decisive move."

Otto glanced at the guards marching alongside the wagons. They didn't so much as flinch at her seditious words.

"Don't worry," Jet said. "Everyone that is a part of my caravan is also a member of the cult. Their loyalty to Astaroth and our mission is absolute."

Otto nodded, only somewhat relieved. In his experience, you could never rule out a spy or traitor in your midst.

"What, exactly, is the plan? Lady White was a little vague on the details."

"The goal is simple." They had fallen a little behind the lead wagon, so Jet flicked the reins prompting the mules to pick up the pace. "One of our members has worked his way up to second minister of the interior, a powerful position that oversees the day-to-day operations of the peacekeepers. Once his immediate superior is eliminated, he will move into the fifth highest post in the empire."

"And you need me to kill this minister?" Otto asked.

"He is protected every moment by a force of twelve, totally loyal guards, the finest warriors in the empire. An ordinary assassin would have no hope of success, but a wizard is another matter. You can kill him from a mile away and no one will know."

That was a bit of an exaggeration, but not a huge one. "Surely someone so important will have at least one wizard among his guards."

"Wizardry of the sort you know is frowned upon. Those born with the ability to see the ether are trained as alchemists and eventually join the lords. It's their way of controlling a potential threat."

So even here wizards were treated as second-class citizens with no real control over their fate. He would have dearly liked to help those that wished for a different life, but had neither the time nor the power to do so, not yet anyway.

"And what is it you wish us to do for you in exchange? I assume it is more than simply passage into the empire."

"I'm looking for an artifact that would have belonged to Lord Cheng called the Heart of Alchemy. I assume you have some idea where I might find such a thing."

"Indeed. I know exactly where you must look. The

Forbidden Garden. Getting in and out of it alive is another matter."

Otto swallowed a sigh. Why weren't these things ever hidden in a place called the Garden of Delights?

◯

"There it is," Jet said.

The caravan had stopped on a hill overlooking the border wall. And what a wall it was. Nearly as tall as the one surrounding the City of Coins and with more guard towers, this barrier would keep out an army. Maybe not one equipped with magical armor like in Colt's Land, but anything less certainly.

Otto couldn't begin to imagine how long it had taken to build and the less said about the cost, the better.

A dirt road led to an open gate wide enough to allow two wagons to enter at the same time. Otto counted fifty spearmen on the ground led by a smaller group armed with swords. On the wall itself, over a hundred archers manned stone watchtowers directly above the gate.

As he watched, another caravan approached, this one consisting of ten wagons and forty guards. One of the swordsmen marched up to the lead wagon and a discussion was held. A pouch was exchanged and after a cursory examination, they were allowed to pass.

Seemed simple enough. Hopefully it went as well for Otto and his companions as it did for the last group.

"I suppose it's time for me to hide," he said.

"That would be best," Jet agreed. "If the head guard dislikes our looks, he may order a closer search. Rest assured, the smuggling compartment has been used many times without being found. Stay calm and all will be well."

His state of mind would have less to do with their success than his silence. A pair of crates were shoved aside and a narrow slot in the bed of Jet's wagon revealed. Otto unbuckled his sword and squeezed inside. When the board was replaced, he found himself in perfect darkness. Lucky for him tight spaces had never bothered him.

The wagon rattled into motion and the die was cast. Soon they would either be in the empire or dead.

Minutes dragged by and Otto focused on his breathing. The air was stuffy and close and soon sweat plastered his clothes to his body. He didn't dare use magic lest one of the lords be around and see his work in the ether.

At last the wagon stopped again. He held his breath and listened. There were muffled voices, but he couldn't make out what they said.

The wagon rattled from side to side and one of the voices went up a fraction. He couldn't say for sure, but it sounded like Jet.

There must be a problem.

He tightened his grip on his sword. If everything went to hell, he didn't intend to go down easy.

A pair of thuds sounded from above and the cover to the secret compartment rattled.

If he did nothing, he would certainly be caught.

Taking a chance, Otto wrapped himself in invisibility just as the lid popped off.

A guard dressed in red-lacquered armor stared at him but gave no sign that he saw anything. At last the guard said, "It's empty, sir."

"I told you," Jet said. "I only use that compartment in Port

Han. Those thieves would steal the fingers off your hand. Hiding your most valuable goods is a necessity."

There was a muttered apology and the guard put the cover back in place. A moment later the crates were shoved back where they belonged and the wagons were moving again. Otto let out the breath he'd been holding and released his spell.

Their rattling journey continued for he knew not how long before the wagon stopped again. This time when the lid opened it was Jet staring down at him.

She smiled her radiant smile. "I thought the game was up before it even began. It never occurred to me that you had the power to simply turn invisible."

"I didn't want to risk it in case a wizard was around to see the magic. What happened?"

"The head guard was a prick. He spotted the bottom of the hidden compartment and demanded that I show him the interior. He must be new here. None of the regular guards look that close. We're out of sight of the wall so you can come out now."

Otto happily climbed out of the tight space. While it might not have bothered him, that didn't mean he enjoyed lying in a virtual coffin. "I suppose I'll have to climb back in should we encounter anyone."

"When we reach Celestial City you will, but until then I think a simple disguise will suffice." Jet pulled a satchel out from under the wagon bench and handed it to him.

Otto pulled out a black robe, a black veil, and an odd, round hat that rose to a sharp peak. He'd never seen such an outfit. "What is this?"

"Traditional mourning garb. You'll be posing as a cousin who recently lost his wife and is traveling with me to the capital to offer your prayer at the Lotus Temple."

That was as good a story as any. He set his sword on the bench and donned his costume. Despite an appearance that seemed odd to his foreign eyes, the outfit was comfortable enough. The veil didn't obscure his vision and the hat even provided a little shade. All in all it could certainly have been worse.

He climbed up beside Jet and she shook the reins.

"How far is the city?" Otto asked.

"If we make good time, about two weeks. As we come closer, the traffic will pick up. If we encounter anyone be sure to stay silent. Your accent will give you away at once."

"And if someone should speak to me?"

"They won't. No one would intrude on someone in mourning."

Otto nodded and settled in for what he hoped would be a boring trip north.

CHAPTER 37

True to Jet's prediction, the few people they encountered on the journey north took one look at Otto's disguise and immediately looked away. Entry into the city had also gone off without a hitch. Otto listened to the whole process from his hiding spot and as best he could determine from the muffled voices, the guards were more interested in Jet herself than her cargo. Nothing like the combination of lust and overconfidence to make a person lax.

On the downside, Jet deemed it wise for him to stay out of sight until they reached her warehouse, a building that also served as the base for Astaroth's cult in the city.

At least the road was smooth. If he'd had to bounce through potholes while stuck in the secret compartment, that would have really been unpleasant. As it was he merely had to deal with heat, stale air, and stiff muscles.

At last they stopped and Jet said, "We're here."

The crates shifted and the secret compartment opened. Otto sat up and sucked in a great lungful of fresh air. Or reasonably fresh air. Smoke and stink battled to offend his nose more. Even for someone used to the foundries of Garen, the smell of Celestial City was a lot to take in.

"I take it you've noticed the unique odor of our capital," Jet said. "You can thank the alchemists. They are constantly experimenting, trying to come up with something to catch their lords' gaze and elevate themselves in the alchemists' hierarchy."

She said it with disgust in her voice, but he couldn't see how their actions were any different than members of any other group jockeying for favor. Even Jet was trying to better her position in the cult. Otto forbore comment on her hypocrisy. She would be neither the first nor the last to lie to herself about her motives.

Instead Otto looked around at the stacks of crates. There was nothing here resembling living quarters. After his time on the road, he badly needed a bath, some decent food, and a good night's sleep.

"I assume you have an actual temple or something nearby," Otto said.

"Of course." Jet crooked her finger. "Follow me."

The two of them moved deeper into the warehouse while the guards remained behind and a pair of burly laborers busied themselves with moving the crates. Jet led him to the right rear of the building and stomped twice on the floor.

A hidden door slid open and a man with wide open, unblinking eyes stared at them without seeming to see. From the glaze over his pupils and lack of breathing, Otto decided this must be his first encounter with a zombie.

"Back, slave!" Jet commanded.

The zombie shuffled down the steps and squished into an alcove to allow them to pass. At the bottom of the steps, Otto started to conjure a light, but before the spell activated, torches burst to life with an eerie green flame. Corruption swirled around the lights and put a queasy twist into Otto's guts.

An effort of will formed a shield of pure ether around him and cut off the nasty feeling. If Jet felt any discomfort, she didn't show it. Perhaps having pledged herself to the demon lord, she was no longer troubled by the unnatural energy. Either that or she'd just gotten used to it.

She led him down a stone tunnel that looked carved rather than natural. Otto ran his fingers along the wall. Yes, this was definitely a hallway. He found crevices where the blocks fit together.

"Did you build this?" Otto asked.

"No." Jet looked back at him. "The warehouse was built on the foundation of another building that burned during one of the purges years ago. We just took advantage of what was already here. It also connects to the building next door, which I own, so we have plenty of space. But I'm sure our leader is eager to meet you."

Otto frowned. "I thought you were the leader of this cell."

"No, I'm the face of the group. Our leader, well, he doesn't blend with the living as well as Lady White. Meaning no offense of course. He understands that under the current circumstances, his remaining behind the scenes is best. Once Astaroth rules the empire, that will all change. And after all, the dead have nothing but time."

Jet led him to another set of stairs down. Otto prepared himself to meet an undead creature considerably less pleasing to the eye than Lady White. Given his limited assets, Otto had no desire to offend his host.

At the bottom of the stairs, the corruption was so thick it took half his power to filter it out. Interestingly, it was all contained within the single large room that looked like a proper temple. There was an altar with a large bloodstain in the center, and two square pedestals that held green flames like the ones above.

A single figure stood behind the altar, his body draped in loose-fitting dark robes. A deep cowl hid his features. Jet offered a deep bow while Otto contented himself with a nod of respect. Damned if he'd kowtow to anyone, living or dead.

Scabrous, rotted hands reached up to pull the cowl down revealing a face ravaged by Otto knew not what. The entire left side was stripped down to the bone. Ragged bits of flesh marked the border between bone and skin.

"So," the dead man said. "You are the assassin Lady White has sent us. I trust you can do what you claim."

Otto bristled at the insult. "One, I am not an assassin. I'm here for my own reasons. I agreed to help you in exchange for you helping me. Second, no one sends me anywhere."

The fleshy part of the undead's face tried to smile with limited success. "Finally, a human with iron in his spine. You and I will get along fine. My name is Marius and I bid you welcome to the Temple of Astaroth. A room has been prepared. Tonight, we meet with my agent at court. Until then rest and recover. Jet will provide you with anything you need."

Otto nodded. "Thank you. Until tonight."

Marius turned his back on Otto and Jet led him upstairs and down a different hall to a closed door. She opened it and stepped aside to let him enter first. The modest suite had only a bed, table and two chairs, and a small trunk. Another door led, he assumed, to the garderobe.

She shut the door behind them and said, "When you spoke up I feared our master would kill you out of hand. He doesn't take well to people questioning him."

"I don't take well to orders or threats, and I assure you, I'm not so easy to kill. But infighting will do us no good. Better for everyone if we complete our business and I leave the empire as quickly as possible."

"Yes, that would certainly be best. I will fetch you water to wash up with and food. Is there anything else you need?"

"No, thank you."

She bowed, not as deeply as she had to Marius, but deeply enough that it wasn't an insult, and left.

Otto sighed and slumped on the bed. The leader of the cult wasn't what he expected, but then that was his mistake. It did make sense that the leader of a cult devoted to the demon lord of the undead, would be undead himself.

○

The combination of tension and exhaustion sent Otto into a deep slumber. He didn't know how much time passed, but when someone broke the ethereal thread he'd placed across the threshold of his room, he sat up and sent ether surging through his body. Any lingering haziness vanished in an instant.

When Jet stepped into the room Otto relaxed a fraction. She carried a tray covered with steaming bowls and set it on the room's small table.

"You might knock before entering," Otto said. "Trying to sneak into my room is a good way to end up dead."

"My apologies. I wasn't certain if you were awake." She bowed then straightened and pointed at the food. "I thought we might dine together."

The beef and noodle soup she'd brought him earlier, while delicious, hadn't been terribly filling. A second meal would suit him quite well.

He moved from the bed to the table and they sat facing each other. Otto breathed deep, savoring the rich scent of roasted meat and exotic spices. Considering he was staying in a temple dedicated to the demon lord of the undead, the food was surprisingly delicious. Of course, he still checked everything for poison before digging in.

When he'd eaten about half his meal Otto said, "Tell me about your minister of whatever you said he did. I can't imagine it was easy to find someone willing to betray the government."

Jet took a sip of wine. "You'd be surprised. Perhaps once honor and dedication had some bearing on who they selected for high posts in the government, but now it's all about patronage. Minister Hu knew someone to get his foot in the door, but he's risen as far as he can on his own. As you can imagine, that doesn't sit well with him. He accepted our offer of advancement with very little coaxing."

"So a politician with a taste for power, shocking. Does he actually know who he's serving?"

She offered a polite laugh. "Of course not. Lord Marius is highly skilled at illusion magic while Hu has no talent for it and thus no clue that the wealthy, eccentric merchant is actually a long-dead demon worshipper. We'll keep it that way until it suits our purposes to reveal the truth, assuming it ever does."

Otto couldn't deny a little discomfort at the idea of trusting someone so quick to betray his current masters, but as long as the minister stayed loyal until Otto acquired the Heart, what happened after was no concern of his.

"How long until the meeting?" Otto asked.

"About an hour. We'll join Master Marius at the house next door as soon as we finish eating."

Otto nodded and did exactly as she suggested. The food was too good to waste.

After mopping up the last of the broth, Jet led him down a different tunnel and up a set of stairs that led to the basement of a fair-sized house. All the usual junk that people accumulated over the years was absent here. Otto's conjured light revealed a fine layer of dust covering the stone floor along with a single set of footprints that went straight to another staircase.

"Looks like you don't use this entrance often," Otto commented.

"No, not very. I usually go in the front door. Only Master Marius comes this way. We've let it be known that he's a bit of a shut-in that seldom meets with anyone."

They followed the tracks upstairs to a beautifully equipped kitchen. The only thing missing was food. He doubted anyone would ever visit the house, but if they did, it would be instantly obvious that no one actually lived here.

Outside the kitchen, they turned left and entered a sitting room where Marius waited. Now he looked like a nobleman, handsome and dressed in fine silks. All fake of course. The half-rotten corpse under the ethereal construct remained visible in his magical sight. But it should be enough to fool a normal human.

"Did you find everything to your liking?" Marius waved Otto and Jet into a pair of empty chairs.

"The food was delicious, thank you." Otto sat and Jet joined him.

The illusion offered a proper smile. "That may be the only thing I miss about being alive. I was quite the connoisseur before I died."

There was some noise from another room followed by the

sound of a door closing. A moment later a servant Otto hadn't noticed announced, "Minister Hu, my lord."

The minister swept in, a long crimson robe flowing behind him. Despite the loose fit, it failed to disguise the massive potbelly hanging below his belt. His face was round, with chubby baby cheeks, and a patch of hair below his lower lip. Otto pitied anyone that had to deal with this creature on a regular basis. He'd rather take his chances with the undead.

"Marius, my friend, so good to see you again." Hu, his voice a high, grating squeal, bowed a fraction, just enough to show respect.

"Minister," Marius said. "How stand matters at court?"

"The same as always. My genius remains unacknowledged." Hu glanced from Marius to Otto and back. "Is he the solution to our problem?"

"Indeed. We're ready to move at any time."

A ripple ran through the ether.

Otto didn't know what spell was unleashed, but something just happened.

He stood and slowly drew his sword. "What have you done?"

"I'm sure I don't—"

Otto put the tip of his mithril blade under Hu's chin. "Don't lie to me, you miserable sack of excrement."

Jet and Marius both scrambled to their feet.

"Otto, what are you doing?" Jet asked.

"Have you lost your mind?" Marius added.

Otto never took his eyes off of Hu. "Didn't you feel the ether shift? Someone cast a spell, a strong one. Since it happened right after this pig arrived, well, let's just say I don't believe in coincidences."

"I'm sorry," Hu blubbered. "One of my aides grew suspicious and followed me. The lords know everything. They came to my office. Made me agree to help."

There was an explosion outside.

"If you surrender, your execution will be painless," Hu said. "They promised me so."

The sounds of battle grew louder by the second.

Otto flicked his wrist, cutting Hu's throat from ear to ear. "We need to go."

As he said it, a squad of soldiers burst into the sitting room.

Otto didn't even think.

Threads lashed out, slicing the men to ribbons.

"How do we get out of here?" he asked.

"The basement or the front door," Jet said.

Shouts came from the front of the house. Whoever was outside must have realized their comrades had been eliminated.

"I don't recommend the front," Otto said.

"We can't use the basement either," Marius said. "If they find the temple, the cult is finished here."

Otto swore, turned to the wall, and conjured spinning threads of ether that sliced a disk out of the wall. Outside, another squad of soldiers waited in the yard.

Marius thrust a hand out and a black mist of corrupt ether rose up from around the men's boots. An instant later they started to scream. An instant after that they melted into puddles of black sludge.

"Where now?" Otto asked.

"This way." Jet led them away from the warehouse toward the city proper.

This didn't seem like the best way to go, but given his complete lack of knowledge regarding the area, he had no choice but to follow. Marius didn't complain either so her choice must have suited him.

Shouts rose behind them.

He risked a look back. Three squads led by a tall figure swathed from head to toe in crimson robes were headed their way. From the way the ether swirled around the tall one, Otto figured it was one of the Lords of Alchemy. Whatever magic he sensed must have come from this one.

They only had a modest lead and the soldiers were gaining quickly.

Marius pointed behind them and the black mist rose again.

The lord countered, throwing a vial that shattered in the center of the corruption. White mist formed, canceling out the demon magic.

"Astaroth take all the lords!" Marius said.

Otto would have happily seconded that had he breath to spare for curses.

They had covered two blocks and the neighborhood grew worse with each stride. Behind them, the soldiers had reduced the gap by half. They needed more than that if they hoped to escape.

"How much further?" Otto gasped.

"Not much," Jet said. "But I don't want to lead them to our safe house."

Otto scanned the streets, searching for inspiration. It struck a moment later. A rickety balcony hung over an alley ahead of them.

"Turn right up ahead," Otto said.

To her credit Jet didn't hesitate.

They turned and ran down the alley.

The moment they passed under the balcony, Otto sliced it free and sent it crashing down behind them. Hopefully it crushed a few soldiers, but even if it only increased their lead, it would be worthwhile.

After leaving the alley, Jet led them down side streets home only to rats and sunken-eyed men and women that looked more dead than alive. Otto had never seen anyone that looked as wretched as those lost souls.

"More of your followers?" Otto asked.

Marius scowled. "Hardly. Even my lord's creations have more will than these soulless dogs."

"They're addicts," Jet said with more sympathy in her voice than Otto had expected. "The lords outlaw alchemical drugs, but that doesn't stop anyone that wants some from getting a fix. I chose this place because the locals are so far gone they wouldn't be able to answer a question if asked."

Otto glanced back but there was no sign of pursuit. It seemed his efforts had thrown them off the trail. Thank heaven for that. Nothing else had gone their way tonight.

Jet stopped in front of a tenement with a rickety fire escape bolted to it. "This is us."

Otto eyed the rungs of the fire escape. "Ladies first."

"I didn't take you for a coward," Marius said.

"You're already dead. I have a lot to live for. I'll fight anyone without blinking, but crashing to my death in a heap of rusty iron doesn't appeal to me."

"Relax." Jet started up the ladder and it didn't so much as creak. "It's been reinforced then aged to blend in. No need to worry."

Otto shrugged and followed her. On the third floor they ducked through a window. He conjured a light and blinked in surprise. The safe house, while certainly not fancy, had everything they needed to be comfortable: plain, sturdy furniture, an iron stove for cooking. All in all, far better than Otto had dared hope for from the outside.

"What now?" Otto asked.

"Now we wait." Marius dropped into the chair. "Word will reach my followers and soon they will contact me. Once we know the situation, we can decide our next move."

Otto settled on one of the beds. The situation might have changed, but his mission hadn't. The Heart of Alchemy was out there somewhere and he meant to find it.

CHAPTER 38

Three days of forced inactivity drove Otto to the edge of madness. While Jet's safe house was well stocked with food and water, it had little in the way of entertainment. Not so much as a book to read or a deck of cards. Even worse, Otto didn't dare use his magic for fear of drawing unwanted attention.

Marius, at least, seemed untroubled by the tedium. The undead cult leader simply found a spot in the corner of the room and sat down. He hadn't so much as batted an eye since they arrived. Otto couldn't help wondering what he was thinking about. Or maybe he could turn his brain off and become truly dead for a time. That would certainly be a handy trick at moments like this. Of course he must still have some awareness of what was going on around him otherwise he'd be totally helpless.

Jet emerged from their modest kitchen with a pot of tea and two cups on a tray. Otto joined her at the table as she poured.

He took a sip and sighed. Jet had missed her true calling.

She should have worked at a tea shop. "Thank you."

She smiled. "Of course. This turn of events has been difficult for all of us. I'm sure when you took Lady White up on her offer, you never expected to be stuck in a safe house on the run from imperial peacekeepers."

"No." He set his cup down. "Tell me about the Forbidden Garden."

"Thinking of abandoning us and taking your chances on your own?"

Otto shrugged. "Killing the minister seems rather pointless now. Unless there's something else you think I can offer, perhaps going our separate ways would be best."

"You wouldn't last a day on your own," Jet said. "You don't exactly blend in here. But let's leave that for now. As for the Forbidden Garden, there's not much I can tell you. Since Lord Cheng died, no one has entered and emerged to tell the tale. At least no one I'm aware of."

Otto swallowed a smile. Where had he heard that before? It seemed the Arcane Lords enjoyed leaving lethal areas behind them. There was probably some horrible guardian like in Colt's Workshop. Hopefully it wasn't as tough as the steel construct, as he didn't have help this time.

"Can you tell me where it is?"

"On the palace grounds. It fills the entire northern courtyard. Probably three hundred yards square."

"Shouldn't take too long to search."

"Someone's coming," Marius said.

Otto nearly jumped out of his seat. He'd been so quiet for so long, Otto had almost forgotten Marius wasn't really dead.

Jet stood and went to the door. "One of our people?"

"One of mine," Marius said.

Jet lowered her head and unlocked the door. A furtive little man hurried in and looked all around like he expected a guard to jump out and grab him.

"How bad is it?" Marius asked.

"Bad," the little man said. "They've been all over the warehouse and through the tunnels. Most of us escaped, but they grabbed eight that were too slow."

"The temple is still secure," Marius said. "I would know were it otherwise. The rest can be replaced. Where did they take the prisoners?"

"Not sure. The lords are running the operation and my contact in the peacekeepers didn't know much. He said they seemed scared, and the lords fear nothing."

Marius stood. "They are wise to fear us. Find out where the prisoners have been taken. If they live, we will free them, if they don't, I will send Astaroth's revenge against those who killed them. We have hidden in the shadows for long enough. For better or worse, the time for subtlety has ended."

"Should we not contact Lady White for instructions?" Jet asked.

"I lead this cell!" Marius said. His dead features were incapable of showing emotion, but the anger was clear in his voice. "If we succeed, I will reap the rewards and if we fail I will answer to Astaroth in Hell. All you need do is obey."

Otto kept quiet and watched. A full-blown uprising in the city would provide the perfect cover for him to sneak into the garden. Whether these lunatics succeeded or not was irrelevant.

Jet took a step back and lowered her gaze. "I meant no disrespect."

Marius seemed to accept her submission, but Otto knew she was lying. Jet didn't approve of his chosen path, but lacked the power to change it.

Marius turned his focus back to the messenger. "Go and learn what happened. I expect an answer by sunset tonight at the latest."

"Yes, Marius." The little man hurried away.

"And what should I do?" Jet asked.

"Nothing for now. You two will stay here until we're ready to free my followers. I must go to the temple and prepare for the attack."

"Sneaking back in will be tricky," Otto said.

"No, it will not." Marius sat back down and closed his eyes.

Otto shifted his perception and watched as a black ghost made of corrupt ether rose out of Marius's body and flew through the ether back toward the warehouse. Fascinating. It was similar to what Otto did when he became one with the ether, only it was all spirit.

"Marius is wrong," Jet said. "If we act directly against the government, with the forces we have now, the cult is doomed. I need to contact Lady White and convince her to order him to change course."

Otto wasn't sure why she felt the need to tell him, but he could play along. "Do you have some way to reach her in the Land of the Demon Binders? That has to be almost a thousand miles."

"There is a way, but Marius is always the one to use it. I'm not sure the shadow birds can be activated by someone without magic."

Now he understood. "I'm not certain it's in my best interest to go against your superior."

"I don't think it's in your best interest to get caught up in a battle with the peacekeepers and lords. Even if you're not a member of the cult, you're still a foreigner here and that's just as certainly a death sentence. Besides, Lady White is higher up than Marius. This isn't a decision he should be making on his own."

Otto weighed his options. Jet had a point, but he didn't plan to join in the actual battle. Marius, on the other hand, might be planning to use him to bolster his meager forces. That didn't appeal to Otto in the least.

"Tell you what. I'll help you send your message and afterwards, you show me the Forbidden Garden."

Jet nodded. "Deal."

J et seemed to think it wise to make their move while Marius's spirit was out of his body, so they set out immediately from the safe house. Otto would have preferred to wait until dark, but as they made their way through streets crowded with the debris of humanity, he realized Jet had been right. Draped in ragged cloaks she provided, they blended right in with the other beggars. The only downside was that he had to carry his sword to keep it hidden.

The handful of men they passed gave Jet hungry looks, but Otto's angry glare quickly turned them away. Like any other predator, they were looking for weak targets. A quick show of strength was enough to convince them to look elsewhere.

"Where, exactly, are we going?" Otto asked when it seemed like they'd been meandering for too long.

"The entrance to the aerie is underground. I've been looking for an access point. Usually Marius goes through the tunnels to a sewer connection."

Judging from the stream of foul-smelling water running down the center of pretty much every street, Otto doubted the sewer extended to this part of the city. He was about to say so when Jet hurried across the street to a half-collapsed building.

"What is this place?" Otto asked.

"Nothing special, but sometimes when a building collapses, it breaks into the tunnels below. The city has been built up throughout the centuries over many levels. You'd be amazed what you can find if you're not afraid to look."

"And you're not afraid to look? Given your position, I would have assumed you grew up far away from places like this."

"Oh, I did, but that didn't stop me from being curious. I regularly snuck off the grounds and made my way to some of the rougher neighborhoods. Astaroth must have been watching over me even then as I could have ended up in some serious situations."

Jet looked around but no one seemed to be paying them much attention. She led Otto around to the rear of the building. A gap had formed where the roof met the ground.

Otto conjured a light and sent it in ahead of them. Not far beyond the entrance a pile of rubble formed a ramp that descended into an even darker hole. Otto sensed no corruption, but then again, they probably had a ways to go to reach the shadow birds.

Once again Jet took the lead, squeezing her shoulders through the gap and starting down the ramp. Otto had to work a bit harder to force his broader shoulders through, but he managed it without dislocating anything. Together they descended into the underworld.

At the bottom of the ramp, they found a tunnel made from two collapsed and crushed buildings. Fascinating, like a second city below the first.

"Do you know where you're going?" he asked.

"I know which direction we need to go, the trick is finding a tunnel that follows the same path."

Not filled with confidence, Otto trailed her through the darkness. Above them, the ceiling seemed solid and thankfully none of the vile water leaked through. The trip was nasty enough without having anything dripping on them.

They traveled in silence with only the occasional rat for company. After a few minutes Jet stopped and whispered, "Douse your light."

Otto frowned but obliged. As soon as he did, a glow became visible ahead of them. "Is that it?"

"No. Where we're going, there's no light."

"Then what is it?"

"Trouble." Eight figures stepped out of the shadows all around them. The ragged, dirty men all had weapons of the poorest quality. Though they certainly looked sharp enough.

Otto reached for his sword and the ether at the same time.

One of the men grabbed Jet and put his homemade knife to her throat. "I wouldn't do that, not unless you want your pretty friend dead."

Otto looked long and hard at Jet and she stared back with pleading eyes. Did he really need her? She would certainly make his task easier. For now he'd play along.

"Very well." Otto released his grip on his sword and one of the others yanked it out of the baldric. Fine as it was, the blade was the least of his weapons. "Now what?"

"Now we take you to the boss. He'll decide if we kill you, ransom you, or…" The man holding Jet licked her cheek, drawing evil chuckles from his companions. "Something else."

When Otto killed these fools, he'd reserve something especially unpleasant for that one. The marauders forced them along the tunnel toward the light Jet had pointed out earlier. Only fifty or so yards further on they emerged into a chamber that looked like it had once been an inn's common room. There were even four crude tables and a bar made of a board across two barrels. Ten men and three women, their bodies all missing at least a finger and sometimes far more, crowded the area.

In the center of the room, a grotesquely fat bald man covered with tattoos and piercings, his left ear missing, sat on a throne made of what looked like human bones. Corruption swirled around him, similar to Marius, but also different. That had to be the leader. Otto had never imagined a human so horrific looking.

"What have you brought me?" the leader asked. "One's a tasty snack, the other not so much."

"Trespassers, boss." The marauder holding Jet shoved her into the room while another forced Otto over beside her. "We caught them in our tunnel headed this way."

The man that had taken Otto's sword hurried over to the leader with it. The fat man touched the hilt and hissed as if burned, confirming Otto's assumption.

The leader shoved his subordinate aside. "Take the cursed thing away."

The marauder looked down at Otto's sword as if believing it truly cursed before tossing it into the rubble that filled the corner of the room.

"Which demon lord do you serve?" Otto asked.

The leader heaved himself up off his throne and stomped over to Otto. "And just how do you know my allegiances?"

"Normal humans don't get burned by mithril."

The fat monster threw his head back and laughed. "True. The wretched stuff purifies corruption. And if you can afford a mithril blade, you must be rich. That is good. We can always use money. Now, what else do we have?"

The leader turned to Jet and sniffed her hair. "The stench of Astaroth covers you. I hoped to catch Marius, but one of his followers will do until our paths cross."

"What is a servant of Golmol the Torturer doing here?" Jet asked. "I thought only Astaroth's followers had interests outside the Land of the Demon Binders."

"You thought that because we wanted you to." The leader smiled, revealing a mouth full of teeth filed to needle points. "We snuck in, quietly, and kept watch. Waiting for our chance to seize what you've built for our own. Though now it appears you've lost what little you had."

Otto crossed his arms and gathered ether around his body. "What happens now?"

"We'll find a cage for you. Assuming someone is willing to pay to get you back, you'll go free. Since I doubt Marius would bother to pay a ransom or even try to rescue an ordinary human, the woman will serve as a canvas. I shall make an offering of her flesh to Golmol."

The other humans cheered.

When they did, Otto lashed out.

Lightning streaked out in every direction. Men and women were struck down, the metal imbedded in their flesh making a perfect conductor for his magic.

A pair tried to flee out the far end of the chamber. Otto bound them in place and turned his attention to the fat monster. He held his hand out and threads pulled his sword to his grasp.

The leader roared and corruption rushed at Otto.

He slashed the mithril blade through the dark cloud, slicing it in half, and disrupting its power.

Otto slapped the flat of the sword to the man's face, drawing a pained howl that was part agony and part ecstasy.

"Don't bother torturing a follower of Golmol." Jet had a dagger in her hand. "They just get off on it."

She strode forward. "When you see your master, give him Astaroth's regards."

Jet slammed the dagger into the side of the cultist's head, driving it in up to the hilt. He collapsed and after a final twitch went still. The corruption surrounding him dissipated, lightening the atmosphere a fraction.

After Jet had cleaned and sheathed her weapon, they walked over to the surviving cultists. Though his spell didn't allow them to move, Otto saw the fear in their eyes. Watching their leader be murdered in front of them probably did a lot to knock the fight out of them.

"We really need to send a message now," Jet said. "Lady White has to know about Golmol's plans."

Otto didn't especially care about the internal politics of Hell, but he did want to complete his business as quickly as possible so they could move on to the Forbidden Garden.

He gestured and a tentacle of ether yanked the bound man to his feet. Up close Otto guessed his age at less than twenty. "We need directions. Tell me what I want to know and you won't end up like your boss over there."

Otto released his head, freeing him to speak. "Whatever you want to know. I only joined this group because I liked the look of the tattoos."

"We should kill him simply for being that stupid," Jet said.

"Let's find out what he knows first. We're looking for a place of corruption dedicated to Astaroth. It should be in this general area. Ring any bells?"

"Sure. I know the place. The boss had us watching it all the time so we could jump anyone that showed up. Not that anyone ever did, at least not as long as I've been here."

Jet shot the man a hard look, but Otto ignored her. "Excellent. You'll show us the way as well as pointing out any guards. If all goes well, you'll have earned your life."

"And if it doesn't go well?" the prisoner asked, his voice barely a squeak.

Otto sent enough lightning into the bound woman's head to make it explode. "Let's hope for everyone's sake that things go well."

☌

As they made their way through the dark tunnels, Otto kept a leash of ether around the neck of their reluctant guide. The last thing he needed was to end up stranded down here when the young man vanished down a side tunnel. Beside him, Jet had been muttering and shaking her head since they left the cult hideout.

Unable to stand it any longer he asked, "What's bothering you?"

She looked over at him as if suddenly remembering he was there. After a brief hesitation Jet said, "Something our guide said. He claimed they'd been watching the aerie for a while and seen no one, but I know Marius has gone twice that I know about to send messages to Lady White."

"How do you know?"

She blinked at him like a fish out of water. "What do you mean?"

"I mean did you join him when he went? If not, he could have gone anywhere and just told you he was going to send a message."

"What? No. Why would he lie to me about something like that? I mean, we're on the same side."

"No offense, but how much benefit of the doubt are you willing to give someone that worships a demon lord? Maybe he's afraid of the orders he might receive. Or more likely Marius plans to seize control of the cult in Celestial City."

"No." Jet gave a vehement shake of her head. "He wouldn't dare oppose Lady White."

"She's a thousand miles away and has her own problems to deal with. If he took over, do you think she could come here and slap him down?"

"I guess not. It doesn't matter anyway. Everything's falling apart. It'll be a miracle if the cult survives the month at this rate."

"Ahem!" Their guide had stopped in the middle of the tunnel and cleared his throat. When Otto looked his way he said, "It's just ahead."

Otto peered through the ether and sure enough a thick fog of corruption filled the air. It seemed like what they were looking for. "Does this look right to you?"

Jet nodded. "It feels right. Like Astaroth is looking over my shoulder. We always came from a different direction, but this is the aerie."

"I can go now, right?" their guide asked.

Jet stalked over to him and cut his throat. When he'd finished bleeding out she looked back at Otto. "He knew too much to remain alive."

Otto shrugged. The young man's death meant nothing to him one way or the other, though her ability to kill someone in cold blood impressed him. "So what now?"

"Um, now we go into the aerie and you send a message to

Lady White telling her about Marius and the Golmol worshipers."

"Okay, but how, exactly, do I do that? Sending messages using birds made out of corruption isn't exactly a skill my mentors have taught me." When she just stared at him in silence Otto finally understood. "You don't have a clue, do you? You asked me to come along hoping I'd figure it out on my own."

"It sounds so much worse when you say it that way. I was desperate! Can't we at least take a look?"

"After you."

Jet took a few hesitant steps toward the aerie. As Otto watched, the corruption grew stronger around her, coating her like a second skin. Moving closer himself, he could now see shapes moving in the darkness. Shapes that did, in fact, look like black birds.

First one then another dove at Jet.

Then another. When their beaks struck her flesh, she moaned and a white patch appeared on her bronze skin.

Otto stayed just at the edge of the darkness, content to watch for now.

After six hits Jet staggered back out of the corruption. Her once flawless complexion now closely resembled one of the undead. The birds had literally drained some of the life out of her.

She collapsed at his feet and peered up. "I saw nothing that hinted at how to send a message. That place isn't meant for the living."

Otto couldn't argue with that. "That's why I wanted you to go in first. Happily, while you might not have learned anything, I believe I have."

Hope blossomed in her face. "Really?"

He nodded and held out his hand to help her up. When Jet was on her feet Otto continued, "Unfortunately, I need some bait."

He shoved her toward the aerie.

Immediately a bird dove at her.

As soon as it separated itself from the darkness, Otto wrapped it in a bubble of ether. With a tentacle he yanked Jet out of harm's way before another of the nasty little beasts could strike.

She glared at him. "You should've warned me."

"Sometimes knowing what's about to happen isn't useful. Now be quiet. I need to concentrate."

Turning the full weight of his gaze on the bird, Otto studied how it interacted with the ether. Every time its beak struck his bubble, it burned a tiny hole that he was forced to seal. The corruption acted like acid, dissolving the ether. The two were antithetical. That was why mithril burned those associated with corruption and made ethereal magic stronger.

Amet Sur, the first and greatest Arcane Lord, had mastered corrupt magic and that meant Otto didn't need to trade his soul to a demon lord to use it. Unfortunately, he was no Amet Sur. On the plus side, he wasn't trying to build an army of undead or melt the flesh from men's bones. He just needed to figure out how to write a message in corruption.

Okay, think it through. How would he have done it if he wanted to send a message through the ether? The same way he created his message sticks. If he could send a ten-word message through the ether, he should be able to send one using corruption. Maybe.

Frowning, Otto conjured a message the way he knew how first. Ten glowing words appeared in his ethereal vision, *Marius planning to attack city, Golmol cultists uncovered in under-*

ground. He compressed them and wrapped them in a bubble. Now, how to attach them to the bird?

Using the ether like a spatula, he gathered corruption and applied a thin layer to his bubble before making a thread and wrapping it around the bird's claw. Lastly, he conjured an image of Lady White in his mind and tried to drive the desire to go to her into the bird's mind.

When he'd done his best to secure the message, Otto released the beast and it vanished into the ether. Whether it went to the Land of the Demon Binders or dissolved, he had no way of knowing.

"I've done all I can," Otto said. He felt as exhausted as if he'd run a marathon. "How long until she replies?"

"I don't know. If Lady White is busy, she might need hours or days. Anyway, she always sends the reply directly to Marius, so we'll only know what she said if he tells us."

"In that case, let's find somewhere nicer to rest for an hour then we'll see about finding the Forbidden Garden."

CHAPTER 39

The Imperial Palace sprawled over a half mile in the city center. The central keep towered seven stories high, a red tile roof and dragon-style gargoyles giving it an imposing look. The hundreds of guards Otto counted patrolling the battlements didn't hurt either. A twenty-foot-high wall, patrolled by yet more guards, surrounded the grounds. None of them seemed to have magical abilities, so sneaking in wouldn't be a problem.

After a two-hour rest in the Golmol worshippers' tavern, Otto and Jet had emerged into bright, almost blinding noon sunlight. When Otto's eyes had adjusted, it was clear nothing had happened during his time underground. That made sense. Marius's power would be strongest after dark. Naturally he would want to wait until night to make his move.

Otto and Jet snuck around toward the northern wall of the compound wrapped in an invisibility spell. No one paid them the least attention. Patrols of soldiers guarded every approach. Even ministers dressed in fine robes were questioned as they neared the solitary gate.

"They take security seriously," Otto said. "But I've seen no lords."

"They'll be inside as well as in the Citadel of Alchemy." She pointed out a smaller but still large three-story fortress surrounded by a faint haze of smoke.

When Otto looked closer the powerful currents of ether became clear. Many people in that building were working magic. Good, if they were busy with important projects, they would be less likely to notice when Otto entered.

Trees towered over the northern side of the wall. Ether swirled around the branches, marking them as no ordinary growth. No guards patrolled this side of the wall either. Clearly the powers that be had no fear of trespassers from this direction. So much the better for Otto.

Satisfied with what he'd seen, Otto tagged the alley where they stood with a single thread. "Okay, let's head back. If Lady White was going to respond, she should have done so by now."

"You're not going in?" Jet asked.

"Not until tonight. I need a proper rest to recover my full strength. Anything less is asking for failure. Plus, I need to know where things stand with Marius. I can't focus on what's ahead of me unless I know what's behind me."

Jet chewed her lip but finally nodded. "I have to face the consequences some time. If I go back with you, maybe he won't kill me on the spot."

As they turned back toward the slums Otto asked, "If you knew the consequences, why risk sending the message?"

"When the government raided my warehouse, I knew my days as a merchant were over. If I lose the cult as well, I'll end up a beggar on the street. Better death at Marius's hand than that. Since I did my best to serve him in life, hopefully Astaroth will be generous in the afterlife."

Otto wanted to laugh, but held his tongue. He seriously doubted a demon lord took intentions into account. Only results mattered, just like in the world of the living.

The pair made it back to their safe house without issue. The streets were busy but calm. Either word of the raid hadn't reached the people yet or they thought little of it. Otto didn't know enough about the empire to guess which.

Jet opened the door and they found Marius pacing while five rugged, armed men watched without meeting the undead cultist's angry gaze. This was the first time Otto had seen Marius on edge. Perhaps he'd gotten a message from his mistress.

The moment Otto closed the door Marius rounded on them. "Where have you two been? As if I didn't know."

"I went to scout the palace grounds," Otto said. "What little I saw of the Forbidden Garden impressed me."

Marius ignored him and focused on Jet. "You betrayed me."

She shook her head. "We're all on the same side. I feared you were making a mistake that would destroy all that we had built. And yes, I said we. You're in charge, but you couldn't have accomplished all you have without me. When I saw the danger of all that going up in flames, I acted to protect it."

Otto admired her courage even if he considered it slightly foolish. "Tell him about the other cultists."

That drew Marius's attention. "What other cultists?"

"On our way to the aerie," Jet said. "We ran into some of Golmol's worshipers. They won't be a problem now, but who knows how many of the other cults have cells in the empire? This bunch were lying in wait. They claimed for some time. How long has it been since you sent a message to Lady White?"

Marius took two strides and backhanded Jet so hard her

legs buckled. "Don't you dare try and turn this back on me. I tell Lady White everything I decide she needs to know."

"Did you get a reply to our message?" Otto asked. He wasn't sure why he tried to deflect some of the attention away from Jet, but her courage deserved some sort of acknowledgement.

Marius's hand shot out and grabbed Otto around the throat. "This is none of your concern, outsider. Keep your mouth shut and you might live long enough to die in your precious garden."

A fist made of twenty threads slammed into Marius's chest and sent him flying across the room to crash into the far wall with enough force to make a spiderweb of cracks. Otto rubbed his throat, but a barrier of ether had prevented any damage.

He drew his mithril sword and stalked over to the undead. "I don't know who you think you're dealing with, but I'm not one of your lackeys to be bullied into submission."

Otto slapped the flat of his blade against the fleshy side of Marius's face. The skin hissed and crackled, forcing Marius to pull away.

"Lay your hands on me again and I'll send you to meet your master." Otto stabbed the wall an inch from Marius's head. "Do we understand each other?"

"Perfectly." There was such hate in Marius's voice that Otto almost killed him on the spot. Only a desire to stay on good terms with Lady White stayed his hand.

The floor creaked behind him.

Otto spun to see the five thugs edging closer, hands on the hilts of their weapons.

"I'll happily kill all of you as well."

"Enough!" Marius said. "Fighting amongst ourselves is doing us no good."

The thugs relaxed and Otto moved to stand beside Jet. He didn't sheathe his sword just yet though.

"I did receive a reply from Lady White. She ordered me to lie low and rebuild in secret." Jet brightened, but only until Marius resumed speaking. "Unfortunately, what I set in motion can't be stopped. Orders or not, the attack will proceed."

"What have you done?" Jet asked.

"I activated the temple defenses. When the sun sets, the black shroud will rise and spread through the city, drawing power as it kills and raises the slain as zombies. While the lords are busy trying to stop it, we will free our brothers and sisters and strike them from behind, slaughtering the most powerful force in the empire. Then we need only march on the palace. With the army of undead I raise, we will seize the city and from here spread across the empire and world until all serve Lord Astaroth."

With that speech, Otto fully understood just how insane Marius was. Once the threat became clear, all the empire's power would fall on the cultists and crush their revolution flat. Of course, Otto planned to be long gone before that happened.

"It seems you have everything worked out," Otto said. "After dark, I'll make my way to the palace and infiltrate the garden. We can meet in the courtyard."

"I wouldn't want to send an ally into such a dangerous place alone," Marius said. "Take Jet with you. She might be of some use."

"And she'd be out of your way," Otto said. "That's fine. Now, I'm going to rest. Barring a peacekeeper raid, I would prefer not to be disturbed."

Otto stalked over to the safe house's only bedroom and after a moment Jet followed him. He slammed the door shut.

Things had certainly gotten complicated. Otto knew when he decided to seek out the pieces of the Immortality Engine that it would be difficult, but so far it had been difficult in ways he never expected.

"Thank you for agreeing to let me come along," Jet said. "Had you refused, Marius would have killed me at the first opportunity."

Otto grunted and dropped onto the saggy bed. "Instead he thinks we'll both die in the garden. That's fine. We'll just have to prove him wrong."

CHAPTER 40

An eerie feeling woke Otto from a deep sleep. He sat up and looked out the bedroom's lone window. The sunset dyed the sky in purple and orange. When his vision shifted to the ether, a blot of corruption appeared in the direction of the warehouse, or more specifically the temple of Astaroth beneath it. It seemed Marius's ritual had begun.

Otto rolled out of the creaking bed and turned his attention to the safe house's main room. Marius had left, the absence of corruption told him that clearly. Whether the thugs had joined him didn't concern Otto. They posed no threat, present or absent.

Back on the bed, Jet slept on the very edge, totally oblivious to what was happening. Otto shook his head. He'd been so tired he hadn't even noticed her lying down beside him. Maybe his subconscious had decided to trust her. She hadn't killed him in his sleep, so he'd take that as a sign of her loyalty.

Or desperation.

Either way, they needed to go. He didn't know how quickly Marius's black shroud would spread, but he didn't want to end up in the middle of the corruption. He reached out to the ether and found his power fully restored. Considerably relieved, he went over and shook Jet awake.

She groaned and opened her eyes. "Time to go?"

He nodded. "Marius has begun. What, exactly, I'm less certain of. But whatever it is, I want to be far away before it gets bad."

She climbed out of bed, hair going every which way, and stretched, her back popping. "I'm ready."

Out in the main room, they found their so-called allies long gone. That suited Otto fine as he had no desire to waste his strength killing fools. He adjusted his sword and led the way outside.

The dark streets were quiet enough for the moment. Following the thread he'd left, Otto turned north toward the palace. As they walked, he asked, "Just how bad will things get?"

"I know little about the cult's magical rituals," Jet said. "Unopposed, the shroud will slowly spread until it covers the entire city. The only things that will stop it are killing Marius and sealing the hell gate he's opened or running out of lives to power it."

"Are we going to have to worry about demons as well as undead?"

"No. The gate is tiny, only big enough to summon corrupt energy. Summoning a proper demon requires far more power than Marius commands. I can't imagine how much time he's spent just to gather the magic needed for this ritual. He's probably been working on it for decades."

Otto immediately ratcheted up his estimation of the danger. In his experience, the longer you spent on a project, the greater the potential for remarkable results. Investing decades on a single ritual was something he couldn't even imagine. Of course, Marius was immortal now, so he had all the time in the world.

They'd covered about ten blocks when the first screams reached him. They were faint but distinct. He couldn't tell if they signaled horror, pain, fear, or something else. He didn't especially want to find out either.

He picked up the pace until they were nearly jogging through the dark. The screams only grew louder despite the increased speed. It almost sounded like the person making that noise was running right toward them.

Otto stopped and turned to face the noise. Light blazed to life around him as he agitated the ether. They were still in the rundown part of the city and none of the locals seemed inclined to stick their heads out to see what was going on. Otto didn't blame them a bit.

Jet grabbed his arm and tugged. "What are you doing? We can't stay here."

"We can't escape either." Otto drew his sword. "Better to face whatever's coming now than when we've run ourselves to exhaustion."

Jet pulled her own dagger, her knuckles white on the hilt. While he appreciated the gesture, Otto expected little in the way of help from his companion.

The screaming was nearly deafening when the creature burst into the light at a full sprint.

Otto didn't hesitate.

A spear of ten fused threads lashed out, reducing the creature's head to pulp, sending it crashing to the ground, and putting an end to its screaming. After all that noise, he'd expected more of a battle.

Otto walked over and looked down at the remains. It had

clearly been a woman once. Her clothes were torn and ragged and her feet bare. Her body had been twisted and distorted. Fingers were transformed into claws, teeth into fangs, and her skin was now rough and gray like stone.

In the distance more screams filled the night.

"What is it?" he asked.

"They're called Screamers, for obvious reasons," Jet said. "I read about them in one of Astaroth's holy books. They serve as shock troops in his army. Running ahead of the main force and slaughtering all that oppose them. I got the impression they were supposed to be tougher."

"Don't let this battle fool you. Against my magic, this one stood no chance, but against an ordinary soldier, I shudder to think what it might have done. Anyway, let's get going. I'd just as soon avoid any more of them if possible."

It ended up not being possible. Otto was forced to kill two more of the Screamers before they reached the alley where his thread ended. Across the way, the Forbidden Garden glowed a dull yellow in the dark.

"With all the undead running around the city," Jet said. "Maybe the garden won't be so bad."

"What do you want to bet?"

Her laugh sounded nervous and brittle which perfectly described Otto's nerves. After the long journey here, crossing the border, running and hiding, it was finally time.

Otto conjured a platform beneath them and they rose slowly toward the palace wall. No shouts of alarm rang out and no guards came running. A quick look revealed that all the guards were clustered around the main gate.

Perfect. Just as he'd hoped, Marius's uprising served his needs well. They landed on the battlements and looked down into the garden. Or they tried to. The thick canopy blocked

Otto's view. They ended up having to walk a third of the way down the wall until what looked like an entrance, really just an arch made up of bent saplings, became visible.

He lowered them down to the ground and they walked slowly toward the arch. There was no barrier beyond the thick growth, yet for all appearances, no gap wide enough to admit a person existed.

Otto stopped and took a deep breath. A shield of ether formed around him. If Jet decided to follow, she was on her own.

Steeling himself, he stepped across the threshold into the garden.

○

Ten strides past the entrance and Otto already knew he was dealing with something beyond even his wildest imaginings. It felt like a million eyes were watching, but when he looked around, he saw nothing save trees. Even the sky was blocked out by the sprawling branches. No bird or squirrel, not even a bug broke the perfect stillness. An odd scent filled the air, faint, like distant perfume. It was floral, but unlike anything he'd smelled before.

"Where do you think the Heart is?" Jet asked.

It seemed she'd decided to join him. Otto had been so focused on what was around him that he hadn't even noticed her.

"If Lord Cheng was anything like the other Arcane Lords, I suspect it will be in the center of the garden. Probably on a glowing pedestal surrounded by lethal traps and monsters."

He looked back at Jet then past her, over her right shoulder. The garden entrance was gone.

"No going back now."

Jet turned then snapped her gaze back to his, panic clear in her eyes. "How?"

That was always the question with Arcane Lords and far too often the answer was the same. "I have no idea. It seems down the path is our only option."

Jet had her dagger out and her head jerked left and right as if trying to watch every direction at once. Otto didn't bother telling her it was a waste of time and that ordinary steel would probably do her no good.

"Try to relax. Your anxiety is stressing me out. Whatever is going to happen will happen no matter how ready we are. All you're going to do is exhaust yourself."

"Easy for you to say. You have magic and mithril to protect you."

"You were free to wait outside."

"For Marius and his undead to show up? No, thank you. I'll take my chances in here. At least the trees don't want to eat me."

Otto wasn't entirely sure that was true. He sensed no malevolence from the garden, but there was definitely something, some presence, that was aware of them. Its nature and purpose eluded Otto, but he would never assume good intentions.

The path made it clear where they were meant to go. Hopefully not directly into a trap. As they walked on, he shifted his focus constantly between the ether and the physical world. Not that there was much difference. Everything in the garden seemed infused with massive amounts of ether. The amount of power in a single tree was more than he could have channeled in a year.

He tried to think how Lord Cheng might have created such

things and immediately gave up. Trying to think like an Arcane Lord was still as far beyond him as long division was a mosquito.

Much like being underground, the constant, unchanging glow made it hard to tell how long they'd been wandering around. Far longer, it seemed to Otto, than it should have taken to reach the center of such a small area. It seemed like they were moving in a straight line, but he couldn't assume his senses hadn't been affected.

He took a deep breath. The perfume was getting stronger and he took that as a sign that they were closing in on their final destination. Not that he had any way to prove his theory, but it was better than panicking. Which was exactly what would happen if he allowed himself to believe they were simply wandering in circles.

Otto's faith was rewarded a moment later when they found a modest clearing directly ahead. A glowing figure of a man in long, golden robes stood in the center of the clearing. On a pedestal made of twisted branches sat a bloodred gemstone the size of Otto's fist. That had to be the Heart of Alchemy. Which made the ghost Lord Cheng.

He stopped just outside the clearing and studied the scene with both his mundane senses and his magical ones. In the ether, Cheng glowed more brightly than the trees. It looked like he was made of pure ether packed so dense he was practically solid. His glowing, golden eyes bore into Otto like a drill.

It was a challenge, pure and simple. Did he have the courage to step into the clearing and face whatever the long-dead Arcane Lord had in store for him?

Otto certainly did. "Wait here."

With that he stepped off the path and into the clearing.

Sensing movement behind him, Otto spun just in time to

watch the trees close in, blocking off the path. Well, no turning back now.

He strode directly over to the ethereal construct and bowed. "Lord Cheng."

"You have come for the Heart," the construct said. "I congratulate you on claiming the Chamber. Lord Colt was always known for the... durability of his tests."

Otto stared for a moment. "How did you know I passed Colt's test?"

"The pieces of the Infinity Engine are separate, but still connected. What happens to one, the other knows. As the Heart's guardian, what it knows, I know."

"Fascinating. I suppose you have a test for me as well. Shall we begin?"

"We have already begun. You noticed the pleasant perfume that fills the air?"

Otto nodded. "I've never smelled anything like it."

"I'm not surprised. I created the plant that gives it off. It is also highly toxic."

Otto touched his chest. He felt no different. "What do I do now?"

"You must make a choice," the construct said. "As long as you remain in the garden, the tree's pollen will protect you from the poison. The moment you step outside, it will activate and you will quickly die. Your choices are simple. Stay here and spend the rest of your life as my companion or take the Heart and pray you can transmute the poison in your body before it kills you."

"That's it?" Otto said, like the test was simple, but in reality, it was probably harder than defeating Colt's steel construct. "I thought I would have to fight a living tree or something."

"That is not my way."

"No, I suppose it isn't. Can you give me any pointers on how to use the Heart?"

"Why do you think a simple guardian like me would know anything?"

"You're a simulacrum, right? You should know everything your creator knew, or close to it."

The construct smiled. "Congratulations. The reward for your perceptiveness is a hint. Alchemy is about transforming a substance from one state to another. That is why it serves as the Heart of the process for becoming an Arcane Lord. When you access the Heart's power, keep that in mind."

Otto frowned at the indirect advice. Still, he suspected he'd get nothing else. When he went to claim the Heart, Cheng's construct made no effort to stop him.

The gem gave off a faint heat and weighed less than a double eagle. Peering at it in the ether revealed a complex matrix of connections far more advanced than anything he had ever contemplated. With the proper knowledge you could probably do just about anything with this thing. Pity Otto lacked that knowledge.

When he looked back, he found a rather nervous-seeming Jet watching him from the edge of the clearing. Since there was nothing more for him to do here, he strode over to her.

"Are you okay?" she asked.

"No, and neither are you." He explained about the poison and how to deal with it. "It all comes down to me figuring out how to use this thing. If I do it right, we live. If not, we die."

"Great. Nothing to it, right?"

Otto remained silent. Transforming the poison would be the most complex and difficult magic he had ever attempted. He'd said it half in jest, but right now, he really would have preferred to fight a tree monster.

⟳

There was no more sense of being watched as they made their way back to the edge of the garden. Beside him, Jet fidgeted, adjusting her hair, then her clothes, then back to her hair. You'd think she was meeting her lover after a long absence. Otto rubbed the smooth surface of the Heart. If he screwed this up, the only thing they'd be meeting was their doom.

The walk out took far less time than the trip in. Or maybe Otto was so distracted the path felt shorter. Either way, when they reached the end he stopped and gathered himself. The moment he moved beyond the trees, the countdown began.

"Wait here," Otto said. "If I survive, I'll signal you to come out and I can repeat the process on you."

"And if you don't?" she asked.

"Then you have to decide if you prefer death or spending the rest of your life in an enchanted garden with only the spirit of a long-dead Arcane Lord for company. You could also wait and hope for Marius to raise you as an undead."

"I'll just hope you succeed."

Otto nodded, filled the Heart with ether, and took the last step forward. He had the briefest impressions of an empty courtyard before pain unlike anything he'd ever known stabbed into every inch of his body. Even breaking through his personal magical limit felt like a tickle compared to this.

Fear and pain being wonderful motivators, he plunged all his senses into the Heart. He followed the crystal matrix all the way into its core and was promptly pumped out like a spurt of blood. Letting his awareness ride the ethereal flow, Otto's consciousness was sent back through his hands into his blood stream.

Once there he quickly found the problem. Tiny flecks of something other than blood filled his body. That had to be the poison. But there was so much of it. Every second more damage was done to the surrounding vessels. How could he deal with all of it in time?

The answer came a moment later. He ran a thread of ether through one of the specks of poison then used a variation of the spell that allowed him to find someone by using their blood. At his command, the ether sought out everything like that fleck of poison.

Instantly, the magic carried out his will. There was so much information his mind could barely comprehend it. Now that he had the poison marked, he needed to destroy it.

No.

What had Cheng's simulacrum said? Alchemy was about transformation. He couldn't destroy the poison, he needed to change it into something else.

Gritting his teeth against the pain, Otto ran a second thread through a red speck that belonged in his blood.

Now. Change!

Power flowed from the Heart into his body. For a moment it was like being one with the ether.

Bliss washed away the pain.

A moment later it was gone, leaving Otto feeling slightly hollow, but still alive. Even better, he didn't feel drained like he usually did when he used too much magic. Having the Heart as an intermediary must have banished the exhaustion. Considering how much he had left to do, he wasn't about to complain.

"You're still standing," Jet said from the edge of the garden. "Did you figure it out?"

Otto's answer got drowned out by a huge roar mingled with explosions and crashes coming from the direction of the palace gate. Sounded like Marius was getting close. Otto glanced at Jet. She wasn't really his problem. He could become one with the ether and return to Port Han in an instant.

He shook his head. No, she'd tried to do right by him and Otto respected that. He couldn't leave her poisoned and trapped and dependent on whatever small mercy Marius could summon.

"Yes, I understand the process. You need to understand that it isn't going to be pleasant."

"I didn't think purging a magical poison from my body would be fun. Are you ready?"

Otto turned to face her and nodded.

Jet took one step past the garden's edge.

Her whole body went rigid.

Otto drew ether through the Heart and sent it into her along with his sight. Now that he knew what to look for, finding the specks of poison took no time at all. Binding and transforming them required a few extra seconds.

Behind him, the crashes had turned to roars while the explosions grew ever less frequent. Sounded like the undead were winning.

He had little focus to spare. Guiding a rush of ether, Otto transformed the poison into blood cells. When he blinked his vision back to his body, Jet looked okay, but her expression was still stiff and fixed in a grimace.

It took him a second to realize she was looking beyond him.

Otto slowly turned to find Marius, flanked by dozens of undead, all humanoid, but also no two exactly the same. It was a veritable banquet of horrors. Surely even Amet Sur would have been impressed by such a selection.

Marius and his entourage stopped about five paces short of

Otto. "So you survived the Forbidden Garden. I must admit I am impressed."

"Thank you. The Cult of Astaroth has been a great help, even if things didn't work out exactly as planned. I'll be heading back to Port Han at dawn."

"You might be, assuming you hand over whatever you found in the garden along with the betrayer cowering behind you."

"Who are you calling a betrayer!" Jet stepped out from behind Otto. "Lady White will have your head for this rebellion."

Marius chucked. "She is a long way from here and in no position to do anything even if she wanted to. I control a third of the city and my forces are expanding by the hour. The emperor, miserable coward that he is, has fled before me. Astaroth clearly favors my path and no one will take this victory from me."

Otto shook his head. "The internal politics of your cult don't interest me. But if you think you're going to claim my prize, then what remains of your brain must have rotted along with your face."

"You're hardly in a position to deny me."

Otto flooded the Heart with ether as Marius sent a wave of corruption rolling out at him.

With the Heart augmenting his perception, Otto sent out a matching wave of ether. When the two forces touched, he transformed the corruption into pure ether.

"Impossible." Marius stared as though betrayed by the person he trusted most.

But Otto wasn't finished. He sent threads into the undead surrounding Marius and repeated the process with the corruption sustaining their existence. Each of the creatures collapsed like a marionette with its strings cut.

"I could do the same to you," Otto said. "But I have no desire to end up on the bad side of a demon lord. Jet and I are leaving. Keep your monsters out of my way and I won't destroy them. Come after me and I'll find you and end you. Do you understand?"

Marius was staring at the remains of his followers, seeming oblivious to Otto.

"Do you understand!?"

Marius jumped as if struck, finally looking at Otto. "I understand. You will not be troubled."

"Good." Otto turned to Jet. "I assume you wish to come with me."

"I certainly do. My place here is lost, but hopefully Lady White will find a position for me."

Otto hadn't seen a single mortal servant in Lady White's home, but that didn't mean there weren't some somewhere. "We'd best be on our way."

Leaving the palace grounds and entering the dark city felt like walking into another world, a world devoid of people. Corruption tainted the ether all around them. This had to be the effect of the black shroud.

Otto used the Heart to purify the ether around them, forming a bubble of protection. As they walked, it didn't seem to be causing any ill effects so his protective bubble must be working.

Out of the corner of his eye, Otto spotted movement, but it vanished as soon as he turned to look. True to his word, Marius sent no undead after them. It took nearly half an hour, but they finally reached a district free of the shroud. Even though it was still dark, the atmosphere felt lighter. A couple dozen people were fleeing the cursed area as fast as possible.

Otto released his spell and Jet left his side and went over to a woman herding a pair of children ahead of her. From the quality of her dress and the gold rings on her fingers, the woman must have come from a wealthy household. They spoke briefly and then she rejoined Otto while the mother hurried off.

"There's a gathering area in the southern trade district. Everyone from the affected districts are heading there."

"Sounds like a good place for us to avoid."

"Agreed. If all the attention is focused on that district, we should head for the western gate. We also need to find you a disguise. You stand out too much as you are."

"Let's just skip the gate and go to the wall. If we find an unguarded section, I can lift us out easily enough. But it's a long walk to Port Han."

"There are supply stops not far from the city. I can secure us a wagon and horses at one of them. Since my credentials have been canceled, getting through the border wall will be the real problem."

"The guards know you there, don't they?"

"Yes, why?"

"Because I doubt word will reach them before we do. I can make you a pass and they won't give a familiar face a second look."

"Sounds like a plan." Jet grinned, seemingly having regained some of her spirit.

Otto just hoped he wasn't being overly optimistic. He didn't make it this far only to fail on the final leg of the trip.

CHAPTER 41

The journey south toward the border had gone smoothly enough despite their lack of guards. Otto was delighted to avoid trouble as it freed him to study the Heart. Not that he learned much as the magic involved in its creation was about five hundred years too advanced for him. Still, he found exploring the crystal matrix endlessly fascinating.

Beside him, Jet reined in the horses at the top of a low hill. In the distance, the border wall loomed, tall and impenetrable. Three merchants had lined up to wait their turn to enter. None of the guards seemed especially alert, so word of what happened in the capital must not have traveled this far yet. That suited their plans perfectly.

Otto pulled a palm-sized disk of bronze out of his pocket and looked at it from both sides. Using focused ether, he'd carved the image of a horse-drawn wagon on one side and a series of numbers on the other.

He handed it to Jet. "Does that look right to you?"

She'd guided him in the process of creating the fake medallion, but a second check couldn't hurt. If she wanted to make any adjustments, this was the last chance.

Jet looked it all over and said, "It looks good. Unless something extraordinary happens, they shouldn't give it a moment's thought. The real trick is going to be getting you through."

"Oh, that won't be a problem. I'll be entering by magic. If the medallion works, I'll be waiting at the inn where we first met."

Otto became one with the ether, sought out the rune he'd carved, and willed himself to it.

A moment later he emerged in a decidedly dustier but still-familiar bedroom. It seemed Hans had followed his orders and kept everyone, including the cleaning staff, out.

Otto stepped off the rune, turned, and drew the ether out of it until it no longer glowed. No doubt he would have to pay a small fee to cover the cost of repairing the floor. He shrugged and strode toward the door.

The instant he opened it, Corina came running and nearly tackled him with a hug. "You're okay! We've been so worried."

Otto looked over her head at Hans and his squad who were seated around a table playing cards. None of them looked especially worried, but then when he wanted to, Hans could show the best stone face Otto had ever seen.

After a moment he disengaged from Corina. "I trust there were no issues during my absence?"

Hans tossed his cards on the table and stood. "Not to speak of. Your brother had a few run-ins with local gangs thinking foreigners would make an easy mark. He quickly showed them the error of their ways. The inn has been as quiet as a grave. The food is delicious and the staff... charming. After dealing with giant animals and spooky boat creatures, we've enjoyed the peace and quiet."

Having seen the lovely ladies on the serving staff, Otto fully understood Han's sentiments. He was also glad the guys enjoyed a little rest and relaxation. After losing one of their own, it probably helped.

"Did you find what you were looking for, Master?" Corina asked.

"Indeed." Otto pulled the Heart from his pocket and held it out to her. "If you want to see something wondrous, extend your sight into it. Just beyond the surface. You don't want to lose yourself in the matrix."

Ether gathered around her eyes and a second later she gasped. "That's amazing! How could you make something like that?"

Otto shook his head and put the Heart back. "I haven't the slightest idea. The time and power required boggles my mind. If you ever think you've reached a point where you have nothing more to learn, remember what you just saw. If that doesn't keep you humble, nothing will."

"What now, my lord?" Hans asked.

"Now I'm going to rest and enjoy some fine food. Jet should be here in three days. If she isn't here in four, we're leaving."

"You're bringing that woman with us?" Corina asked, her distaste plain.

"We'll be dropping her off in the Land of the Demon Binders. I'd like to speak with Lady White again as well. Don't worry, it won't take more than a day."

"Would you like me to send a messenger to let Axel know you've returned?" Hans asked.

"Please do." Otto stretched and yawned. How long had it been since he slept in a comfortable bed? He couldn't remember, but he was looking forward to doing so again.

‿

Otto poured his focus into the Heart of Alchemy. His vision flew down one passage of the crystal matrix after another. The ether, tinted red by the Heart, seemed more alive and potent than ever. It was intoxicating and at the same time disappointing. Enthralling as the magic was, it didn't actually teach him anything. Much like channeling his threads through mithril, the Heart served to augment his current abilities rather than granting him new insight.

Several hard raps on his bedroom door drew him from the depths of the crystal. He had no idea how long he had been exploring the artifact. Not that it mattered as he had nothing else to occupy his time while he waited for Jet.

He stood, his back and knees protesting that he'd been sitting there for far too long. Beyond the door he found Hans waiting. "Messenger, my lord."

Otto went to the outer door and found one of the scantily clad serving girls waiting in the hall. She bowed. "You have a visitor. She asked me to let you know of her arrival."

That had to be Jet at last. He tossed the girl a silver coin. "Thank you."

She bowed again and hurried away.

"Hans, pack our stuff. We'll be leaving shortly. Meet me downstairs when you're done."

Otto left his subordinates to prepare for their departure and went downstairs to the common room. Given the sun pouring in through the windows he made the time around midday. He hadn't been working for quite as long as he thought.

Jet was sitting alone at a corner table. Otto joined her and waved off an approaching servant. He had no desire for a final drink.

"You had no difficulties at the border?" he asked.

"None. As you guessed, word hadn't reached them yet. Your fake medallion did the trick."

"Nothing like an undead attack to slow the flow of information. Is it still your wish to visit the Land of the Demon Binders?"

Jet sighed. "I have no other choice. Returning to the empire is a death sentence. I had to leave most of my wealth behind so staying here isn't going to work."

"As you wish. I hope to speak with Lady White myself, so it's not out of our way to deliver you."

"You have my thanks." She offered a seated bow.

Hans and the others joined them shortly and after settling up with the owner, they left for the docks. The ship looked to be in perfect condition and they set sail not long after boarding.

Despite his success, Otto wouldn't miss the Celestial Empire. All he wanted now was to return home, complete the Chamber, and find out about the final piece of the Immortality Engine.

CHAPTER 42

A group had gathered near the helm of the ship. Otto got the impression Captain Wainwright didn't appreciate the company, but he also had sufficient wisdom to keep his opinions to himself. They'd been sailing for a week and were supposed to be getting close to the Land of the Demon Binders. Really close in fact. Yet the sense of foreboding was gone as was the creepy fog. No monstrous humanoid creature came out to greet them as they eased closer.

Otto turned to the captain. "Are you certain we're in the right place?"

"Unless the stars have changed position while we were in Port Han. According to the measurements I took this morning, our destination is only ten miles due north."

Otto had no reason to doubt the man's competence at this late date. He'd gotten them safely to their destination halfway around the world. If that didn't give you a boost of confidence in someone's abilities, nothing would.

"What do we do?" Axel asked.

That was an excellent question. Unfortunately, Otto hadn't the slightest idea.

"What do you think?" he asked Jet.

The woman shook her head. The situation seemed to have left her as surprised as the rest of them. "Something must have happened. If The Voice isn't here and no one is maintaining the barrier, I can only imagine the worst."

In a nation of demon worshipers, the worst might be pretty bad. It might also offer an opportunity.

"Take us in," Otto said.

"Is that wise, Master?" Corina asked.

"Time will tell."

Captain Wainwright turned the wheel, adjusting their course and bringing them in line with the port. Or so they hoped. Having sailed through that soup of a fog left them with only a guess as to where the precise location of the city was. At least this time they could see it coming.

An hour later Corina grasped his sleeve and said, "Wow."

Otto couldn't argue with her assessment. The port city lay directly ahead of them, its glory undiminished by obscuring fog. Black spires jutted up into the sky. Shorter buildings surrounded them like mushrooms at the base of a tree.

No wall protected the city from the surrounding wilderness. No doubt the unearthly aura kept any ordinary animals from wandering in. Anything else would quickly end up dead and transformed into a demonic host.

An explosion shook the air and a mushroom cloud of blue flames shot up into the sky.

"Those are the unholy flames of Abaddon," Jet said. "There must be a major battle going on."

"Who would be stupid enough to invade a country ruled by demon cultists?" Corina asked.

"Oh, I doubt it's an invader," Jet said. "Most likely the cults are warring amongst themselves. Usually, the nine High Lords keep a relative peace broken by only the occasional murder. But sometimes more serious conflicts break out."

"How much do you want to bet this has something to do with events in the Celestial Empire?" Otto asked.

Jet shook her head. "Marius's actions have shifted the balance of power. The other cults will want to weaken Astaroth's power to restore it. Since Lady White is in charge of the cult's operation in the empire, she will be forced to bear the consequences."

The ship was only a hundred yards from the dock now. If they were to turn back, now was the time. Otto chewed his lip as he weighed his options. He had what he came for. Making a run for home was the safe move. But on the other hand, if he rescued Lady White, she would make a powerful ally.

"Orders, Lord Shenk?" Captain Wainwright asked.

"Take us in. Tie up at the farthest-out dock. Hans, prepare the squad. Axel, you're on security detail. Have your archers use their mithril arrows. Anything approaches the ship that isn't with me, kill it. No mercy, no hesitation. Clear?"

Axel nodded and started shouting orders.

"What about me?" Corina asked.

"You'll stay and help Axel." When she didn't complain Otto turned to Jet. "You'll come with me. I need someone to guide me to Lady White's tower."

Jet winced. "I've never actually been there. We only met once in Port Han and that was via magic. That's where she inducted me into the cult. We've never actually met face to face."

So much for that brilliant idea. If Lady White was taking the brunt of the assault, they could probably just follow the fighting right to her. That was as good a plan as any. The city didn't look all that big, so the search shouldn't take too long.

◯

Otto led Hans and the others he'd selected for the shore party down the ship's gangplank and up the dock. The explosion of demonic blue flame had come from a position a little to the left of where they docked. He angled that way even as more explosions rocked the city and filled the air with the stink of brimstone.

Sounded like Lady White was putting up a fight. That was good. He'd hate to go to all this trouble only to find her dead.

"Shall I send out scouts, my lord?" Hans asked.

"No. We stick together. The team is small enough as it is. Besides, there's plenty a scout would miss that I won't. Just keep your eyes peeled for anything headed our way. And keep your swords out."

Following his own advice, Otto drew his sword.

The first neighborhood they passed through, assuming that was the right word for the collection of low stone building clustered around a five-story tower, showed signs of recent battle. The most obvious of which was a claw mark five feet up one of the walls. Otto would hate to run into whatever made that.

The main thing lacking in the city was people. They hadn't seen a single one, not even a body. Surely someone must live here other than demon worshippers.

When Otto posed the question to Jet she said, "There are ordinary people in the country, but only demons, undead, and mortal worshippers live in the city. A regular person with no magical protection would quickly end up a monster's meal or a husk for a demon spirit."

"Lord Shenk," Hans said.

Otto turned to find a beast charging towards them. It was filled with corruption. Whatever the beast used to be, it clearly housed a demon now.

At Otto's command, a twenty-thread lightning bolt crashed into the beast, blowing a hole in its side and slamming it into one of the stone buildings. Despite the grievous wound, the beast climbed back to its feet.

A second spell blew its head to bits and finally put it down for good.

"Let's keep moving," Otto said.

Another two blocks and the roar of flames grew louder. Smoke filled the streets, reminding Otto of his first visit. He summoned a gust of wind that blew the smoke away and revealed a magical battle unlike anything he'd ever seen.

Lady White crouched behind a berm of earth and stone, the warbeast she'd made from the giant cat thing he'd traded her for access to the city beside her. The beast had taken a fair share of damage. One of its legs was gone from the knee down and its skull showed through in places where the flesh had been burned away.

On the opposite side of the street, five figures in crimson robes hurled fire blast after fire blast at her. It was a standoff, but he doubted she could hold out for long outnumbered like that.

"Circle around," Otto said. "When I distract them, attack hard from behind."

Hans nodded and led the guys around to the right.

"What should I do?" Jet asked.

"What can you do?"

When she didn't reply he shrugged and said, "Stay out of the way and keep a lookout. If anything else heads our way, let me know."

"Okay."

A few minutes later he spotted Hans sneaking up on the cultists in red.

Otto channeled ether through his sword and lashed out. Thirty threads' worth of lightning, nearly his maximum output, arced out into the cultists. The attack hammered them one after another.

The first died instantly.

The second fell and went still.

The rest were only stunned.

But that was all Hans needed.

He and his men waded in, hacking and stabbing until nothing was moving.

Lady White stood, looked his way, and smiled.

They met halfway between their positions and before Otto had a chance to so much as offer a greeting, she hugged him. Of all the reactions he'd expected, that wasn't one of them. Her body held the chill of the grave but also the curves of a beautiful woman. The result was an incongruous mix of sensual and repulsive.

At last she stepped back. "Astaroth must still favor me if he sent you to my aid. I thought to never see you again."

"That makes two of us. I came primarily to deliver your follower." Lady White looked over his shoulder at Jet and seemed to dismiss her immediately. Otto cleared his throat and continued. "I also hoped to discuss undead and how best to control them. But now I'm thinking our best move is to leave this place, quickly. Do you have a secure location where we can talk?"

Lady White stretched, straining the fabric of her thin dress before focusing once more on Otto. "Nowhere is safe for me here. Astaroth's High Lord has cast me out of the cult. Abaddon's followers were selected to hunt me and my familiars down. I'm down to my final warbeast and he's not in very good shape. I would be grateful for transportation elsewhere."

"I can arrange that." Otto whistled. "Hans! We're heading back."

The good sergeant trotted over, mithril blade still bare in his hand.

Lady White shivered and moved away. "Could you put those swords away for now? Being surrounded by so much mithril makes me nauseous."

"You'll just have to bear it," Otto said as they set out. No way would he leave the others unprotected in the corrupt land. He'd lost one man on this journey and he had no intention of losing another.

Lady White glared at him, but her expression quickly smoothed. She needed him and she knew it. More importantly, she knew Otto knew it as well.

The little group set out at a quick march back toward the docks. The sooner they put some distance between themselves and the cursed city the better.

They managed six blocks before Lady White said, "They're coming."

Otto sensed it a moment later. Concentrated corruption headed their way, four of them it felt like.

A gout of blue flame came roaring in only to be turned aside by Lady White's magic.

"Run!" Otto said.

They broke into a sprint, abandoning all stealth for speed. Fortunately, the docks weren't that far away and soon the ship was visible ahead of them. Even better, Axel had his archers on deck, bows at the ready.

Otto waved and pointed over his shoulder.

Axel nodded and said something to the scouts. Seconds later arrows arced over their heads.

No more fire blasts exploded.

The moment Otto made it up the gangplank, the crew cut them free of the dock.

"Keep watch." Otto sent thirty-four threads through his sword and formed them into a huge arm that pushed the ship away from the dock and out to sea.

He fell to his knees, drained by the exertion.

꩜

When Otto finally forced himself to his feet, the ship had put on half her sails and they were making good time away from the cursed land. On deck, Lady White and a cowering Jet stood on one side, while everyone else gathered on the other side and watched her warily. Perfectly understandable given that she was an undead demon worshipper. Still, Otto couldn't have this tension the entire trip home.

He made his way to a spot near the main mast, halfway between the two groups. "Hans, Axel, Corina, Lady White, if you'd be so kind as to join me."

When all four had met in the middle Otto went on. "Everyone, Lady White is my guest on this voyage. Please treat her with the proper respect. You have nothing to fear from her."

"What about that?" Corina pointed at the warbeast.

"Rest easy, child," Lady White said. "It will do nothing without my permission. The poor thing has been through a rough time and needs to rest."

Corina bristled at being called a child, but she remained silent which Otto appreciated. "Shall we descend to my cabin and discuss our arrangement further?"

Before Lady White could respond, something hit the ship, sending it lurching to the side. Otto sprawled on the deck but quickly regained his feet.

He looked up at the crow's nest. "What was that?"

"Can't see anything!" the lookout shouted.

"It was Dagon's guardian," Lady White said. "I didn't think they would dispatch it after I left. It seems the High Lords really want me dead."

Otto frowned. "Dagon's guardian, you mean that thing that pulled us into port last time?"

"Correct."

"Something's coming right at us!" the lookout shouted.

Sure enough a long shadow was bearing down on the ship. They had about five seconds before it hit them again.

"Hang on!" Captain Wainwright said as he frantically turned the wheel.

The ship turned hard to the right.

Otto used threads of ether to brace himself.

"It missed!" the lookout called. "It's turning back!"

"How do we kill it?" Otto asked.

"It's a demon fused with a mass of corpses," Lady White said. "It's already dead."

"Can you control it?"

Lady White shook her head. "The bound demon serves Dagon. It would never heed the commands of a follower of Astaroth."

Otto snarled away his annoyance. He considered and rejected using the Heart. This thing had so much corruption in it, he doubted he had the power to transmute it all into pure ether even with the artifact's help.

He peered closer at the approaching monstrosity. While the corruption ran through its entire being, there was a core at its center. It was as close to a heart as he expected to find.

A desperate plan formed. "Axel, get your archers ready. When I force it up, have them shoot mithril arrows into it."

"How many?" Axel asked.

"All of them!" He turned to Lady White. "I'm going to need your help."

"What do you want me to do?" she asked.

"Be the bait. Stand at the rail and expand your presence. Call it to the surface."

He hadn't thought her pale skin could get any whiter, but it did. "You want me to challenge Dagon's guardian? I'm strong, but I can't defeat that creature."

"I'll deal with it. You just need to coax it to the surface."

"Thirty yards!" the lookout called.

"Quickly!" Otto hustled her over to the rail rather more firmly than he'd intended. If she took offense at his rough handling, she had no time to complain.

Lady White raised both hands and corruption poured out of her. It reminded Otto of a warrior flexing before a fight to try and intimidate his foe. Compared to the darkness at the guardian's core, Lady White's power seemed a weak imitation.

"It's rising!" the lookout called.

In an explosion of water, what looked like an amalgam of a dead whale, a giant squid, a shark, and a few other random beasts Otto couldn't begin to recognize burst from the sea twenty feet from the ship. A scattering of burning red eyes all focused on Lady White.

For a moment Otto considered throwing her over the side

in the hopes that the beast would spare the rest of them, but he dismissed the idea at once. She was too valuable a potential ally to waste.

"Axel!"

Bows twanged and mithril-tipped arrows soared out, hammering through the creature's thick hide with ease. The magical metal burned away the corruption around them, but it hardly made a dent.

Now that they were in place, it was Otto's turn.

He tapped the blade of his sword, connecting his magic to the arrowheads.

Now the hard part.

With every drop of ether at his command, he drove the arrowheads deeper into the demon beast. It thrashed and howled, spraying the ship with water and bits of rotten flesh.

The flesh started moving on deck.

Otto had no power to spare. "Hans! Deal with those things!"

The soldiers hurried out, stabbing the fleshy slugs with their mithril weapons and flinging them overboard.

Otto continued to force the arrowheads deeper.

Only feet separated the tips from the creature's core.

With a final grunt of effort, he drove them home.

The core dissolved and when it did, the amalgam broke. Pieces of different creatures fell off, splashing into the water until at last the whale corpse that served as the primary body sank out of sight.

Otto blew out a long breath and staggered back to lean against the main mast. At this point, staying on his feet took every bit of his focus.

A moment later Hans was there, slinging Otto's arm over

his shoulder. Corina joined him a second later, taking the other side.

Otto glanced at Lady White. "Join me in my cabin. We still have matters to discuss."

She gestured at her warbeast to remain behind and trailed along behind Otto and his companions. When he'd settled into his chair and dismissed Hans and Corina she asked, "What do you have in mind?"

"An alliance. You're clearly no longer welcome in your homeland. Yet having been cast out of the cult, you still retain your power. That makes you useful. Especially your command over undead."

"As to my power, that comes directly from Lord Astaroth. Unless I displease him, I'll continue to wield his might. The High Lords are another matter. They rule the Land of the Demon Binders with an iron fist and any failure is severely punished. I may well be the first to escape that punishment. You mentioned the undead before. Why the interest?"

"Before I tell you, I want you to swear an oath on your true name to not betray me, my companions, or the New Garen Empire."

Her bloodred lips curled up. "You don't trust my promise?"

"You're a demon worshipper. No offense, but that doesn't make you the most trustworthy of allies. But your talents will be useful in what I think will be the final phase of my mission. In exchange for your oath, I give you my word that should your former countrymen come for you, I will be there to help."

She studied him, clearly uncertain, but equally short on options. While she might survive on her own for a time, eventually that time would be cut short.

At last she said, "I swear on the name Alice Young to not betray you, your companions, or your empire."

The corruption shifted around her, bands of darkness wrapping around her heart and head. He'd never seen such a reaction. It had to be something to do with her unique nature. He made a note to ask Lord Karonin about it.

"Satisfied? Now will you tell me what you plan?"

"While I have no proof, I believe the next leg of my journey will take me to the Dead Lands. That haunted place is filled with undead. Who better to help me on my journey than someone that worships the lord of the undead? I'd like to drop you off on the coast and have you search for Amet Sur's capital. I can meet you there once I finish researching the final item's location."

"And what's in this for me?" she asked.

"Safety? A place at my side as an advisor to the second most powerful person in the empire? You'd be surrounded by enough wizards and soldiers that no one would ever dare make a move against you and if they did, they'd be doomed to fail."

Her smile broadened. "I like the sound of that. Very well, I accept your terms, but I will never call you master."

Otto smiled back. "As long as you keep your oath and serve my cause, I don't care what you call me."

He didn't add that the first thing he planned to learn was how to use her true name to compel her obedience. Oath or not, she was still a demon worshipper.

CHAPTER 43

O tto studied the bleak landscape of the Dead Lands. It appeared devoid of life, or unlife in this case. That made the sheltered cove Captain Wainwright selected as their temporary anchorage perfect. Once they escaped Dagon's guardian, the journey had continued without a hitch. After everything that had happened, no one complained about the stretch of quiet.

At least no one complained to Otto, who spent hours every day hunkered down in his cabin with Lady White learning necromancy. The magic fascinated and frustrated Otto in equal measure. Everything she knew about demons and undead was filtered through the teachings of her cult. Translating that into something useful to a wizard took more time and effort than he expected.

But if he ended up having to spend any amount of time in the Dead Lands, the lessons he learned might make the difference between survival and death.

Now his time of study had come to an end. It was time to drop his teacher off and see if she could find Amet Sur's capital. Otto didn't even know the name of the city, only that it had a huge black pyramid that served as the first Arcane Lord's palace. How hard could it be to find a city with both a portal and a pyramid?

As the anchor splashed down Lady White came to join him at the ship's railing. "So this is where we part company."

He nodded. "I don't have any advice for you. I assume some of the locals are capable of speech. If you can compel them, they might be able to guide you to the city."

She drew in a lungful of air and let it out slowly. That had to be a habit from when she still lived. "This place is rich in corruption. I will be at home here. Assuming I can find this city you seek, how do I let you know?"

Otto took two items out of his pocket. The first was one of the thin crystal sticks he'd prepared. The other was a gold coin engraved with an empowered rune. "Snap the crystal and you can send me a ten-word message. I can then teleport to the rune."

She accepted the items and slipped them into a pocket of her robe. "Sounds simple enough. What's the time frame?"

Otto shrugged. "It takes as long as it takes. We'll be a month minimum returning to port. After that I'll need time to recover and prepare for the next leg of the mission. Probably three months minimum."

"I'll do my best to be ready."

The crew had one of the ship's dinghies ready and Otto escorted her to the boat. Her warbeast loosed a soft growl at him but Lady White swatted it on the nose and it fell silent.

He turned at the sound of pounding boots. Jet was running across the deck towards them.

When she stopped, she said, "I want to go with you."

"No," Lady White said. "You're still living, with all the

weaknesses that come with that condition. There's no food or potable water out there. And I can't stop every time you need to sleep. Go with Otto and rejoin me when he does. If you still wish it, we can petition Astaroth to grant you his blessing then."

Jet's face fell but she bowed. "As you command, Lady. Good luck."

Otto used his magic to steady the dinghy and Lady White climbed aboard with her warbeast. The unlucky sailors selected to ferry her to shore inched as far from the beast as possible without leaving the oars. Otto didn't blame them even though Lady White was by far the more dangerous of the pair.

When the dinghy had moved away from the ship Jet said, "I'll be below deck if you need me."

She sounded depressed, but Otto doubted anyone else on the ship would share her feelings.

CHAPTER 44

Otto couldn't begin to describe his happiness when Lux's port appeared on the horizon. How long had they been gone? A bit over a year if he wasn't mistaken. It felt like longer. He'd once heard a veteran of many battles describe life in the army as long stretches of boredom broken up by moments of sheer terror. That described the last year really well.

As the ship eased up to the dock Hans came striding over. "Orders, Lord Shenk?"

"We're heading home, Hans. As soon as we're tied off and our gear's unloaded, it's straight to the portal and Garen. I haven't desired a home-cooked meal this much in a very long time."

"I second that." The sergeant grinned. "We really did it, didn't we? We made it to the Celestial Empire and back in one piece. Most of us anyway. That's a story I can tell my nieces and nephews. I can tell them, right?"

Otto laughed. "You certainly can. I suspect Captain Wain-wright plans to tell every captain in the city."

Axel and the scouts were coming up on deck, their packs slung over their shoulders. Corina was behind them and the rest of Hans's squad, each of them heavily laden with their and Otto's gear, brought up the rear.

"I need to talk to Captain Wainwright for a moment," Otto said. "I'll meet you on the dock."

Hans saluted and went to join the others.

For his part, Otto strode across the deck to the helm where the captain was busy shouting orders to his men who were equally busy tying off the sails and doing other things Otto didn't understand.

"Lord Shenk," Wainwright said. "You've made my career with this journey. I can't thank you enough for letting me command such a historic voyage."

"You guided us there and back," Otto said. "I could ask for nothing more. I may not have need of you and the ship for some time. Do you have plans?"

"I'm going to write a book about the trip." He laughed at Otto's expression. "With what you've paid me, I have plenty of wealth to hold me over for years. When you need us, me and the *Sea Star* will be ready."

"Good enough. But I will thank you not to mention where we dropped off Lady White."

Wainwright nodded. "I will be circumspect with the details. When I'm finished, perhaps you'd like to read it before I hire a printer."

"That sounds like a good idea. Farewell, Captain."

"Smooth seas, Lord Shenk."

Otto climbed down the gangplank and joined the others. The group set out for the portal at a brisk walk. It seemed they were all as eager to get home as he was.

〇

After a good night's sleep in his own bed and so much food he could barely walk, Otto set out for the palace. It was time to put the Heart of Alchemy in place. He also needed to check in with Allen and Sin. He didn't hold out much hope that they would have found any assassins, but you never knew.

The chill air and quiet streets of Gold Ward soothed him after the heat and crowds of Port Han and the Celestial City. No one looked at him as a potential target here either. Until he left, Otto hadn't appreciated how nice it was to be known and feared.

At the palace gate, the guards on duty snapped to attention and hastened to raise the portcullis. As it clanked up Otto asked, "How fares the emperor?"

The men shared a look then the elder shrugged. "We see little of him, but the rumors are that he's shaken off his melancholy. At least he's attending court again."

Otto nodded his thanks. He'd get a full report from Draken later, but it was nice to hear his friend had beaten his depression. Nothing like getting betrayed by someone you thought you loved to sour your mood.

He crossed the courtyard and entered the main keep by a side entrance. A handy guard directed him to the library. When he arrived, he found Wolfric seated in a leather chair, book in hand, and a glass of brandy at his elbow. The familiar scent of paper and leather brought a smile to Otto's face.

"Good morning, Your Majesty."

Wolfric jumped and peeked over his book. "Otto!"

He leapt to his feet and embraced Otto like a brother. Fortunately, there was no one around to witness the inappropriate reaction.

"I had word you were back, but I didn't expect you this early. You look tired."

"I am, my friend. But I couldn't wait to put the second piece of the engine in place. Would you like to see it?"

Wolfric smiled. "Indeed, I would."

Otto pulled the Heart out of his pocket and held it up to glitter in the light. "Here it is. The Heart of Alchemy."

Wolfric looked the Heart all over but made no attempt to touch it. "I thought it would be bigger."

"Its power is considerably greater than its size. Shall we go put it in place?"

The question was largely rhetorical and they were soon on their way to the basement room where the Chamber of Eternity rested.

"Are you well?" Otto asked as they walked through the quiet halls surrounded by a squad of royal guards. "I know Jade's betrayal was a hard blow."

"It was and I am. Annamaria has been a great help. So has Abby."

Otto glanced at his friend and tried to imagine what his wife and supposed daughter had to offer the emperor. He hadn't even taken time to say hello when they got back.

"How did they help?"

"Annamaria helped by showing me that kindness and friendship were still a thing. And Abby's innocence warmed the chill in my heart. She's started walking, you know. The sweet thing."

Otto was pleased that the two of them were good for something besides making his life difficult.

At the sealed door Otto deactivated the wards protecting the room and entered. The guards remained outside. The seven-foot glass cylinder looked exactly as he left it after saving Wolfric's life. In his pocket, the Heart grew warm as if knowing that it was close to its partner piece.

Otto ran a loving hand over the smooth glass. The moment over a year in the making had come at last. Using a tendril of ether, he lifted the Heart up into the mithril tripod at the top of the Chamber. The moment the red crystal made contact, the mithril changed shape, wrapping around the Heart like vines locking it in place.

Any doubts he might have harbored were washed away.

Otto breathed out a sigh of satisfaction. Two pieces down and one to go.

CHAPTER 45

A phantom pain ran through Valtan as he paced in his private library. It wasn't physical pain, but a tremor that ran through the ether. The tremor held a unique pitch, one he'd felt only once before, when his former love, Karonin, had been chosen to make the transformation to an Arcane Lord.

How he wished he could have gone back and stopped her from agreeing to the offer. Or better yet, never making it at all. He hadn't fully understood what the transformation meant. After he saw what it did to the sweet, eager young woman he'd fallen in love with, Valtan knew the engine could never be used again. It was then he'd begun planning his ultimate betrayal. The horrors his fellow Lords had committed before he figured out how to stop them had only driven home the importance of his act.

And now someone else had assembled both pieces of the engine. Otto Shenk was moving far faster than he'd ever dreamed possible. It seemed like the young man had a single thought and it drove him every moment of every day. How well Valtan recognized that drive. Every great wizard had it.

Now all he needed was the final piece of the puzzle. Once he got that, only a miracle would stop Otto from becoming the most powerful wizard in the world. And there would be no one capable of sending him to the netherworld. He would rule for all time, slowly becoming the worst sort of despot. Valtan had seen it all before. Somehow, he had to keep the past from repeating.

And the only tool he had, Eddred and his companions, wanted to give up the fight. Well, Eddred did anyway. Uther wanted only revenge, but in its own way, that was as problematic as Otto's quest. Hate, anger, revenge, all they brought was suffering.

Valtan drew himself up to his full height and projected his consciousness into the ether.

A moment later he formed an illusion of his body in the center of a modest village on South Barrier Island. He found Eddred puttering in an early spring garden. A pair of little girls crouched beside him, pointing and asking questions. The former king smiled and answer, seeming happy.

The girls spotted Valtan and fled toward a nearby cabin. Eddred turned and his smile faded. "Lord Valtan. Have you come up with a new strategy? It's been nearly a year."

"No. But Otto has returned and completed the Immortality Engine. He's closer than anyone has ever come since I banished my former comrades. In another year, he'll be unstoppable. Will you help me stop him before then?"

"Can he be stopped? We've tried everything you suggested and only made matter worse. Maybe it would be better to stay out of it and see what happens. He's only one man in the end. He can hardly destroy the world on his own."

"Do not underestimate the power of an unbound Arcane Lord. He may lack the power to destroy the world, but that doesn't mean he can't make life miserable for much of it."

Eddred stood. "What do you suggest?"

"Go to the City of Coins."

Eddred turned away in disgust.

"Hear me out. Hire mercenaries and travel into the desert. I have magic you can use to keep the undead at bay. I know where he's going. You can beat him there and seize the item he seeks. It will buy time at least. Bring it to me and I can protect it. If you can kill him, so much the better."

"If you knew where to find the artifacts, why not send us to find them to begin with?"

"Knowing where they are and claiming them are two very different things. All of them are protected. The danger is immense. If there were any other way to stop him now, I would gladly try. But this is the best I can come up with. Will you go?"

After a long pause Eddred said, "Very well, but after this I'm done. I want to live out the rest of my life in peace."

"Thank you, Eddred. The whole world would thank you if they knew the threat they faced. I will prepare a map and transport it to your ship. The sooner you leave the better."

Valtan vanished before Eddred had a chance to change his mind. If this worked, it was only a half measure. But a half measure was better than nothing. Deep inside, he feared he was only sending the king to his grave.

Even so, the chance had to be taken.

EPILOGUE

Otto allowed himself another full day of rest before heading to the hidden tower to report his progress to Lord Karonin. During his absence, it seemed Abby had learned some self-control as she didn't scream nearly as much. And thank heaven for that. A brief conversation with Edwyn confirmed everything was progressing as well as possible with the business. As far as he could tell, his being gone for a year had done the empire not the least harm.

He found that both encouraging and a little depressing. It seemed he was no longer essential to the running of things. In truth, it was more of a relief. It let him move forward without having to worry about his base falling apart.

So after a fine breakfast he became one with the ether and traveled to the tower. When he appeared in the unchanging chamber, he found his master's smiling, disembodied face filling her magic mirror.

He bowed. "I apologize for my long absence."

"Your idea of long and mine are vastly different. More importantly, you succeeded."

His brow crinkled. "How did you know?"

"When you placed the Heart in position, a ripple ran through the ether. I felt it even this far away."

The burst of power had been so overwhelming up close, Otto hadn't realized how far it extended.

"The pig Valtan would have sensed it as well. He will grow desperate now. You must be prepared for him to make all efforts to stop you."

"He's trapped in Lords. What can he do from there?"

"I don't know," she said. "But under no circumstances can you underestimate Valtan. We did, and look what happened."

Otto nodded. He had no intention of underestimating anyone. "And the final piece?"

"The final piece isn't a piece at all." Seeing his confusion, she continued. "You must recover the instructions on how to weave the ether. Amet Sur kept it. He called the directions the Sanguine Scroll. It's far more than just a manual. He hid many of his greatest secrets in the scroll. You can't succeed without it. Even I don't know all the spells necessary to complete the transformation. Why are you smiling?"

"I'm just pleased that I guessed correctly. My assumption was that Lord Sur would have wanted to keep the final piece under his personal protection. I've already sent an agent to locate his capital. My plan was to travel by portal with a search force, but now I wonder. If any undead snuck through, Garen would be in trouble."

"Have no fear," she said. "Undead can't use a portal."

Otto's eyes widened. "Of course, the mithril."

"Exactly. Amet may have had uses for his creations, but even he didn't fully trust them. In fact, you can use the portal to generate an energy field that will repel undead for a great distance. There's a book in my armory called Undead Creation and Domination. You should study it before you set out. But don't take too long. The less time Valtan has to plot, the better."

"One more question if I may. Do you know how to use someone's true name to control them?"

"You've been dealing with the demon binders."

"Yes." Otto told her everything that had happened. "I don't trust Lady White. If there's some way to make sure she can't betray me, I'd like to take advantage of it."

"I've always thought giving power to your true name was a stupid idea, but they use them to make contracts with demons and amongst themselves. I suppose it must work for them despite the disadvantages. You need to prepare a gold amulet set with a mithril band in the center."

An image of the amulet formed in the mirror where her face had been. He memorized the design.

"And when I've made the item?"

"Return here and I will guide you through the process of empowering it. Make haste, Apprentice. At this late juncture, any delay could mean failure."

Otto nodded, his mind reeling with the work ahead of him. Determination steeled him. Whatever it took, he would find the scroll and gain the power of an Arcane Lord.

And nothing—not Valtan, not Eddred, not Lady White— nothing would stop him.